A KING SO SAVAGE

THE SAVAGE DUET BOOK I

APRIL MORAN

The Savage Duet
Book One

Crush~Conquer~Protect

A KING SO SAVAGE

The Savage Duet- Book One

Editing by: Kendra's Editing and Book Services

www.kendragaither.com

Cover Design by: Dragonfly Ink Publishing www.dragonflyinkpublishing.com

For James, always.

And for those of us who loved The Beast... even when he was being beastly.

PLAYLIST

https://open.spotify.com/playlist/2lzbmToAtco0A2Z2WvtJnl?si=80b692c514ed4c18

"Creep" • Radio Head

"Prisoner" • The Pretty Reckless

"Call Me Little Sunshine" • Ghost

"Psycho" • Puddle of Mudd

"The Hand That Feeds" • Nine Inch Nails

"Flesh and Bone" • Blackberry Smoke

"It Ain't All Flowers" • Sturgill Simpson

"In The Dark" • Reignwolf

"Animal" • Badflower

"Cold" • Chris Stapleton

"Lipstick" • The Venice Connection

"Cold, Cold, Cold" • Cage The Elephant

"Skin And Bones" • Foo Fighters

"Change (In the House of Flies)" • Deftones

"Kill4Me" • Marilyn Manson

"Wild Horses" • Bishop Briggs
"Do Your Worst" • Rival Sons
"How Do You Love" • Shinedown
"Never Tear Us Apart" • INXS

PREFACE

I saw her.

I wanted her.

I took her.

The money is just an excuse. Her brother's debt? A convenient justification for my obsession. She's been mine since the day I laid eyes on her.

Taking her captive stirs up a storm. Her depraved brother wants her back. My own half-brother is determined to snatch my kingdom from me, and my men lust after the woman I've stolen. And she looks at me with reluctant, angry desire every time I touch her.

And I touch her every chance I get. She's so bright and shiny—a pretty toy I can break and put back together again and again. She may be my prisoner, but she's got my black heart locked up tight.

Well, I won't need that useless lump of muscle and tissue if I lose her. I won't need anything except the blood of our enemies dripping from my hands. I'll rip the heart out of any man who dares hurt her and place it at her feet.

Crush~Conquer~Protect

When it comes to my wicked little lamb, my personal motto means everything.

I'm Kingston Vaughn Winter.

And Ava Bella Blue is mine.

CHAPTER

ONE

"Wake up, little lamb."

Snuggling deeper into sleep, Ava frowned. "Go away," she mumbled.

The same deep voice spoke again, the cajoling lilt missing. It was now harsh. Accusing. And like someone calling out across a vast ocean, the words wavered and rolled.

"Goddamn it, Oliver. You gave her too fucking much."

"The hell I did. Neil said the dosage was precise for her weight. Isn't my fault she went down like a stone when it hit. Good thing, too. Made it a lot easier getting her pretty ass on the jet. She was out the entire time we were in the air."

Brow furrowed, Ava shifted restlessly, searching for a more

comfortable spot on the pillow. A pillow possessing all the softness of a rock.

Dosage. Was she sick? Maybe she was at the hospital. But why would she be at a hospital?

That's where people go if there's been an accident, silly.

God. Whatever drugs they'd given her were really strong. She could barely string two thoughts together. And her head… it pounded with a fierceness that stole her breath.

Ava tried burrowing back into the darkness, but a disturbing realization was slowly niggling its way in. Her arms were frozen, leaving her immobilized and helpless.

Was she waking from one of her night terrors? Possibly. It had been a while since the last episode, but stress from her recent move could have triggered a reoccurrence. She was always so exhausted in the aftermath of a night terror, the dreamless, terrifying moments in the dark completely draining her.

"Damn, she really does have a fine little ass, doesn't she?" Someone with a rough voice commented.

She couldn't possibly still be asleep, not with her head pounding so fiercely. And it couldn't be a night terror. This was too real but also foreign. She was living it but that didn't make sense.

What a strange dream this is…

"Keep your fucking eyes to yourself, Oliver."

The warning emanated from beneath Ava's head and, puzzled, she turned toward it. Was it wrong to think *that* voice represented something resembling safety? It didn't sound like it belonged to a man who cared about anyone's safety, much less her own.

The blood vessels in her head thumped in agreement.

Danger. Danger. Danger.

Greedy lust was apparent in every syllable when the other man replied with an ugly laugh, "Come on, King. I'm just saying the girl's got a fine ass. Tell you the truth, my cock loved every second of her squirming before the tranquilizer took effect."

"Motherfucker. If you touched her while she was unconscious, I'll slice your throat myself. Brother or not."

That voice... that one sent chills through Ava, even as she inexplicably gravitated to its owner. Smooth cruelty lurked in its depths, swirling just below the calm surface. It reminded her of a fierce rainstorm on a dusty summer day, tiny droplets of water lashing and stinging until everything was washed clean again. The low rumble of it was familiar and frightening. Soothing yet terrifying.

Ava shifted her body, swimming toward a tiny sliver of light far above her. Something was very *wrong*. The ocean surrounded her. Deep. Inky black. Suffocating. A storm raged until the water weighed her arms down. She couldn't move them... couldn't breathe. Her heart pounded in time with the blood in her head.

"Open your eyes, Ava..." The sing-song nature of the command was contradicted by the man's steely tone.

Ava slowly blinked. Her face was crushed into someone's chest, the crisp fabric of a man's tailored suit silky against her cheek. She caught the sharp spiciness of cologne. Fresh like the sea air. Alluring but tinged with notes of peril.

A summer storm come to life.

Beware the storms at sea...

Ava's eyes popped open then screwed shut again. The dim light burned her pupils. She knew in that moment she was not dreaming. This was terrifyingly real.

"There you are," the man crooned, his voice a mix of silk

and darkness. Muscled arms tightened around her. Strong and unyielding. Holding her captive. "Come on, now. Open your eyes for me."

Ava let out a distressed moan. She was incapable of following that command for longer than a few seconds, and that was scary. Her headache swelled, banging with sharp thumps behind her eyes and into her brain. It hurt so bad.

She wiggled in a futile experiment at escaping the arms holding her so tight. But struggling was impossible. Terror built, gathering strength and forming as a scream in the back of her throat.

When she opened her mouth, nothing poured out. Just a silent cry she could hear only in her own head.

"Paulie. A glass of water for Miss Blue," the man holding her snapped. "Now."

There was rustling and lowered voices, but Ava could not make sense of their words. She was so foggy, her brain firing off bits of information too overwhelming to comprehend. A metallic taste permeated her mouth, leaving it dry as cotton. Heaviness weighed her down like a ton of bricks heaped upon her chest.

How had she ended up here?

Am I awake?

Ava took a deep breath, forcing herself to focus. Her head thumped with the effort.

The last thing she remembered was stepping into the elevator. The hotel located in Savannah's historic district served as a temporary home until her new apartment was ready. It seemed safe enough with its mix of tourists and business people.

When she smiled shyly at the handsome man already on the lift, he grinned in return before asking her, "Which floor?"

"Four," Ava had replied.

The man leaned forward, stabbed the appropriate button with a manicured finger, and...

Blank.

It was all a blank. What happened next? Brow crinkling, Ava trembled in delayed reaction as the cobwebs began clearing. She opened her eyes, blinked again, then shut them tight once more.

"Let's sit you up," the owner of that beautiful voice murmured.

Strong hands moved Ava until she was sprawled sideways in what was obviously a man's lap. She was cradled like one would hold a doll. Settled into a position which left her legs dangling over a pair of muscular thighs. Beneath her buttocks, something hard and unyielding twitched in response to her involuntary movements.

Ava's eyelashes fluttered, her head tilting back. Her gaze became more focused as she stared up at the man holding her.

He was beautiful. Achingly, dangerously beautiful.

He possessed finely molded features, his skin lightly tanned and boasting a razor-sharp jawline shadowed with dark stubble. High cheekbones. Full, sensual lips, which now quirked upward with a hint of cruelty as Ava studied him in dazed confusion.

A mop of dark hair, so dark it was almost black, lay styled into well-groomed waves. Any girl would want to run her fingers through such luxuriousness with the express purpose of ruining its perfection.

Lifting a hand to do just that, she discovered her limbs wouldn't cooperate. After a few seconds, she gave up with a little sigh of defeat.

A swirling myriad of dark blue and black fighting for dominance, his eyes were hypnotic and framed by thick, ebony-hued eyelashes.

He peered down at Ava as if he already knew every one of her secrets. As if he knew all her dreams and desires and it was his fervent mission to crush each and every one of those fragile petals into dust beneath a brutal fist.

His face was strangely familiar. Ava was sure she *knew* him. But how? Maybe he was a doctor. Here to administer emergency care.

Only, he didn't look like a doctor. At least, not like any of the ones she'd encountered before. He looked like a terrible, dark angel sent to torment her.

Besides, would a doctor hold her in such an inappropriate manner?

Would an angel?

Attempting to place his features from memory made Ava's head swim. Whatever they'd given her as medication was now making her nauseous.

"Free Miss Blue's hands, Oliver," the man murmured while returning Ava's dazed stare. She did not realize her eyes were watering until he gently whisked the tears from her cheeks with a calloused forefinger.

I'm restrained? That explained why her arms did not work. Awareness rushed in as the man shifted Ava within the cradle of his lap. She was being held so tight. In fact, he gripped her as though she was something highly treasured. Something valuable.

Or maybe he was simply preventing her escape.

From the corner of her eye, Ava saw someone step forward. She did not know his identity, but a sharp pang of fear stabbed her gut. His face was wavy as her eyes continued adjusting to the room's light.

The man holding her called him "Oliver."

I don't know anyone named Oliver...

But she recognized him, even if she had no clue who he actually was. It was *him...* the man who smiled at her in the hotel elevator.

Oliver's grin was callous as he stepped forward, a razor-sharp switchblade held with casual indifference in his right hand. Light blue eyes regarded Ava with curiosity. Chestnut dark hair fell over his brow in an almost endearing manner. There was a strange gleam in his penetrating gaze. He wanted to hurt her. He would, too, if given the chance.

Fear clawed its way up Ava's throat, panic flapping around the walls of her chest until she couldn't breathe. Everything within her demanded she escape. Get away.

Save yourself...

Sensing Ava's unease, the man whose lap she was sitting on again tightened his arms around her. Squeezing with subtle threat, he snaked a large hand between her bare legs. Hard fingers dug into the soft flesh of her inner thighs. With a gasp of shock, she tried closing them, but he merely chuckled at her efforts.

"Settle, Miss Blue."

There was the likelihood of being sliced into bits by either the man holding her or his partner, but Ava froze in place at the softly spoken command. Wild tremors rushed through her body as she processed the man's hands touching her with such intimate brutality.

Oliver snatched up Ava's wrists and, with a smirk, sliced through the zip-ties. An older man, with a headful of salt and pepper hair and calm brown eyes, shoved past him and thrust a glass of water at her. His smile was warm and oddly out of place.

"Thank you, Paulie," her captor murmured, his chest rumbling against Ava's shoulder as she automatically grabbed the glass. It was cut crystal, so heavy and chunky she nearly dropped it. With nerveless fingers, she somehow cupped it within her palms.

"I'm sorry," she croaked in a scratchy voice. Then her lips pressed into a firm line. Why was she apologizing? It wasn't her fault her hands were numb. Staring at her wrists, she dumbly registered the faint red lines etched into her skin. The zip-ties left a mark despite her apparently being unconscious while restrained.

Plucking the glass away from her nerveless fingers with an audible sigh, the man held it to her lips. Although Ava's brain protested being treated like a helpless invalid, she gratefully drank until the glass was lowered and set aside.

Wait. Should I have drunk that so quickly? What if it's drugged, too? What if they poisoned me? Stupid, stupid, stupid! I just swallowed it down without any protest...

"It's only water, Miss Blue." The man holding her spoke quietly, his breath tickling her cheek. His fingers loosened their hold; however, it was infinitely more disturbing when he began stroking her. Softly. Confidently. As though he knew she required soothing and this was the most effective way of handling her. "Besides, I've already drugged you once today."

Those fingers coasted and brushed over the skin of her thighs, smoothing away the marks they'd already imprinted.

Ava wanted to grab his hand and make him stop but didn't dare.

"Where am I?" Her hoarse words came out all soft and wobbly. Weak.

That was a mistake. She could not show weakness in this den of lions and hyenas. Not with this pack of creatures waiting to rip her apart. Not while she sat like a prize in the ironlike basket of their leader's lap.

"Don't leave our guest drowning in suspense, dear brother." Oliver's eyes raked over Ava with insolent desire. He took a seat in an overstuffed leather chair opposite the desk, one leg crossing over the other.

Ava shuddered. Her gaze darted around the room in an attempt at making sense of her current situation. Things were slowly coming into focus, the blurred edges sharpening and stabbing her awareness with unrelenting violence.

The space was huge. Cavernous. It was obviously an office of some sort. Books lined the walls along with several sets of floor-to-ceiling windows draped in sumptuous drifts of black brocade. The drapes were closed so Ava could not determine if it was day or night.

Everything was both lavish and restrained—the hues and décor a harmonious, gothic-like blend of rich fabrics, ornately carved dark wood, and black iron sconces.

Another man, younger than the one named Paulie, stood along the wood-paneled walls. Like the others, he watched her intently. He was handsome, with light blue eyes, built like a mountain, and just as threatening.

"Shut the fuck up, Oliver," the man holding Ava said. Tipping her chin up with a forefinger, his lips curved, revealing brilliant, even white teeth. "You are here, little lamb. With me."

He was so savagely dazzling that Ava could only blink in dazed wonder. His presence commanded her attention. Demanded her focus. He was seriously gorgeous.

But something terrifying lurked below the perfect surface of his features. Something Ava uneasily recognized. This man was dangerous. Calculating. Intelligent and, perhaps most frightening of all, patient. It emanated from him like an expensive cologne. This man would plot and plan and wait in plain sight while destroying his enemy with a friendly smile.

He reminded Ava of a predator waiting to strike. A hunter

stalking its next meal. A lion ready to devour a lamb once it settled down from its fright.

She was that lamb.

"I don't understand," she finally whispered when it seemed he was waiting for an answer. "What is this place? And who are you?"

"Don't you remember me, Ava Bella Blue?" the man murmured, cupping her jaw within his huge hand. Blunt fingers dug into her skin, forcing her to meet his gaze. "I'm crushed. Because you see, I never forgot you. I've dreamed of this moment for ages. And now, you are here. As beautiful as I remember. And even sweeter than I dreamed."

The cruelty in that grip and the jewel-like depths of this man's eyes sent fear trickling down Ava's spine. Recognition rushed through her like a rogue wave. It was enough to make her sick. Hot bile rose in her throat, burning and sticky. With great difficulty, she swallowed it down.

"You are friends with my brother," she acknowledged in a whisper. "And my father... my father worked for you."

"Ahh, you *do* remember me." His grin widened while those cruel fingers tightened just enough to leave a faint mark along her jawline. "Although I wouldn't say your brother and I were exactly friends. Would you?"

Ava did not answer. How could she when her mind was in a whirl?

Kingston Vaughn Winter.

King.

A man who showed no mercy to those who crossed him. A man whose shadowy reputation as the ruler of Bitter Springs and everything surrounding it had only deepened over the past ten years. A man whose rise to power was both mystery and legend. At the age of thirty, Kingston Winter had a fortune at his fingertips, a city under his heel, and an endless list of people who wanted to see him dethroned.

Ava first met him when she was fifteen. Kingston was six years older and already a mysterious figure. Tall. Dark. Obviously handsome. Painfully intelligent. With his own father dead, Kingston came around their house often. Maybe he was unnaturally interested in their family life. Maybe he was simply making sure Ava's father, a successful estate lawyer, handled his affairs properly. Or maybe he enjoyed escaping the frantic whirl of college life during his senior year. Ava wasn't sure. But he was a frequent guest of her father's, and she always carefully avoided him.

Because there was something unnerving in the way Kingston watched her back then. He would smile as if he knew a secret he would never tell. An air of blatant sexuality clung to the man, and Ava remembered her girlfriends giggling over what it would be like to kiss Kingston Winter.

He was every teenage girl's fantasy.

Admittedly, Ava had often fantasized about him. Wondered how firm Kingston's lips would be against hers. If his large hands would be rough or gentle. And she wasn't sure why, but she was certain his touch would be brutal. Savage. Forbidden, but worth it. In her innocence, she recognized Kingston's appeal and found it both confusing and infinitely fascinating.

But that was years ago. Before the man holding her became one of the most feared men along the eastern seaboard. He was a ghost of sorts. A monster strolling in to wreak havoc then sitting back so he could admire the carnage left behind.

Now, she wondered why she was within his grasp.

Ava sat up straighter, and Kingston's grin melted as she tried inching away. Those blue-black eyes darkened with interest, coming alive as she began pulling herself together. She recognized that glint. It was the desire to hunt. And he liked seeing her scared.

"You're right. You and Carson aren't exactly friends. You probably never were beneath that veneer of civility you showed one another." A thread of disdain coiled through the words. "We're not friends either, so tell me why I'm here, Mister Winter."

"Oh, I do love a woman with a bit of backbone. It makes breaking them all the sweeter. And you will address me as 'Sir', from this point forward, little lamb."

It was foolish, maybe even reckless, but Ava's anger surged. Half-turning, she pushed at Kingston's wide chest with her palms. "You don't scare me, Kingston Winter. I knew you back when that handsome face of yours sported a pimple or two."

The man simply laughed at the show of bravado and then actually preened for her benefit. "You think I'm handsome? Did you all hear that? Miss Blue finds me attractive."

"Those drugs must have affected her eyesight," Oliver drawled.

"You're just as ugly on the inside as Carson. Just as cruel." Ava grit her teeth at being the butt of their jokes. "And none of you scare me," she repeated stubbornly, but the words trembled almost as badly as her body did. She nervously bit the nail of her index finger, worrying it with tiny nibbles. It was an awful habit she indulged in when stressed out.

"I'm the one you need to worry about." Kingston sobered, his laughter dying away. Tugging her hand away from her mouth, he held her wrist hostage. "And truth be told, Ava, you should be terrified."

A dismissive flick of Kingston's hand resulted in Oliver obediently rising from his chair. Coming around the desk, he wrapped his hands around Ava's upper arms, yanking her off Kingston's lap and onto her feet.

Her legs were weak, the muscles refusing to cooperate. She fell against him and let out an involuntary yelp when Oliver squeezed with unnecessary roughness. He jerked her closer alongside his leanly muscled body, and although she struggled, she was no match for his strength. He dragged her until she stood on the opposite side of the enormous desk. Like an inmate brought before the warden and presented for punishment.

Kingston's eyes narrowed on Oliver. "Careful, little brother. Bruise her and I will reciprocate."

Oliver nodded. "Got it." His grip loosened imperceptibly, and Ava sagged in response, her cheeks red with embarrassment for her weakness.

The aura of power in the room was achingly apparent. Each man wore an exquisite suit, the expense evident in the quality of the tailoring. They looked as though they'd just stepped from the pages of a men's magazine.

In contrast, Ava still wore a pair of distressed jean shorts and the black tank top she'd thrown on that morning. Her sandals were missing, leaving her uncomfortably barefoot, and the elastic band used to bind her hair was gone as well. Instead of a neat ponytail, dark blonde waves tumbled down her back in a snarled mass.

Even more distressing was the fact her purse and cellphone were nowhere to be seen. No doubt, those items had already been disposed of.

Ava was certain she resembled a bedraggled doll. Something inside her wanted to smooth her hair into place. Straighten her tank-top so the strap was no longer falling off one shoulder. Put some shoes on.

But the spark in Kingston's eyes sent a clear message. He liked her state of dishevelment. Enjoyed seeing her mussed and confused. Why was that?

Why had he abducted her anyway?

Oh, God. Panic rose in her throat again. Had anyone missed her? Was anyone even searching for her? Was Drake wondering what happened to her? They'd only gone out on a few dates so the handsome young lawyer probably had no idea she was even gone. And her bosses at the small publishing house in Savannah… would they miss a new employee who wouldn't report for work for another week?

Ava tried swallowing down her terror. This situation was dire. She needed her wits about her, for she was truly in a den of beasts.

Oliver gripped her tighter when her knees wobbled. Whatever drugs they'd used were affecting her balance.

"Why am I here?" Ava demanded in what she hoped was a strong voice. Staring at Kingston across the width of that gleaming, dark mahogany desk, her teeth clenched when he ignored the question. For some reason, the spot on the inside of her thigh where he'd previously touched her began throbbing. Like a heartbeat. Or the pounding of drums. The imprint pulsed with maddening insistence until Ava shifted her legs together.

Kingston noticed her discomfort. His lips quirked upward as he pulled a thick, dark blue file from one of the desk drawers. Opening it, he thumbed through the sheaf of papers it contained. One page was withdrawn, and he held it up, perusing the figures laid out in neat columns.

"Your brother owes me a great deal of money," he finally said in an emotionless tone.

"That is his misfortune. It has nothing to do with me." Her eyes darted everywhere, making note of items on the massive desk. The things that could be utilized as weapons. The glass she drank water from. An ink pen stand with a base of solid black marble. An hourglass made of black iron and translucent glass. The sand was iridescent like it came from pulverized fairy wings. On the corner closest to her was an unusual paperweight, the intricately cut edges catching and reflecting light from the chandeliers.

Two of Kingston's men waited against the wall with arms crossed. They stood like sentries in a palace, their relaxed stance indicating they hardly feared an attack coming from her.

Kingston smiled with the barest hint of amusement. "It has everything to do with you, little lamb."

Ava shook her head, hating the way the odd endearment rolled off his tongue like a caress. "If you think Carson will ever pay a ransom, you're mistaken. I am worth nothing to him. Less than nothing, actually."

Oliver leaned in, his mouth so close to her ear that Ava cringed. "I wouldn't say you are worthless, Miss Blue."

"Oliver." Kingston's voice was a whip crack of warning.

Oliver threw up one hand in a supplicating gesture. "Just assuring our guest she is valuable."

"She knows." Kingston's brow rose high. "Don't you, Miss Blue? And you know I will use you to erase your brother's debt."

"How much does he owe you?" Ava bit out. Her older brother had essentially abandoned her not long after their parents' deaths during her sophomore year of college. In the years since, she'd studied hard, worked menial part-time jobs, and scrimped on essentials to conserve the meager allowance from her portion of the inheritance.

Carson, on the other hand, lived the high life in their once grand family home. He partied with lower-level criminals and whores, indulged in illicit drugs, and gambled away the possessions their parents left behind. When they died in the car accident, he was granted full access to all the accounts. Ava knew, if he could have managed it, he would have spent her money as well. It was a small blessing that her mom and dad restricted her own access to the inheritance. She couldn't gain full access until she reached the age of twenty-five.

That particular estate provision was in place to keep the two of them from spending every dime. It was supposed to protect them until they were more mature in handling the large sum of money. It did little in dissuading Carson, however. While Ava was careful and frugal with her allowance, Carson was the opposite. He blew through the money as though it were pennies the moment he had full access to his portion.

Kingston appeared neither sympathetic nor sorry as he rose from his chair and made his way around the desk to where she stood. He was so much taller than Ava remembered and impossibly broad. His hands were big but elegant, the fingers capped with neatly trimmed nails.

Ava flinched when he lifted a lock of her hair and rubbed it between his fingers. "How much," she whispered again, dreading the answer. This whole situation was so unfair. Why should she be held responsible for Carson's greed and stupidity?

"Just a little more than two million. Two-point-six to be exact."

Ava swayed. For a second, she thought she might faint. How had her brother managed to rack up such an astounding debt?

Kingston took her elbows, cupping them in the palm of his hands. "Steady, Ava Blue..." he murmured. "Don't worry. You are worth every cent Carson owes me, and I do intend on collecting."

The thought flashed through Ava's mind that she could jerk away from his grasp. She could fight. And scream. "This must be some kind of dream," she choked out. "It is, isn't it?

I'm going to wake up any moment. I'll be in my bed. And you will have been just a bad dream."

"This is certainly no dream, Miss Blue." Kingston grinned wolfishly. "More like a nightmare. And for you, it's just beginning."

CHAPTER

TWO

*A*nd the lion,
  he roars from pain,
    Thorns pricking every side.
It never eases
for a tortured king.

Kingston's gaze did not waver from his new acquisition as he released her and returned to his seat.

Ava Bella Blue was exquisite, even in her disheveled, half-drugged state. As a teenager, she'd been lovely. Now, nearing the age of twenty-five and having grown into her body, she was fucking gorgeous.

She frowned, digesting his words. What she faced was truly the nightmare every woman dreaded. Of course, she had no real idea what lay ahead of her now that she was within his grasp, but the girl was smart. She must possess some inkling of her new future.

Her body, her sweet innocence, would be exchanged for her

brother's debt.

She was absolutely right in asserting her brother would not pay for her safe return. Kingston never considered the possibility Carson would resolve his debt. In fact, the man stubbornly refused to pay. This meant Kingston now entertained alternative measures as a way of recouping his losses.

After receiving intel that Carson also had plans of selling his own sister off to the highest bidder, Kingston sprang into action. He'd simply snatched her up before Carson could. And, *fuck.* All the ways Ava Blue could pay off her brother's debt kept flashing through his mind.

"What will you do with me?" Ava asked weakly.

He should probably let her sit down, but Kingston experienced a perverse need to see just how strong she was.

"What do you think I will do?"

She sneered at him then, an action so bold and unexpected, Kingston nearly laughed aloud with delight.

"Something perverted and disgusting, no doubt," she snapped.

"Uh-oh, King. She's got your number," Oliver snickered.

Kingston curled his hands into fists despite his amusement. Sometimes, resisting the urge to beat his half-brother into a bloody pulp proved difficult.

Leaning back in his chair, Kingston leveled his gaze on Ava. "Whatever you are imagining is tame compared to reality."

"Will you make me work off my brother's debt? Have me scrub floors? Polish furniture?" Ava's moss-green eyes narrowed. "Wash your clothes?"

Kingston's head tilted. "It would take a hundred years to work off the debt in that manner. No, there are other ways. The fact you are a virgin is highly advantageous."

Ava sucked in a breath of outrage. "My sex life is none..."

she faltered in a search for words then finished stubbornly, "I'm not a virgin."

"We can easily find out the truth." Oliver laughed. "I volunteer for the task."

There was no mistaking the fear sparking in Ava's eyes. She shuffled sideways in an effort to place a greater distance between herself and Oliver. She was scared to death of his brother, and Kingston couldn't blame her.

"I do not tolerate liars, Miss Blue. My investigation into this matter was very thorough." Kingston rested his chin upon steepled fingers. "I know everything about you. I know Carson was a sadistic brother who bullied and tormented you from the time you were children until you broke off contact with him after your parents' deaths. I know you love romance books. The ones where the hero rescues the girl and declares his undying love after killing off the villain. Those are your favorites. Your favorite color is green and you adore dogs."

Ava bit her lip, her eyes darkening at the mention of Carson and his cruelty.

Kingston continued, his eyes never wavering from Ava's face as she stared at him in horrified fascination.

"I know how much money you spend every month for your economy cup of coffee at the corner gas station. I know you distanced yourself from your childhood friends after your parents' deaths. You concentrated on obtaining a Master's in English Lit, which left no time for sororities or frat parties. And I know the most wicked thing a man has ever done with you occurred on your eighteenth birthday. Your brother held you down while three of his friends mauled you. They paid one hundred dollars each for the privilege of sucking on your pretty nipples. A travesty, if you ask me. You are worth so much more."

"H-how do you know about that?" Wild panic swept Ava's

features as her secrets were laid bare. She seemed to shrink into herself with the reminder of that dark, stormy night and her brother's brutal betrayal.

"Because Carson offered me the same opportunity. I refused. You see, I couldn't trust that it wasn't a trap. Maybe even an ill-advised attempt to set up a case for bribery." Kingston shrugged.

He recognized Ava's desperation. She would attempt an escape. An impossible feat, considering she was inside The Den. No one left these grounds without his express permission.

Ava's fists clenched. Angry, helpless tears tracked down her cheeks in silent rivers. Her gaze darted about the room, seeking an exit that wasn't there.

Kingston's eyes narrowed on her. "Do not make me restrain you again, Miss Blue."

The quiet warning hung in the air. Trembles racked Ava's body. She fought to remain still, despite her obvious terror.

"Do you plan on selling me to lowlifes like yourselves?" she finally sneered in a voice hardly more than a whisper. "You think you're such big men, but you're not. You're nothing but animals. All of you. Disgusting, greedy pigs. No different from Carson and his band of cretins."

The soft disgust in her tone sparked a nerve within Kingston. He expected the hate and revulsion, but he didn't like hearing it spoken aloud.

"You will keep a civil tongue, Miss Blue."

"Fuck you," she shot back before adding derisively, "Sir."

"Naughty girl." A smirk twisted Kingston's lips.

"Carson might be a guy I might wanna hang out with. Friends with benefits and a little sister to pass around." Oliver laughed, but Kingston's hard stare shut him up fairly quick.

"One more word, little brother," Kingston said softly, "and

I'll cut *your* tongue out, serve it up on a silver platter, then watch you eat it."

Oliver dutifully nodded, although resentment flashed in his pale blue eyes. His half-brother hated him, but the old adage of keeping your enemies close served Kingston well. Having Oliver on a short leash meant tracking his moves was a hell of a lot easier.

Kingston's attention returned to Ava. There was an unshakable air of courage around her. It clung like the faint aroma of her sweet perfume. Honeysuckle and roses mixed with foolishness and bravery. A heady concoction for a beast like himself.

"Here is what you may expect, Miss Blue. You will remain here at The Den as my guest while I remind your brother of his debt." Kingston saw her tears, but they did not sway him. He really did not care if she was frightened. Having her terrified only worked in his favor. She could be easily controlled through that fear. "If he once again ignores my demands to repay the debt, then you shall be sacrificed."

"Sacrificed how?" Ava recklessly demanded.

"Do you really want to know?" Kingston's head tilted at Ava's hesitant nod, and his glittering eyes raked her form. "There are so many options. I can either auction you off or keep you for myself. I've not yet decided. Or, perhaps I'll share you with those who deserve a reward for their loyalty." His voice lowered. "A lamb thrown to the mercy of beasts."

Ava's shoulders slumped momentarily, but she quickly shook off the defeat. Raising her chin, she glared at him, those green glittering eyes so bright they practically shot sparks.

Kingston almost admired her for that. For standing so strong. So proud. So stoic in light of her predicament.

The next instant, he fell back in stunned astonishment as

Ava launched herself across his desk, fingers aiming like daggers for his eyes.

Kingston quickly turned his head, resulting in a scraping of her hand down the side of his neck. The marks left behind were dull red lines due to her lack of fingernails.

"Bastard!" Ava snarled, teeth bared behind the curvature of her plump lips. Her actions caught everyone by surprise. Even Oliver gawked as the girl scrambled across the desk's polished surface, finding purchase on her hands and knees.

Ava grabbed the first item within reach, the cut crystal paperweight. It was the size of a large apple, carved into a stunning replica of a lion's head, and a perfect fit for the palm of her hand.

With a low, feral growl, she swung wildly, somehow catching Kingston with a glancing blow across his upper cheek. The sharp edge of the lion's crystal mane sliced through his flesh, leaving behind a perfect half-moon-shaped wound nearly an inch long. It immediately welled up with blood.

The fact she injured him did not stop her attack. The girl seemed intent on braining him with the desk ornament.

"For the love of God," Kingston hissed beneath his breath. With the quickness of a lightning strike, he grabbed both of Ava's hands, squeezing with brutal intent until she dropped the paperweight with a low cry. The makeshift weapon hit the gleaming wood surface with a dull thud, rolling off the edge of the desk and landing on the soft rug underfoot.

He then jerked Ava forward until, with a pained, breathless "oomph", she lay sprawled on her belly.

She twisted and squirmed, trying like hell to escape his grasp, teeth snapping at anything within reach. Those sharp teeth caught him a moment later on the inside of his wrist, and he grunted in surprise.

"Oliver! Jack!" Kingston barked as his prisoner fought like a wild animal. "Don't just stand there like fucking idiots. Grab her legs."

Oliver shook himself from his stupor and jumped forward. Grabbing at Ava's legs, he was rewarded with a heel to the underside of his chin.

Meanwhile, Jack scored a knee to his abdomen that had him sucking in a breath of pain.

"Fuck!" Oliver swore before bursting out into laughter. "She kicks like a goddamn mule."

Eventually, the three men managed to flip Ava onto her back.

While Jack and Oliver each held a leg, Kingston gripped Ava's wrists in one large hand. The other tangled in the mass of her hair. He gave it a sharp tug and she squealed in furious pain.

"Calm the fuck down, Miss Blue. Before you experience something to really get upset about."

She glared up at him as he loomed over her from his side of the desk. Effectively pinned, she still would not relent in her efforts to break free.

Oliver panted, his chin already turning red with a bruise. "It'd be easier wrestling a wet cat."

"Will you just hold her, damnit? Use whatever means necessary," Kingston said just as Ava twisted her head toward his wrist. The snap of her teeth echoed as he stayed just beyond reach this time. The spot where she'd gotten him moments before was bleeding now, but it was a minor wound. He'd suffered much worse in the past. This equated to the bite of a tiny mouse to a lion's paw.

That slice on his cheek, however? That was another issue entirely. Blood oozed down his face and the area was throbbing. There would definitely be bruising. Possibly even a scar.

Giving another jerk to her hair, Kingston smiled with satisfaction as her eyes filled with tears. Then his hand slid to her throat, squeezing slightly while he bent over her.

"Last warning, naughty girl. Calm the fuck down or suffer the consequences."

"Go to hell, you perverted monster!"

Her weak snarling was adorable, but Kingston had reached the end of his patience.

"King…" Paulie said in a quiet panic upon seeing Kingston's jaw clench. "Don't do it."

The older man's warning was ignored.

Releasing Ava's throat, Kingston transferred his grip so he could hold her down with both hands. Stretching her arms above her head, he squeezed so hard the throbbing of her pulse hammered against his thumbs.

Fuck, she smelled delicious. An intoxicating perfume of sweet flowers and fear clung to her hair and skin. Kingston breathed deeply so it could permeate his lungs.

"Stop struggling before you hurt yourself," he muttered, but Ava only fought harder with a desperate frenzy. She jerked and twisted her body, trying to yank her hands from Kingston's grip until suddenly there was a loud pop.

The scream filling the room was heart-wrenching. It wobbled, high and clear before fading away into hysterical sobs.

"Damnit, King." Oliver grinned. He still held one of Ava's ankles, and now he yanked it toward the far edge of the desk. Exposed in such an obscene manner, her lightly tanned legs shook violently. "If we're starting the torture, sign me up for that shit." Oliver's free hand ran up the inside of Ava's bare leg until he reached the juncture of her thighs. "I wish Malcolm was here to see this. The things we could do to her. She wouldn't be so sassy then, I can tell you that."

Cupping Ava through the material of her shorts, Oliver

grinned while rotating a palm against her sex. "King can have your pussy while I fuck your mouth. Would you like that?"

Ava stared back at Oliver with blank, pain-filled eyes. Kingston doubted she even comprehended Oliver's words, but he did not contradict his brother's assertion. Hell, at this moment, in his own fury at the damage she'd inflicted, he wasn't positive he'd stop Oliver from following through on his threats. How sick was it that the imagery his brother's words conjured was making his dick hard?

Perhaps Ava required punishment as a way of enforcing good behavior. Well, maybe not an actual fucking, but a spanking at the very least. And he should let Oliver administer it. Let Ava see what she truly should be afraid of. And of whom.

Kingston was almost relieved that Malcom, who usually served as Oliver's preferred righthand man, was out of the country on a job. It was always a volatile situation when those two worked in tandem. Their cruelty complimented each other, but Malcolm had the edge for sheer brutality. He was the man Kingston sent on those jobs when someone required a bit of torture before death.

"What do you say, King?" Oliver flicked the button of her shorts with a forefinger. Then he inched her tank top up with that same finger until her bellybutton was exposed. His hand splayed across her bare abdomen, holding her in place. "Should we get our dicks wet? Or save her for a disgustingly rich buyer?"

Kingston frowned, that annoying twinge of disturbing possessiveness returning full force. The unwelcome sight of his brother's hands touching Ava was unnerving. And it was turning his vision hazy red with rage.

She's mine. No one else should be touching her. Not like that. Not if they want to live.

His eyes tracked from the top of her head to the other side

of the desk where Oliver still gripped her ankle. Jack held her other foot captive, his oversized fingers gingerly wrapped about the slender bones. His face was a study of indecisiveness, but like a good soldier, he waited for Kingston's instruction.

"Let her go," Kingston said, his voice murderously quiet. His reaction was irrational, especially since he commanded that she be restrained in the first place. "Both of you, let her go before I start chopping off goddamn hands."

Jack released his grip immediately, but Oliver's face revealed his surprise. He hesitated before shoving Ava away in disgust.

The girl's legs immediately pressed tight together. Bending her knees, she half-rolled onto her side, curling up into a fetal position. Her arms were still stretched above her head, her wrists manacled in Kingston's hands.

"Maybe you won't get the full amount if she's broken, King, but it sure will be damn fun getting her to that point," Oliver said. "You know we can do whatever we want with her and still make money."

"Of course, I fucking know." Kingston's hands slid under Ava's shoulders and her knees. Tugging her across the desk, he scooped her up into his arms. It was the second time he'd held her in such a manner and he liked it. He liked it too much.

Even while crying and holding her hand tight against her chest, Ava still resisted him. Coming alive, she struggled against his grip, arms flailing wildly while she sobbed incoherently.

Kingston swore beneath his breath, even as her stubbornness thrilled him.

"Would you rather I allow my brother to have his fun, after all? No? Then best stop your squirming, Miss Blue. Although I'm enjoying it more than you can possibly imagine." His whispered confession sent a tremor through her slender body. "In fact, I find your attempts to free yourself as pleasurable as the sight of those pretty tears running down your cheeks. Now, be a good girl and let me tend to your injury."

Ava turned her face into his chest. A whimper of pure terror escaped her throat, but she ceased all movement. She cradled her wrist, pinning it between his chest and hers.

Kingston spared a glance for his men. Jack and Paulie were back in their positions along the paneled wall while Oliver flopped once again into a leather club chair. Glaring at Kingston, his mouth pulled into a snarling pout but he said nothing else.

"Paulie? Have Doctor Abbot meet me in the north cell."

"The cell?" Paulie frowned in disapproval.

Kingston's arms tightened around Ava, realizing just how fragile she truly was. He could snap her bones like twigs. "Yes, the cell. Until I have an answer from her brother, it's where I will keep her."

CHAPTER

THREE

*These worlds collide
in a heartbeat.
And little earthquakes find names.
Lust. Madness. Want.*

KINGSTON'S personal physician tended to his new prisoner while he blotted his cheek with an expensive handkerchief.

Ava Blue was a stubborn little thing. And that surprising spark of fierceness she revealed was intoxicating as hell. Maybe she wasn't so docile, after all. Maybe she was more of a she-wolf clothed as a lamb.

Doctor Neil Abbott snapped his medical case close. Rising from the chair beside the cot, he made his way to Kingston. "Nothing broken. Just a bad sprain. I've placed it in a splint as a simple precaution, but she'll recover quickly. Don't let her put any pressure on it for a few days, at least."

"Thank you, Neil." Kingston glanced past the man to where

Ava was curled up on the narrow cot. The lighting in the cell was low, but he could see she was still weeping. Fuck if she hadn't also bitten her bottom lip until it was bleeding.

Neil rubbed the back of his neck. "Are you sure about this, Kingston? I mean, she isn't the type one locks up in a dungeon."

"It's hardly a dungeon," Kingston said, gesturing around the space. "There's a nice bathroom, a bed, a lamp. I even had the heat turned up so she doesn't feel the chill of the stones."

Neil scowled. "It's underground, has a solid wood door with a small, grated opening, no windows, and manacle rings embedded in the walls. Classic dungeon."

"Agree to disagree." Kingston shrugged. "Check on her tomorrow, will you?"

"Fine. You're sure you don't want me to put a stitch or two in that cut? It will probably scar." Neil had tended Kingston first, placing surgical strips over the slice to his cheek before Kingston directed his attention to the girl curled up on the cot.

The bite mark on the inside of his arm was insignificant, and Kingston refused treatment for it. Fuck, he wasn't a pussy.

"It's fine. What's one more scar, anyway?" Kingston waved the doctor away.

"I gave her a sedative. A mild one, since she was already tranquilized earlier today. She needed something to take the edge off the pain of her wrist." Neil shifted his feet, obviously uncomfortable, but continued with a sigh when Kingston's eyebrow lifted high in question. "And the other shot you insisted upon. I gave her that, too. Never mind I've serious problems with the ethics of that. She begged me to help her escape. To call the police."

"You refused, so does it even matter?"

Neil shook his head. "I cannot in good conscience sanction this, King. This is some serious shit."

"And what other option is there? The bastard refuses to pay up, and that cannot be allowed. Not with the enemies I have. Go soft on a debt and my reputation is fucked. Besides, it's not like I've stolen her away from paradise. She's surviving on the edge of fucking poverty while her brother blazes through their inheritance. He's racking up IOUs up and down the coast. And to top it off, he wants to use her to pay those debts. I just beat him to it by grabbing her first. What's wrong with protecting my investments?"

"For one thing, you don't need the money. Not when you're richer than the devil himself," Neil argued. "It's a fucked up situation. You know my loyalty is yours, but I am *really* not okay with this."

"You don't have to be okay with it. You just have to keep your mouth shut. And Neil? A word of advice. You're my closest friend. But don't ever think you have the right to dictate how I handle my business affairs." Kingston smiled, but it did not reach his eyes.

Once the doctor exited the cell, Kingston stalked closer to the cot. Ava was curled into a half-moon shape, her body hidden by clean, white sheets and a fluffy down comforter. It was still a bit chilly down here. He would turn the heat up a little more.

He'd never abducted a woman before, and this particular dungeon cell was only used when indulging his own pleasure with willing partners. Everything he enjoyed when it came to sex was consensual.

Until this girl.

Nothing with her would involve consent. Nothing he intended on doing would be welcomed. And while there was a chance Carson Blue would repay the debt, Kingston prayed he wouldn't.

Because he'd wanted Ava the moment he'd laid eyes on

her. Not sexually, of course. Fifteen years old, all coltish legs and budding breasts, her body hinting at maturity, she'd been too young then. Maybe it was wrong to want her, but he didn't care then and he didn't care now. He waited for her to grow up. Waited for her to fall into his lap. Waited until her stupid, cruel brother provided the catalyst so Kingston could rightfully take her.

Now she was his, and he still wasn't sure what should be done with her.

"You can't do this to me." Ava's voice was soft and a little slurred from the drugs. "It isn't right."

Kingston sat on the edge of the cot, admiring how the glow of the lamp transformed her features into something magical. Tucking the bloody handkerchief back into his pocket, he smoothed her hair away from her face. "No, it isn't."

"You can still let me go."

Kingston chuckled. "No, I can't."

She tried curling even tighter into herself, her left arm coming up across her chest in a protective manner. The splint was huge on her: a contraption of metal bracing and medical wrapping that swallowed her tiny wrist. A tear rolled down her cheek, and Kingston experienced an urge to lick it off her skin. To taste the unique flavor of fear and sweetness. His mouth watered with the thoughts of what else he could taste of her.

"I'm a poor return on your criminal activities, Mister Winter. You'll never get that kind of money for me." Her pretty green eyes were fogged with pain and tranquilizers but still glittered with distrust. Seeing the cut on his cheek, and the accompanying bruising, she sucked in a breath as if surprised by her own ability to wound a man.

When he leaned closer, her thick sable lashes fluttered shut and her throat convulsed as she swallowed.

How intriguing to discover a smattering of pale gold freckles on her otherwise flawless skin. Those little flakes danced across the bridge of her reddened nose. He wanted to count each one with endless kisses.

"You'd be surprised what men will pay for a sweet little thing like yourself, Miss Blue."

"You can't just sell people, you know." She sniffled.

He smiled at her naivety. "Of course, I can. People do it every day. Heads of State. Kings. Princes. Presidents. Judges and politicians. They buy and sell what they want just like they do on the New York Stock Exchange floor. Flesh is a valuable commodity, Miss Blue. Some more valuable than others."

"My father liked you. Did you know that?" Her voice was growing increasingly drowsy. "He liked you better than he did his own son. But then again, I don't think he ever truly liked Carson so that's not saying much. Dad worked himself half to death for you. But you don't care about that, do you?"

Kingston's teeth clenched at the reminder of Garret Blue. The brilliant attorney was the reason his father's estate had settled so quickly.

The man never complained when Kingston requested their dealings be held in the library of the Blue family home. Garrett must have known how lonely Kingston actually was. How he craved the normalcy of family life. He'd even made friends with Carson before realizing the young man despised him for the close relationship Kingston formed with his father.

"It hardly matters now that both of your parents are dead," Kingston said coldly, despising the ache which suddenly seized his heart.

Ava's eyes grew darker with pain. Her bottom lip trembled. She tugged it between her teeth to stop its wobbling. But her chin still quivered, and driven by something he didn't quite understand, Kingston stretched a hand toward her face. To comfort her or scare her even more, even he wasn't sure.

Ava shrank away, tucking the sheet closer with her uninjured hand.

Her instinctive response angered Kingston more than it should have.

He gripped her chin, forcing the sheet to fall away. Hard, cruel fingers dug into soft flesh, and Ava responded with a whimper that sent lust zinging through every cell of his body.

"Don't do that again, little lamb. Don't ever avoid my touch. Until your brother repays his debt, *if* he repays, you belong to me. I will touch you as I please. Whenever I please." Releasing her chin, he trailed his hand down her throat and over the swell of her breasts. "And you will allow it."

Ava choked on a sob but did not move. She lay frozen, eyes wide. A scared little bit of sweetness waiting to be ripped apart.

"There is bottled water on the table beside the bed, and you will find the bathroom fully stocked with everything necessary to clean yourself up. A robe and nightgown are hanging on a hook behind the door. Food will be brought in for you later." Kingston withdrew his hand and rose from the bed. "Get some rest now. You'll need it."

He quickly exited the cell, pulling the heavy door shut with a loud clang. The lock was engaged and the key deposited back in his pocket.

As he strode down the wide, stone-lined corridor, he could not help but hear Ava's little wail of sorrow. It echoed off the cold stones and Kingston's pace increased.

"How's our guest?"

Oliver entered Kingston's study and thew himself into one of the chairs. Shifting his body, he propped one leg up so it dangled over the arm.

"She'll survive," Kingston replied. "I'll remind you again that she's none of your concern."

"Aww, come on. I'm the one who snatched her out of that hotel elevator. I deserve some credit, don't you think? A reward even, for doing it so efficiently and without detection. And all by myself, if I gotta point that out."

"The fewer people involved with this, the better. Remember, there is a certain clientele who will be offered the chance to bid on her."

"I haven't received compensation," Oliver said sullenly.

Kingston leveled a glare on his half-brother that would have dropped any other man to his knees. "You will be paid for that bit of work."

"You could just let me have her for a couple of hours," Oliver suggested with a drawl. "Give her to me as payment. Hell, I'll even fuck her ass so she doesn't lose value as a virgin."

Kingston's teeth clenched. Goddamn Oliver. He didn't have time to babysit the man and keep him from raping their captive.

"If anyone fucks her, it will be me. Stay away from her, Oliver. I'm warning you. This isn't negotiable."

Oliver grinned. "Catching feelings for your little hostage? How'd you ever resist her when you were hanging out at her house, pretending to be friends with her brother? Sucking up to her father so he'd clear the estate faster than a Kardashian takes off her clothes. I imagine Ava Blue was a hot little piece even back then. Prancing around in some kind of sexy cheerleader uniform. Wearing those innocent white cotton panties trimmed in eyelet lace. Tell the truth, King. She gave you such a hard-on, you probably jacked off twenty times a day fantasizing about her."

Kingston settled into his desk chair and popped open a small humidor containing a few of his favorite cigars. He refused to let his brother get a rise out of him, even if the needling was beyond tiresome. "I won't deny it. I wanted her. Even if her brother was a back-stabbing asshole who hated my guts behind all his smiles."

He cut the end of the cigar before igniting it with a custom-made lion's head lighter. A gift from a man he assassinated only the year before.

"He had his reasons," Oliver smirked. "One of his friends wanted to screw his baby sister behind his back."

"Carson never cared enough about Ava to worry about her safety. Even then, he was only interested in exploiting her. He's a bullying piece of shit." Kingston blew a ring of smoke into the air. He never spared Oliver a glance. "I respected her father so I stayed away from her. That's all."

"Ah, yes. The saintly, dedicated, *honest* Garett Blue. The father we should have had. Some people get all the luck when it comes to parents. You and I? We got the worst of the worst."

That was certainly true. Alan Winter was a complete bastard. When his second wife shot him before turning the gun on herself, it was generally agreed the world was a better place without him in it.

Kingston did not blame Oliver's mother for killing the man. His father was an abuser of women, children, and animals. There was nothing redeeming about him. Nothing whatsoever. Kingston only wished his own mom had been alive to see the man's demise.

A clever criminal, his father concealed money and assets behind legitimate fences the DA could never tear down. But the benefits of Alan's death took a while in trickling down. While Kingston finished college with only the barest of necessities provided and Oliver shuffled through the Bitter Springs foster care system, his father's fortune languished in limbo. Nothing could be released as long as authorities investigated his criminal activities.

That was until Kingston dismissed the attorney his father employed and placed Garret Blue on retainer instead. It was a wise decision. Within a year, Kingston became heir to it all. Every penny of Alan Winter's fortune and the secrets to his unlawful schemes were left to his oldest son.

Which explained why Oliver hated him so much. Being dependent on Kingston for financial support infuriated his little brother.

"She's a fucking feisty little thing. Caught you off guard, didn't she?" Oliver laughed. "If you could have seen your face when she clocked you with that paperweight... It was fucking priceless."

"Have you sent Carson the message?" Kingston's stare was cold and unattached as he regarded Oliver over the expanse of the desk.

"Right after I snatched her." Oliver chuckled, still amused by his brother's injury and the cause of it.

"I want his response the instant it comes in."

Oliver smirked again. "No doubt, you do. You know, there are a few of us who'd like to sample her if you decide to keep her. Once you've gotten your fill, of course. Don't deny us that, King."

"I might give you pups a taste." Kingston blew a ring of cigar smoke in Oliver's direction. "Maybe. We'll see how things play out. If Carson pays up, I'll return her untouched. Well, relatively untouched. Honestly, I have a feeling he won't pay a damned dime."

Oliver's laughter was cruel. "Hell, King, you're more than likely right about that. I think that girl is as good as ours."

"Mine, Oliver," Kingston reminded him calmly, fists clenched at the thought of his brother with Ava. "Ava Blue is mine. Maybe I'll share. Maybe I won't. We'll see."

The whispers are so loud
They drown out all reason

AVA SHOOK the cobwebs of sleep from her eyes and swung her legs over the side of the cot. Her wrist hurt, but she ignored it while she examined her surroundings.

It was definitely a cell.

Her eyes darted around the space, heart galloping as apprehension strummed inside her bones.

The cot she was on was placed in the middle of the cell, the iron headboard flush against the wall. A small table was beside it, the lamp upon it emitting a soft glow. On the wall opposite the cot, iron rings set higher than her shoulders were embedded into the wall. Matching chains with attached manacles hung from them. They were not rusty, but they appeared authentic enough.

The rings were the perfect height for a person to hang between.

Ava sucked in a breath at the track of her thoughts. Her panicked gaze skittered away from the implements.

Ohmygodohmygodohmygod.

This was real. She was Kingston Winter's prisoner. Imprisoned in a cell somewhere deep in the bowels of God only knew where.

She *was* his captive.

As soon as that terrifying reality sunk in, practicality washed over Ava. She must settle herself. Think things through. Find a solution to the problem at hand. Reason a way out of this.

Remain calm. Collected. Focused.

First things first. What were the chances of escaping this cell? Because she wouldn't waste time hoping Carson would rescue her.

Other than the lamp, she did not see anything useful as a weapon. There was a wooden chair, but it was constructed as sturdily as the table. Both were heavy, chunky pieces of furniture she'd never be able to lift high enough to inflict any meaningful damage, especially with an injured wrist.

Which you brought about on yourself, remember?

Maybe there was something sharp in the bathroom. A razorblade. A nail file. Anything with a pointed edge would give her a small advantage.

When Ava stood, the room spun like a kaleidoscope. Bracing herself against the wall resulted in a sharp pain lancing up her arm.

Snatching her hand back, she cradled it against her chest and closed her eyes until the pain receded to a dull ache. The dizziness eased. Being drugged and injured placed her at a severe disadvantage. No matter. It would not stop her from getting out of this mess.

She continued exploring the cell. Her stomach growled, reminding her she'd not eaten since the morning of her abduction. How many days had it been? Two? Three? Not knowing the passage of time filled Ava with anxiety. Her life revolved around punctuality. Schedules. Lists. Calendars. The lack of time awareness sent her adrift.

Floundering and lost.

It appeared no one had entered while she slept. Kingston's promise of food had not yet been fulfilled. How long had she slept after the doctor administered that sedative?

Making her way to what must be the bathroom, Ava swung open the door and immediately covered her eyes. She needed a second of adjustment and spent a few moments blinking before she could truly see.

The brightly lit room was startling compared to the shadowed austerity of the cell. In direct contrast, this was a huge, luxurious space of expensive ivory marble and gleaming fixtures. A built-in wall niche held thick white towels and various toiletries. An oversized soaking tub stood alone in one corner while an expansive shower built from marble slabs took up a quarter of the entire space. A separate door revealed a private toilet.

It was a bathroom suitable for royalty. And it made no sense it existed within this dungeon.

Stepping to the double sink area, Ava turned the handle and cupped her hand. She drank straight from the faucet. The water was icy cold, which was not surprising. It was also sweetly refreshing and contained no hint of the metallic, rusty taste one might expect.

Splashing her face with icy water she glanced at her reflection in the enormous mirror.

"Oh, God," Ava breathed in dismay.

Her dark blonde hair was a hornet's nest of tangles. Within her deathly pale face, her eyes appeared twice their normal size and were hazy with apprehension. A scrape on her chin was a reminder of how hard she'd landed on Kingston's desk. That uncharacteristic show of temper goading her attack only proved how easily he could overpower her.

And blood was smeared down her neck. Not her blood. His. A sense of pride swelled inside her chest. It was foolish, of course, to think she'd actually seriously injured him with that spontaneous attack, but at least she'd given him a reason to wonder if she would do the same again if given a chance.

Ava cast a longing glance at the shower stall. She quickly abandoned the thought of cleaning herself up. No way was she shedding her clothes. Not when someone could be watching her every movement on a secret camera system.

She could see no evidence of that in this bathroom, but it did not mean cameras weren't there. It was a worrying thought, but a more pressing matter was making itself known. She must relieve her bladder and the need was growing urgent.

A close inspection of the toilet room did not reveal tiny blinking red lights or anything resembling a camera lens. Not that it mattered at that point. It was either use the facilities or soil herself.

Very quickly and with as much grace as she could muster, Ava tended to business. An almost hysterical giggle escaped her as she finished. That was probably the fastest she'd ever peed in her entire life. Surely, it was some sort of world record, at least among women held as hostages.

When she exited the small room, she hurriedly washed her hands. It was disturbing that the soap carried the divine scent of rosemary and lemons and the hand towel was soft and luxurious.

Why waste such expensive touches in a dungeon bathroom?

Ava shook away those thoughts and got back to the business of escape. A quick examination of the items on the shelves as well as the cabinetry beneath the double sinks only revealed more toiletries, toilet paper, and towels.

No razors.

Nothing appeared suitable for use as a weapon. Unless she removed the tank lid from the back of the toilet. Maybe she could bash someone in the head with it, but the thought of wounding anyone in such a brutal way turned her stomach.

"Stupid idea, Ava," she muttered. How would she even lift the lid and hold it aloft with her injured wrist? "Stupid. *Stupid.*"

The only option was the lamp... It would be awkward with only one hand but not impossible.

Ava made her way back to the cot in the cell. Examining the lamp, she discovered it was made of intricately forged iron creating a series of interconnected circles. It mimicked the iron rings embedded in the walls, and that thought made Ava's hands tremble. The lampshade was creamy ivory and a delicate contrast to the rustic design.

Hefting it up in her good hand, Ava considered the possibility of what she envisioned.

It might work, even though the lamp was heavy and unwieldy. If she removed the shade and broke the lightbulb, leaving it screwed into the socket, it could even serve as a sharp object.

Good to know if her plan to bludgeon a person failed.

Ava removed the lampshade, setting it aside. She then snatched the cord away from the wall, wrapping it around the lamp's base so it wouldn't pose a tripping hazard. The room plunged into darkness with only the bathroom light illuminating the space.

Just where she intended to go once she escaped, Ava had no clue. But she wasn't about to sit meekly on that damned cot and wait to be sold into slavery.

Crossing the cell, she stood on tiptoe trying to see out of the small, grated window of the door. The door itself was solid wood and braced with thick bands of iron. There was some kind of wooden slide in place on the window which prevented a person from peeking in or out. It refused to budge when she pushed it with her fingers.

A low moan rumbled in Ava's chest. Even if the slide were open, she would not be able to see the exterior corridor unless she stood on top of something. Stretching herself to her full height resulted in her line of sight being level with the bottom of the window.

She could drag the chair over, but if someone pulled the slide and checked the room before entering, they would immediately notice its absence and be on guard.

With a huff, she sank back against the wall. For this plan to work, she must be in place and ready to crack the lamp over the head of the person as they entered. They must be unaware she waited to ambush. Which meant lurking behind the door, waiting an indeterminate period of time for the unlucky person to walk through.

Did she have the strength to do it? To lay in wait and attack? Was this even a good plan or was it fueled by desperation?

"Stop and think, Ava," her mother always said. Jocelyn Blue was steady, rational, and thoughtful, and her only daughter inherited many of those same attributes.

Ava rarely made foolish decisions. Although, grabbing a

paperweight and attempting to bash a man's head in wasn't something she'd carefully thought out.

She was careful and almost rigid in her methodology when overcoming obstacles in her path. It was how she survived the excruciating trauma of her parents' deaths and her brother's cruelty and neglect and still maintained a spot on the Dean's List with a perfect 4.0 GPA.

She'd gone into auto-pilot mode back then—surviving until she graduated. Living life one step at a time without the guidance and love of her parents.

It was now a life of loss and a sense of not belonging anywhere anymore.

"Wait, Ava," she said to herself with a deep breath. What if Kingston strolled through that cell door? Her plan would likely fail. He was so much more powerful and cunning. And he expected her to attempt an escape. She would be at his mercy.

What if he turned the lamp on her and beat her with it?

With a little exhale of defeat, Ava returned to the cot. It was better that she wait. Give Kingston a reason to believe she was resigned to her fate. She would outwit him.

At the first sign of complacency, she would act.

She replaced the lampshade, plugging the lamp in and pulling it back to the middle of the table.

Then Ava sat on the cot, the fingers of her uninjured hand tracing the lines of the metal brace on her wrist.

Her lips tightened as she recalled begging to be set free. The doctor tending her wrist ignored her, simply telling her everything would be all right. He'd given her two shots and everything turned hazy soon after.

Ava scoffed. *Yeah, right.* Everything would turn out just peachy-keen. She was held captive by a savage king who did not care who he destroyed as long as he recouped his money.

Ava's bottom lip trembled. She bit it hard... ignoring the

pain from where she'd chewed it earlier. Damn it, she hated being so weak, but she was truly terrified. And with her life in Kingston's hands, it probably would not last long.

Moving back against the surprisingly fluffy pillows, Ava drew her knees to her chest and gingerly laid her arms on top of them. Then she rested her head against them, breathing deep in an effort to calm herself.

But a million thoughts were running through her head and none of them were good. The hopelessness of her situation was overwhelming. She would not be rescued. No one knew where she was. Carson would not pay a ransom. Why would he? He hated her for reasons she'd never understood.

She might never escape this cell. Because she was smaller and weaker than the animals surrounding her and the one back home who placed her in this situation, to begin with.

Worst of all, she feared the gleam in Kingston's eyes when he stared at her. He wanted her. And Ava knew she could not fight him off if he decided to take what he wanted.

She was crying soft, quiet sobs when the lock on the door jangled. The sound of a key scraped. Metal against metal. The deadbolt turned with a quick, rolling tumble of iron.

Jerking her head up, Ava wiped away her tears as the door swung open and Kingston entered the room. Another man Ava did not recognize followed him in. He carried a silver tray.

Kingston stared at her as the man set the tray on the bedside table.

"Thank you, Cal. That will be all. I'll notify you when to retrieve things." Kingston's voice rumbled, and the entire cell seemed to shrink in size.

Ava turned her head away so he could not see her face.

"Sure thing, boss."

The man retreated, the door clanging shut with an obnoxious bang.

Locking her away as if *she* were the wild animal rather than the monster holding her prisoner. Her heart hammered with both fear and the first licking flames of rage.

"You did not follow my instructions. I told you to clean yourself up."

Ava did not deign to turn her head to him. "Clean or dirty, does it really matter? You'll do what you want, regardless."

Kingston let out a slight exhale of breath. That sigh of frustration was telling because it verified her assertion.

"You would feel better." His voice moved closer, and Ava squeezed her eyes shut against the terror. "I know how much you enjoy bubble baths."

"You don't know anything about me," she choked out. "But let me guess. You spied on me every time you met with my dad. You crept around the hallways. Followed me. Snuck into my room and went through my personal things. Maybe even stole some of my underwear. Classic stalker behavior. Did you put your eye to the bathroom keyhole and get yourself off? Watching me when I was naked?"

His hand stroking her hair startled Ava. With a low shriek, she scrambled away, launching herself off the cot. Maybe he didn't lock the door. Maybe she could dart around him... lock him inside his own damned cell.

He snagged her by the arm before she could get very far and hauled her up against him. Hitting that solid wall of muscle knocked the breath out of her. The arm he gripped so tightly was also the one with the injured wrist.

Stars swam before Ava's eyes as Kingston's hand moved until it lightly encircled her wrist, metal contraption and all. He squeezed gently, and the resulting pain was a scathing reminder of how helpless she was. How hopeless.

Powerless.

Ava met the blue fire of Kingston's gaze, a tumble of

confusing emotions swarming through every vein she possessed. Like an angry hoard of bees, those emotions stung and buzzed until she was dizzy from the bombardment.

She hated Kingston so much in this moment. Hated the thick tousled waves of his dark hair. Hated the chiseled perfection of his features, the dimpled chin shaded with a hint of stubble, and the full, pillow-like softness of his lips. Hated that his hard hands sent a dark thrill streaking through her like a bolt of fiery lightning. She hated the thick, sooty eyelashes that swept down concealing his lust as though she couldn't handle the thought of what he truly wanted from her.

The cut on his cheek and the bruising around it only added to his perfect, rugged good looks. And she hated that, too.

"Stop making me hurt you, Ava. Behave yourself before I'm forced to do much worse."

"Worse? What could be worse, you fucking monster?" She cried out without thinking. Of course, he could do worse. He could do so many cruel things, and no one would hear her screams down here. And even if they did, they would never come to her rescue. Not when they were loyal to this man.

"Are you tempting me, Ava?" Kingston's lips twitched with humor. "I'm happy to show you just what I'm capable of. To show you what a *fucking monster* I truly am." With a free hand, he smoothed her hair out of her face and then... *oh, God...* brushed a thumb over her abused bottom lip. "You're bleeding."

He carefully smeared the blood across her lips, coating his thumb in the bittersweet fluid before bringing the digit up to his own mouth. He tasted it, grinning like a lion sipping fresh cream.

"Sweet as honey, little lamb. Your blood. Your tears. Even your sweat. All aphrodisiacs to a man like me. If you hope to emerge from this situation with your sanity intact, I suggest you stop provoking me with these little episodes of defiance. More importantly, you should refrain from using any variation of the word 'fuck'." His grin widened even more. It was mean. Heartless. Beautiful. "It's giving me all kinds of filthy ideas."

Ava hoped his enormous hand would not tighten any more on her fragile wrist. Still, she could not help but sneer, "Obviously, you are a psycho or something."

He smirked, mocking her words. "Or *something*. Want to find out? Keep testing me. I dare you, Ava Bella Blue."

The threat of violence in his tone was a sponge absorbing Ava's defiance from her bones. She sagged in his grip, and that was enough of an answer for Kingston. He released her so she sank back onto the cot, but remained looming over her. Those blue-black eyes pinned Ava in place, glittering like black diamonds scattered across a summer sky.

"You will eat," he commanded, "then you will bathe. I'll assist you."

Ava bristled. "I don't require your assistance. And I don't want your *help*."

He simply smiled and sank onto the chair beside the cot. Leaning over, he lifted the gleaming silver dome away from the tray of food. "I know. And I don't care what you want, Miss Blue. Haven't I made that abundantly clear?"

CHAPTER

FIVE

*H*ands bound
    Hair tangled
       And cherry lips bruised red
Says you're mine.

KINGSTON RELISHED Ava's sharp inhale of breath. She was furious and terrified, and he realized just how much he enjoyed that combination in her. It was heady. Arousing. Addictive.

He shouldn't like it so much. After all, Ava was his prisoner and, until he heard from her shitty brother, she would be nothing more. But that did not mean he wouldn't play with her while she was within his grasp.

Earlier, he'd watched Ava carefully when she'd believed no one could observe her movements in the main cell. While the camera system recorded her every move, Kingston tracked her actions in real time. When she picked up the lamp, raising and lowering it as though mimicking a blow to someone's head, he could scarcely control his glee. Perhaps a savage creature existed behind that meek lamb veneer.

But then, she'd replaced the makeshift weapon with an air of defeat. And when she began crying as though all was lost, Kingston buried the stirrings of sympathy deep within his gut.

Ava glanced at the tray of food. It contained her favorites. A sandwich of roasted turkey and Swiss on wheat toast—mayonnaise only and no mustard—a salad of spring greens with fresh strawberries and poppy seed dressing along with an ice-cold bottle of Cheer Wine. The soda was one of Ava's guilty pleasures. Something she rarely indulged in as she usually preferred water with her meals and she rarely drank alcohol.

Ava's lips tightened in a way Kingston recognized as discomfort. She didn't like the fact he knew so much about her.

"My chef made your favorites," Kingston said, unrolling the napkin to reveal plastic utensils. Even the plate was plastic.

"You've thought of everything, haven't you?" Ava said accusingly. Picking up the fork, she tested the tines, bending them as far as they would go without breaking.

"Yes." Kingston could see the wheels turning in her mind. She was thinking about how she might attack him with a plastic fork. If it injured him badly enough, she could make a run for it. He chuckled and said, "You won't get far, Ava. Even if you managed to stab me in the eye with that fork, I'd still catch you. So, instead of entertaining silly notions of escape, you should eat. Who knows? Tomorrow, I might decide you don't deserve a meal at all."

Ava threw the fork down onto the tray and scooted back until she was flush against the cot's iron headboard. Surrounded by fluffy pillows, she glared at him as though he'd betrayed her. "I'm not hungry."

Her stomach growled, belying her words. She pushed her

fist tight against her belly as if hoping she might silence her body's protest.

Kingston regarded her for a long moment. "After your bath, then."

Ava's fist relaxed, dropping to the bed beside her. Her fingers twisted nervously in the coverlet, her relief almost tangible. "Yes. After."

Rising from the chair, Kingston held out his hand. "Come along."

Ava's eyes widened as she stared up at him. At six foot two, he knew his height would be intimidating to a woman of her size. She was a slender thing but also perfectly proportioned with sleekly toned limbs and a flat stomach. The top of her head barely reached his shoulder.

She ignored his outstretched hand, her brow furrowed. "What?" Her eyes landed on the spot inside his wrist where she'd bitten him, the reddish-hued teeth marks against his tanned skin.

"Bath first, food last." Kingston snapped his fingers as if summoning a favorite pet. The sharp sound echoed in the quiet of the cell. "Now, Ava. My patience grows thin."

"You don't mean..." Her voice was thin with incredulous horror.

"It's precisely what I mean. I assume you did not bathe earlier due to your injury, so I will help you. Once I've drawn your bath, we'll wash your hair."

"Wash my hair?" She repeated Kingston's words as if making sense of a foreign language.

"Let's get you in the tub."

"*Tub?*" Ava shrank away until she was in danger of tumbling off the far edge of the cot. "I-I'm not taking a bath with you in the *same* room!"

"You prefer a shower then? Perfect. I've showered once

today, but a second won't hurt. Probably easier, anyway. I can soap you up all at once."

In the next instance, Ava scrambled off the bed, darting from corner to corner like a butterfly confined in a glass box. Kingston observed in silent bemusement as she sought to escape. Just where in the world she thought she might go, he had no idea.

Then she sprinted for the bathroom, slamming the door behind her with a thundering bang. There was a panicked sob of relief as she barricaded herself within the luxurious room.

Kingston was in no rush as he approached the door separating them. It did no good to flee him, especially within this cell. The only lock was on the main door. And he held one of the two keys to that deadbolt within his pocket.

Leaning a shoulder against the thick door, Kingston rapped lightly with his knuckles. "Little lamb, little lamb, let me come in..."

"Go away!" Ava cried in response to the macabre taunting. *"Go away!"*

"You can't keep me out, Ava." He could tell she had her weight pushed against the other side, her uninjured hand tightly gripping the knob in case he tried turning it. "There's no lock on this door, and even if there were, I'd tear down any obstacle between us with my bare hands. Now, voluntarily open this door and let me run your bath. Every second you hesitate only adds to your punishment."

"Punishment?!" she screeched in outrage. "You are insane... I'm not letting you *punish* me for rational behavior. Anyone with half a brain would do whatever necessary to escape you. You cannot punish me..."

Kingston laughed softly. More than inciting his lust, she was actually beginning to amuse him. "Oh, but I can. And I will after we've dispensed with this bath business. Don't you want to wash away the imprint of my brother's hands upon your skin?"

There was a moment of silence, then Ava blurted out, "Yes! His and *yours*. I want to erase you both. One is as bad as the other."

Scrubbing his chin, Kingston experienced a twinge of anger. He was a bad man, this was true, but Oliver was sadistically cruel.

And Kingston didn't like being lumped in with his brother.

"Open the door. Now, Ava. I'm done asking. It will go worse for you if I'm forced to break it down."

Something in his tone must have frightened her into being somewhat reasonable. The bathroom door's knob turned, then it inched open just a little.

The moment Kingston stepped through the threshold, a heavy bottle of shampoo flew through the air. It struck a glancing blow to his temple and bounced off. Next, a bottle of conditioner hit him in the chest. A chunky bar of soap struck his midsection a split second later.

Through the barrage of toiletries turned into weapons, Kingston saw Ava positioned in front of the built-in nook. She went through the items systematically. Throwing each one with the precise aim of a professional baseball player.

Tears streaked down her cheeks, but there was also that same grim determination he'd witnessed in his office. She was fierce and scared and half-wild, and the thought of taming her made Kingston's dick harder than it had ever been for a woman.

Instead of dodging the missiles, he strode straight toward her and halted her in mid-throw. Grabbing her uninjured wrist, he held it tight.

"Let me go, you bastard," she seethed while twisting and turning. "Let me go this instant."

"No chance of that now, little lamb." Kingston chuckled low in her ear. Spinning her around, he pulled her arms behind her, her wrists anchored in one large hand at the small of her back. Using his body, he shoved her flush against the wall and held her there. "I warned you how much I love it when you struggle. Now, you must deal with the consequences."

He gave her heart-shaped rear a couple of rapid slaps with the palm of his hand. Then, as she processed the sting of those unexpected strikes, he wrapped his arm around her waist. He pushed against her with a low growl of appreciation as she yelped in surprise.

Firm and round, her ass was made for spanking. And if she didn't watch herself, she'd get the full force of his hand on her bare bottom.

Ava stopped moving when his cock rubbed her backside.

"You can't do anything with me... You can't do... *that,*" she choked out. "Not if you expect to sell me off."

Kingston considered her words, squeezing her wrists harder than he probably should. "It is a conundrum, I'll admit. Especially when I wonder what fool would pay more than two million dollars for a woman. Perhaps I'm setting myself up for failure."

"Well, you're the idiot who took me to force repayment of a debt. So, now who's the stupid one?" Ava turned her head from the heat of his lips brushing her ear.

"Perhaps we should see what you are worth?"

She froze in place, her body crowded by his, his larger form swallowing hers. He could take what he wanted from her, but oddly enough, he hesitated.

Reluctant admiration for this girl curled inside Kingston. She was bravely foolish, even while teetering on the very brink of a breakdown.

He was fascinated by her, never imagining she would be

like this. She'd always been meekly obedient. A quiet, sweet girl. The perfect daughter. The favorite of her parents and a despised younger sister to her older brother. She could do no wrong and had been doted on since birth.

A true princess. Tormented by her cruel prince of a brother.

And a tiny part of Kingston hated her for having the things he'd been denied in life. Attentive parents. Security. A sense of belonging.

Love.

"There's one way to discover if you are worthy of erasing your brother's debt," he murmured, settling his mouth in the curve of her neck. Her scent was of desperation and honeysuckles, her hair a soft tangled mess brushing his cheeks. When he licked her, his tongue tracing from a spot below her ear to the round softness of her shoulder, Ava whimpered.

"Please, don't."

Kingston's lips curved. "Beg me. Maybe I'll listen."

The cruel taunt galvanized Ava. She almost succeeded in jerking free of his grasp, but Kingston's arm tightened around her waist. When he slowly released her hands, she immediately gripped his arm.

"Go to hell," she raged, digging her nails into his muscled forearm as it pressed harder against her stomach.

The sting of it made him laugh.

But most of all, it made him hard.

"Not without experiencing a slice of Heaven first." He spun her around and saw the startled confusion in her eyes. "There are so many ways I can take from you, Ava. And none of them diminish your value as a virgin." He brushed his knuckles over the soft curve of her cheek.

Her teeth sank into his index finger.

Kingston did not even flinch. Instead of shaking her off, he bent his head to the spot where her neck met the slope of her shoulder. The need to tame her was a roaring fire in his blood. The desire to dominate surged into an overpowering lust.

He bit her there, his teeth finding the softest part of her. Although there was sure to be a mark left behind, he carefully avoided breaking the skin. He only wanted to bruise her, not maim her.

Ava screamed.

The moment her teeth released him, Kingston raised that same hand and wrapped it around her throat.

Squeezing until she hovered on the edge of choking, he leaned away and stared into her eyes. Eyes now dark green and hazy with pain.

"Wicked little lamb," he drawled, smearing the blood from his finger onto the skin of her throat. "Do that again. I dare you. Because I have a particular contraption that will solve this problem. Once I strap it on you, it will keep that mouth of yours completely open and make biting impossible. Then I'll use that sweet hole for my pleasure until I come down your throat. Do you understand me?"

Kingston waited until her head bobbed in an almost imperceptible acknowledgment. For good measure, he flexed his fingers in case she doubted he meant every word before slowly letting her go.

Ava stumbled backward, catching herself against the edge of the vanity counter. Coughing, she rubbed her neck and watched him as warily as one might a lion on the prowl.

Bloodied, disheveled, injured, and terrified, she looked like she'd been in a battle. In some respect, she had. But there was no winning the war in this case. Kingston would emerge victorious every time.

"Now, back to the business at hand," he stated calmly, turning on the tub's faucets. "Remove your clothing, Ava. Don't make me strip you. Knowing how Carson has treated you over the years, I can't imagine you would enjoy that sort of thing. I'm happy to oblige if you want it handled that way, but you should know something. I don't do gentle. I will hurt you and enjoy every minute of it."

The reminder of her brother's cruelty had her eyes widening with remembered fear. And Kingston knew a sudden urge to find that man. To break him in two. To make him suffer. To make him pay for the things he'd done to Ava in their years of growing up. He only knew half of Carson's mistreatment of his little sister, but it was enough to exact revenge on Ava's behalf.

Why he cared was disturbing on its own.

She likely considered resistance but, instead, Ava briefly closed her eyes. A shudder of defeat racked her body with the realization of her helplessness. She would be compliant—at least momentarily.

"I won't give you the pleasure of ripping my clothes off." With a shaky hand, Ava undid the button to her shorts, then shimmied out of them. Next, she pulled the black tank top over her head, tossing it aside. Now clad only in a pretty pair of silky black underwear and matching bra, she straightened to her full height and glared at him.

Kingston tested the water's temperature, his eyes roaming her delightful body. The fullness of her breasts encased in lacy material made his mouth water. "All of it." He motioned with an impatient hand, fingers twitching with the urge to stroke her skin.

"Creep," Ava muttered beneath her breath as she undid the front clasp of the bra. She hesitated for a second, then let it drop. The underwear was next, and when she was completely nude before him, Kingston approached her once more.

She trembled but did not move as he ran a hand across her collarbone and down to the peak of one breast. Her nipples were tight buds of pale pink, contracting both from his perusal and the coolness of the bathroom.

"Your punishment and my taste of paradise," he murmured while tweaking her flesh between bloodied fingers. Her moan of despair filled the room as he pinched the peaks harder. When he cupped her other breast within his palm, smoothing it with a soft caress, she swayed unsteadily against him. Fear and hunger were taking a toll on her body, leaving her pliable and accepting in the numbness.

Before he changed his mind, Kingston bent over her, sucking one nipple into his mouth. Laving the tip with his tongue, he savored the sweet taste of her flesh.

Ava cried out in alarm, arching her back.

It was like waving a red flag at a bull.

Confirmation that she wasn't completely immune to whatever had sparked between them.

She's fucking exquisite.

His cock was hard as stone, straining against the zipper of his suit pants. Somehow, Kingston restrained himself from doing anything more than tasting her breasts before stepping away.

Catching her chin in his hand, he forced her to meet his gaze.

"Goddamn, Ava. I would fuck you right here on this bathroom floor if it wouldn't cost me two million fucking dollars."

Her face flushed an enchanting pink, embarrassment and dazed arousal staining her skin. She looked good enough to eat alive.

"You disgust me," she replied woodenly, her chest heaving with the words. A curious light in her eyes indicated confused desire and hatred for her own body's betrayal.

Kingston knew the truth, however. She'd liked his mouth on her. She couldn't hide that fatal revelation.

"Better watch your fucking mouth or I'll put it to good use." He ran a thumb over her bottom lip and then forced it into her mouth. Daring her to bite him. "Maybe you would like that, after all. Maybe you want me to shove myself past these pretty lips. Feeding you my cock." The action of his thumb mimicked his words, thrusting and withdrawing until her lips closed around the digit with an agonized groan of surrender to his persistence. "Fucking your throat until you choke on me. I'd make you swallow every drop of cum I unload into this beautiful mouth. Is that what you want, Ava Blue?"

Ava shook her head, her green eyes wide and glassy with the filthiness of his words. Smiling, Kingston removed his thumb from her mouth, then slowly sucked it as though savoring her.

Ava hesitantly covered her body with crossed arms. Confusion flooded her features and she stood awkwardly under his perusal.

Kingston clucked his tongue in mock dismay.

"Don't you dare hide from me. I own you for the time being, and I like looking at my property. Drop your hands this instant or I'll bind them behind your back."

A fierce battle of wills erupted. Ava's eyes flared with rebellion, but eventually, her arms dropped to her sides. She stood like a statue awaiting placement, rigid and unbending. A chess piece in an age-old game.

A lowly, lovely pawn for the moment.

"Get in the tub," he finally said.

When she brushed past him, Kingston admired the perfect globes of her ass. They glowed a faint pink from the swatting he'd given her a few moments ago. How beautiful she would be with his handprints marking that pale skin.

A strip of soft, blonde curls adorned her pussy, and she quickly turned away in a belated effort to hide that part of her.

Ava's body was made for sin. One crafted specifically for fucking. The curves of her hips called for a man's hard hands, those long legs designed for wrapping around a man's waist as he plowed deep inside her.

How many of her brother's friends had seen her beauty? How many had stroked the perfection of this girl's body? Kingston knew there'd been at least three men present that night in Judd Vanderhoff's bedroom with Carson standing guard and collecting the money. It stood to reason there were more incidents like the one Kingston had declined to attend.

Although she was definitely still a virgin, there was no denying Ava had suffered abuse. And her parents had been woefully ignorant of Carson's actions.

But the tragedy of Ava's past would not keep Kingston from recovering the money he was owed. If anything, he believed she would be more pliant and complacent in accepting her fate. She was already preconditioned for exploitation. Already submissive to it.

And Kingston would use that to his advantage.

There would be no problem recovering every cent of the money her brother owed him. The men extended an invite to make offers would throw away ungodly sums for the chance to own such beauty. And she would do as she was told.

Ava settled into the tub, sinking low into the water as the faucets continued running. Kingston retrieved the bottles she'd hurled at him, setting a few on a low bench by the tub. The rest were returned to the shelves.

She sat with her knees drawn up to her chest, arms resting atop them with the injured one being favored. Staring straight ahead, she watched the flow of water from the faucets as if mesmerized.

When Kingston pulled the bench closer and sat on it, she did not acknowledge his presence. For a long moment, neither said a word. Ava's gaze remained fixated on the water, and Kingston's eyes were glued to the lush creature he'd stolen.

Turning off the faucets, he dipped a large sponge into the water, lathered it with body wash, and smoothed it across her shoulders. Silently, he worked, washing her back and her arms, which she steadfastly refused to remove from around her knees.

Gathering her hair into a mass within his fist, he tipped her head back. With his gaze locked on hers, he washed her throat, erasing his bloody handprint. Soapy water cascaded over the bruise where his teeth had marked her.

"I hate you," Ava whispered fiercely.

Kingston's lips quirked as he forced her arms apart. She chewed her bottom lip as the sponge drifted over her chest. Across her plump breasts. Encircling the rose petal-pink areoles. Down the center of her body to her flat belly. The muscles there quaked as he washed her, his gaze fever bright with needy lust.

"I know, little lamb. I know."

CHAPTER

SIX

*B*ut my heart knows better
It twists and squirms
Excited by cruelty
Ruled by the savage

AFTER BATHING HER, washing her hair, rinsing her clean, and drying her off, her captor unceremoniously and with a great show of detachment, dressed Ava.

Now curled into a ball on the cot, Ava's good hand tightened into a fist. Pulling the virginal white nightgown closer around her body, a tear slipped down her cheek when she remembered how Kingston bathed her.

It was an unimaginable violation. Made worse by the way her skin warmed beneath his hands. The sponge glided over every inch of her body. He never broke eye contact with her while forcing her legs apart so he could cleanse her even there.

Her thighs clenched at the memory of the sponge passing so carefully over those private areas. A shameful tingle shuddered through her. Why the violation affected her like this was a confusing tangle. She *hated* him. Hated how effortlessly he controlled her. Hated how weak she became when he touched her. The man was a sociopath. It sickened her that even a hint of attraction existed between them.

He tidied up the cell while she huddled on the cot, her knees drawn up to her chest. Why lower himself to such menial tasks? The man was as rich as the devil himself and just as cruel. He could afford a hundred servants to clean up. He probably had dozens upon dozens just waiting to be told what to do.

Maybe he didn't trust any of them around her. Her jaw tightened. Kingston was smart. He wouldn't chance letting her slip through his fingers now that he had her.

"Sit up."

His rough voice startled her. She'd become so lost in her thoughts she hadn't realized Kingston's attention had turned to her once more.

"No," she said in soft defiance. It was foolish, provoking him like this. But she could not be an obedient little toy. She wouldn't make this easier for him. Nibbling on a fingernail, she watched him warily.

Kingston sighed heavily. Her refusal was obviously a disappointment but one he must have expected.

"I welcome the opportunity to make you obey, Ava. It excites me, if you must know the truth." He spoke so casually he might have been discussing the weather. "Making you do the things you don't want to do. Forcing my will upon you. Even when you fight me, I find myself intrigued. Every bit of it makes my dick hard." He was close enough to touch her now. A huge palm stroked her hair although she tried ducking away. "So, keep defying me. I want you to. Because I will likely give in and fuck you. I'll risk losing the money, but having you force my hand will make that loss easier to bear."

Ava sat up as he commanded. "What do you expect? That I will smile pretty and act like we're dating? Ignore the fact you abducted me? Drugged me. Injured me. Violated..." her voice cracked. "I'm not a little doll. Or a puppet you can control. You may have me trapped at the moment, but I will escape." Her eyes narrowed. "Even if I must kill someone to make that happen."

Kingston's head tilted.

"That fire right there—that sweet, little flame beneath an otherwise meek exterior. That will certainly be your downfall," he mused, sitting on the edge of the cot. Capturing her chin in his palm, he studied her. "It's absolutely fascinating. Mostly because I don't recall ever seeing you so bratty and defiant. Never knew you to stand up for yourself. Or to fight back."

"It was ten years ago that my father worked for you," Ava replied sullenly. "And even if you were Carson's friend, our own paths rarely crossed."

"If you want me to admit I watched you, I did, indeed." He grinned. A Devil's grin containing zero shame. "All the time, although I shouldn't have. I wondered what you would do if I kissed you. Made those virginal white panties of yours wet for me. I wondered if you would push me away or pull me close."

Ava's thighs quivered at the thought of Kingston touching her. "My dad would have had you arrested. He *should* have had you arrested. My parents could not have known how much of a monster you were. What an animal you would turn out to be."

"They liked me well enough. If anything, they should have paid more attention to their own son's activities and his treatment of you." Kingston tilted his head to indicate the tray of food still waiting for her. "I want you to eat something now." A twist of a smile transformed his lips. "Other than your own fingernails, that is."

"I cannot eat." Ava grimaced at the mention of her nervous habit. "I don't expect you to care, but the thought of food is nauseating."

"A side effect of the drugs. You need something in your stomach." He pulled the tray onto the cot until it was between them. "Shall I feed you?"

"Shall I bite your fingers off if you dare try?" Ava replied in a sweetly acidic tone.

Kingston chuckled. "Didn't you get a big enough piece of me earlier? And have you forgotten what I'll do if you attempt it again?" He wiggled the index finger marked by her teeth. It was a wound much worse than the nip along the inside of his wrist. "Should I worry about rabies, my fierce little lamb?"

Ava did not answer. The reluctant admiration in his tone confused her. Why did it sound as though he were inordinately proud she'd injured him? Her thoughtless actions should have resulted in rage. Not approval.

He reached out with that same hand, blunt fingers stroking the bruise now forming along the crook of her neck. Marks in the shape of his teeth. "Now, eat."

Ava snatched up one half of the sandwich and took a bite. Her stomach roiled in protest, but she swallowed it down and took another.

"How long have I been here?" Ava asked around bites of the sandwich. She hated to admit he was right about the nausea subsiding.

Kingston consulted a very expensive-looking wristwatch. "Time does not matter to you, but it's been three days since you arrived here at The Den."

"And you intend to keep me prisoner until my brother pays you." It was a statement, not a question.

Kingston's eyebrows rose. "Or until he doesn't."

Ava's lips tightened. "Then you'll sell me off if he doesn't come up with the money."

"It's no worse than what he intended."

Ava's gaze shot to his. "What do you mean? Carson and I have not spoken in more than a year."

"Do you think I'm the first to think of using you to cover his debts?" Kingston replied smoothly. "The difference is I will take great care in vetting all interested parties. Your brother would simply take the highest bidder. I'm not the only man he owes money, Ava. I just happen to be the one he owes the most, and my prime interest is in seeing that debt paid."

"Carson would not..." Ava choked out in horror. "We may not be close and he's an awful person, but he would never do that to his own sister."

"You sure about that?" Kingston's smile was cruel. "Sibling relationships can be so complicated."

Ava said nothing. In truth, she knew Carson would go to any length if it meant maintaining his lifestyle. He might even sacrifice the sister he hated for reasons she never understood.

"You're getting the picture now, aren't you?" Kingston tenderly tucked a strand of her wet hair behind her ear, but Ava was not fooled by his mock gentleness.

"You won't get away with this," she whispered, shrinking back from him. "People will be looking for me."

"Like your new employer at the Savannah Literary Society? You already sent her an email saying how much you regret not being able to take the job. A sudden family emergency will take you away indefinitely. That weak loser you dated back in Bitter Springs? Drake Cornerstone received your text two days ago. The one where you told him you want a fresh start in Savannah. You asked him not to contact you as you would be extremely busy over the next few months. And besides, there was never any real chemistry between you. Don't worry, you also apologized for breaking it off in a text." Kingston smiled angelically. "Minor acquaintances will be dealt with as they arise, but Ava, darling, no one will be looking for you. However, take heart in this. If Carson pays the money, I'll release you. My involvement in your life will be done, and I won't care what Carson does with you at that point. Maybe you can convince him not to hand you over to the other men he owes money."

Ava's chin tipped higher with the realization of Kingston's words. He had effectively erased her existence while revealing a frightening bit of information. Her brother would use her as payment. Even if this particular debt was satisfied, he still owed other people. She might have to relive this nightmare a second time.

No matter who held her prisoner, she was no longer safe.

"I'm going to be sick," she calmly announced as the small bites of sandwich boiled up into her throat. And she must have looked sufficiently green because, without a word or even a moment's hesitation, Kingston swooped her up into his arms.

He had her positioned over the toilet just seconds before everything came up. As she retched, she became vaguely aware of Kingston crouching beside her. His broad shoulders almost blocked out the light fixture overhead. Indeed, there was barely enough room in that separate toilet room for the two of them.

He hovered. Rubbing her back. Murmuring sympathetic assurances. Holding her hair as she vomited. Tending to her as though he were the most considerate, loving boyfriend in the world.

The thought made her even sicker.

Pushing him away with her injured hand, she ignored the shooting pain and shrieked, "Don't touch me! God, don't you dare touch—"

"Let me help you," he replied calmly as though she were not a hysterical mess.

Ava's stomach heaved again as she began crying. It was truly her lowest point since this whole ordeal began. On her knees before her enemy, vomiting helplessly while he fisted her hair into a loose ponytail.

"Go away," she groaned in a singsong voice full of defeat. "Goawaygoawaygoaway…"

Kingston paid her no heed, of course. The devil stayed at her side, although he did fall silent. When she finally collapsed in exhausted despair, he simply stroked her back, holding her hair away from her face.

When he helped her back onto her feet, his hands were gentle but firm.

Ava had no strength left to fight when Kingston murmured in a soft voice that did not accept defiance, "Let's get you cleaned up. Then it's back into the safety of your cage, little lamb."

SEVEN

L*ittle lambs fight back*
    Winning the battle
      Losing the war
  Casualties of greed

AVA'S OUTBURST apparently disturbed Kingston. He frowned while she brushed her teeth in short, jerky movements, a flicker of reluctant concern lighting his dark blue eyes.

Wetting a cloth, he washed her face. While he was gentle, Ava did not trust that for a second. Even in her dazed state, she sensed the violence in the hands tending to her.

"I'll send Doctor Abbott to see to your wrist and give you something else for the pain. There's medication which will also settle your stomach," Kingston said, his arms full of the towels from her bath as well as her dirty clothing. "I'll leave the food in case you'd like to try eating again. And I'll have Chef prepare your favorite soup for your supper."

Ava curled up on the cot. "Of course, you know what my

favorite soup is, don't you? You know everything there is to know about me. Even things I have no awareness of." Her voice came out wooden and flat.

Kingston's lips tightened but he did not respond. He simply gathered up the silver tray and dome, aware of their usefulness as weapons. Then he exited the cell, locking the door with a decisive click and leaving Ava alone once more.

"Asshole," she whispered beneath her breath.

As she lay there, gathering her strength and wits for what seemed like the hundredth time since she woke up in that man's hard lap, she realized something. Something Kingston had not considered.

Perhaps he'd thought her too incapacitated, or too innocent to consider something so devious and calculating, but he'd left behind the glass bottle of Cheerwine.

The soda bottle was perfect. Heavy enough to bludgeon someone over the head, small enough to be easily handled. And if it broke, the jagged glass would prove much deadlier than a lightbulb stuck in a lamp socket. Or a desktop paperweight.

Ava's spirits lifted as she stared at the bottle, her mind racing with plans. There was probably no hope of using such a weapon on Kingston, but perhaps it would work against the doctor. The element of surprise would be in her favor, provided the man came alone during his next visit.

I can do it when he comes in. Take the key and lock him in here. I can find a way to the outside and I'll run.

Never mind she would escape wearing nothing but a thin nightgown. Never mind she had no money. No identification. She didn't know where she'd been taken or what state she was in. It was possible she was no longer within the United States.

Without the means to see outside, all those things were unknown elements. But it would not stop her from trying.

And once she was free, she would take the remaining money from her inheritance and use that to disappear. She would go somewhere far away from the clutches of both her brother and the handsome psycho determined to sell her for his own gain.

But if she intended on succeeding, she must eat something. Going so long without food was affecting her. At the moment, her head was so fuzzy. There was no telling when she might be given another meal. And if she were caught in this escape, Ava had no doubt Kingston would withhold all comforts until she fell in line and did as he commanded.

Picking up the sandwich, Ava forced herself to nibble on the corner and chased that bite with a swig of soda. Heaving a deep breath, she willed her heart to stop racing and her stomach to settle. She must calmly consider what might be encountered once she was past that cell door.

There could be others in the corridor. There could be more locked doors preventing escape. But no matter what obstacles she faced, she would not stop until she was free.

She could do this. She *must* do this.

There was no other alternative.

After drinking the entire bottle of Cheerwine and eating the sandwich, Ava dozed fitfully. Several hours passed before the key scraped in the lock.

She was as ready as she ever would be.

Gripping the bottle tight, she leaped from the bed and ran on bare feet to stand beside the door. Raising the makeshift weapon high overhead, she waited until the man's head appeared.

It was the same doctor who tended her previously with a

kind smile and gentle hands. Remorse tickled her insides but that sentiment was quickly shoved aside. She must be ruthless.

He came through the portal, set his bag on the floor, and turned with the intent of locking the door behind him.

Ava struck without mercy, swinging the bottle down as hard as she could muster. It did not shatter like she'd hoped, but Doctor Abbot groaned and staggered back, holding the crown of his head. The keys fell from his hand, landing with a clatter on the stone floor.

There was a momentary pang of remorse, but Ava brushed it away and quickly grabbed the keys. The next instant, she darted around the doctor and swung the door shut behind her.

Her hands shook as she quickly tried the keys in the lock until she found the right one.

"Wait, Miss Blue. Please, don't run from him..." Doctor Abbott implored from inside the cell. "You don't know what he will do..."

Ava ignored him, locking the door and reveling in the sense of accomplishment flooding her.

I did it! I actually did it!

But there was no taking a victory lap just yet. She still needed to escape the building.

The corridor was long and dimly lit. Iron sconces like the ones in the cell adorned the stone walls, and the air was chilly and damp. It was also eerily quiet.

"Which way should I go?" Ava muttered. Neither end of the corridor looked promising as a way out. Taking a deep breath filled with adrenaline, she made a split-second decision and took off in the direction she hoped would lead to freedom.

Damn Kingston for taking her clothes. Wearing a nightgown certainly was a disadvantage when eluding pursuers.

She almost cried with relief when she rounded a corner. There was a set of stone stairs. The thick, dark grey slabs led to a small landing and a door matching the one to the cell. It had to be the way out.

The door opened easily, and the contrast between the dark, cold corridor and the room she fell into was startling.

It was a brightly lit space, old world but modernized with sleek furniture and gleaming light fixtures. It appeared to be some sort of small foyer. Maybe a mud room. Another door existed on the far side of the space, and through the glass panes, Ava could see a well-maintained lawn in the last bloom of summer. The tree line of thick hardwoods was adorned with fading green leaves. Some already carried the first blush of fall color. Rolling mountains were visible on the horizon, and Ava's heart seized with panic.

This prison was far from the flat, sandy coastline of Georgia or her hometown of Bitter Springs in New York. But the terrain appeared similar to upstate where her family once had a summer cabin in the Adirondacks.

There was a security keypad on the wall by the door. Ava ran to it but did not bother attempting to input a code she did not know. Fumbling with the deadbolt lock, she flung the door wide open, fully expecting a siren blare of alarm.

There was only a steady, low-key beeping indicating the door had been opened. With a frantic glance behind her, Ava rushed outside.

The first thing she realized as she sprinted across the lawn was how cold it actually was. Clad only in the thin nightgown and a pair of panties, the chilly air cut straight through to her bones. But she did not care. She was free. And if she could reach a nearby road or a neighbor, she would beg for their assistance. Call the cops. Report Kingston Winter for what he'd done. Then she would disappear into anonymity.

There was no driveway or anything in this area, which would indicate a heavily used portion of the grounds. It was nothing but a wide expanse of lawn and distant trees. Curious to see just what she was escaping, Ava glanced over her shoulder to see the rear of the house.

It was a mansion. No. It was far more than that. It was literally a castle. An imposing structure of turrets and grey stones. Its massiveness made Ava dizzy. The door to freedom had opened into a side yard and, from where she stood, the full glory of the building was apparent. Multiple terraces extended away from the house, spread out to take advantage of the views and the terrain. One terrace contained an infinity-edge pool. It was so enormous it might have been lifted from an exclusive five-star hotel and plopped into the space here.

The whole of it was beautiful. Frightening. And sinister.

But nothing surpassed the horror of seeing Kingston. He leaned casually on the low stone wall of one terrace and simply waited until she saw him. Even from this distance, Ava recognized the flash of his smile in the encroaching twilight.

He found her escape attempt amusing. Or perhaps that was just the expression he affected right before torturing and killing his captives.

Ava froze in place like a deer caught nibbling in someone's garden. For a long moment, the two of them simply stared at one another. Then Ava's heart pounded within her chest again and the blood in her veins screamed at her.

Run!

Ava whirled away, sprinting for the trees. Once she reached that thick section of forest, she would hide and creep out later when it was safe.

If she didn't freeze to death first.

"Little lamb," Kingston called out, his tone mocking and laced with excitement. "There are wolves in this forest. And the biggest one is coming for you."

Ava ran faster, chest heaving as she finally reached the

trees. She crashed through the forest, weaving through elms and oaks. The undergrowth was not too thick but still cut at her feet, the rock-studded terrain forcing her to slow down occasionally. It seemed she ran forever before, eventually, she came to a halt in a little clearing and leaned her shoulder against a slender elm.

Gulping in huge breaths of air, she rested. Sweat dotted her brow despite the cool air. She listened carefully for any signs of pursuit, but there was only her own labored breathing and the trilling of sparrows settling into their nests for the night.

Ava glanced down at herself. Low branches had ripped several holes in the gown she wore, and one capped shoulder was torn until it hung off her arm. There was also a cut on her knee, courtesy of a tumble over a half-hidden rock ledge. The fall jarred her injured wrist, and she knew once the adrenaline wore off, it would be very painful.

She should keep running, although she had no idea which way led to safety. The density of the woods was foreboding. Glancing up at the darkening sky, a frisson of fear tingled throughout her body. She would soon be alone in this cold forest. In the dark. With no compass to point a way out.

"Have you had enough excitement for one afternoon?"

Kingston's voice rumbled from behind her.

With a shriek, Ava spun around. He stood at the edge of the clearing. Not a single strand of his dark hair was out of place. His clothing was crisply pristine and bore no evidence of a mad dash through the forest. It seemed he had materialized out of thin air. Or maybe straight from the pages of a GQ magazine.

The one thing striking Ava the hardest, however, was the gleam in his sapphire blue eyes. He looked both hungry and triumphant. The waning daylight glinted off the steri-strips closing the cut on his upper cheekbone.

Her vision swam at the sight of it and *him.* This man

enjoyed hunting her through the forest. And his obvious skill at it was terrifying.

"Stay away from me," Ava choked out, holding out a hand as though she could ward him off.

"I don't think I'll do that. In fact, I plan on coming even closer. Hoping you'll run again so I can keep chasing you. It's quite exhilarating."

"You're crazy!" Ava shouted.

"Yes." He laughed. "Crazy to think you wouldn't try escaping so soon. What a surprise you are, Ava Blue. A blood-thirsty, murderous, wicked little lamb."

Murderous? I couldn't have actually killed Doctor Abbott. I did not strike him that hard. Regret swelled inside her. She truly had not meant to hurt the man too badly.

"I'll kill you, too, if you don't let me go," she bravely declared, pushing away the remorse at taking another man's life.

Kingston's head cocked. "Do you think you killed Neil?" He chuckled, striding toward her as Ava backed away. "Oh, don't worry. You did not harm him too badly. His pride took a beating more than anything." Those cold, dark blue eyes swept her, taking in the ripped gown and the blood seeping through the material from the cut on her knee. "Do you like being hunted like an animal, Ava?"

She refused to answer as he sidled closer, but her feet automatically moved in the opposite direction. Back, back, back until she stumbled and caught herself against another tree.

"I like hunting you," he admitted with a wicked grin. He began rolling up the cuffs of his dress shirt, revealing muscled forearms. Ava swallowed hard at the implicit threat of violence conveyed by such a simple action. "I like chasing you, hearing your frantic breathing. Knowing you're scared of me. I like knowing I'll catch you. And I really like what happens next."

Internally, Ava was already coiled into a tight spring, ready to bust out running again. Being lost in the woods was a far better alternative to being caught by this man. She feared her reaction to him. So much so that she questioned her own sanity. What sane, normal woman would enjoy being caught by a madman?

"What happens next?" she whispered, dreading the answer but morbidly curious. Her mouth was dry with fear mixed strangely with excitement.

His lips curved with amusement.

"Punishment."

EIGHT

C ome into my arms again
And let me set you free
While the stars shine bright.

Kingston laced his hands behind his back, studying Ava closely.

She truly was prey at this moment. Lust, anger, and that annoying bit of admiration swirled together in his gut while he contemplated what he would do once he got his hands on her. Of course, he could not fuck her senseless like he wished, but there were other ways of ensuring she obeyed him.

The chase left him with an aching need to conquer. And this girl, this little bit of a girl who continued defying him would now experience a taste of his wrath.

"If you can escape this little clearing, Ava, I'll show a bit of mercy. When I recapture you, as I undoubtedly will, I'll conduct your punishment here. In these woods where no one will hear your screams. But if you cannot get past me, we'll see to matters back at the main house. It's all up to you."

Ava's eyes were such a bright green, they glowed in the twilight. Dark blonde hair tumbled over her slender shoulders, and her hands clenched into fists at her sides. That virginal white gown he'd purposefully dressed her in was ripped, dirty, and bloody, but Ava somehow still managed to give off the air of a goddess.

He wanted to sink balls deep into her and never come up for air.

"Which will it be?" he asked evenly.

Kingston knew her intention immediately. Knew which way she would run probably before she even realized it herself. Instead of darting in the opposite direction of where he stood, she sprinted to the left.

As she made her move, Kingston snagged an arm around her waist, hauling her back against him.

"Not quick enough." He laughed softly in her ear as she pounded his chest and shoulders with her good hand in a frenzied attack. She landed a couple of blows to his chin, but the strikes certainly did not hurt. If anything, they inflamed his appetite.

His rough hand coiled in Ava's hair, pulling so tight the strands were in danger of being yanked out by the roots.

"Stop. Let me go this instant," she gasped in pain.

His chuckle was a sharp rasp in her ear. "Make me. Go ahead. I dare you to try."

"You're a bully." She snarled as he reeled her in closer. "A monster. A pitiful coward forcing yourself on someone who despises you."

"Yeah?" His drawl was unconcerned. "Maybe. But one thing's certain. I'm gonna fuck that sass right out of you if you keep this up."

His threat did the trick. Ava's lips clamped shut.

With efficient brutality, he untangled his hand from her hair, grabbed the torn sleeve of the gown, and ripped it free.

"My wrist..." Ava moaned as the strip of cloth was wrapped around her hands.

"Should have thought about that before. Did your wrist hurt when you bashed my friend over the head with a bottle? Did it pain you when you were running from me? Running from the safety of your cell?"

"You maniac," Ava breathed in outrage. "Safety? I'm not crazy enough to think I'm *safe* as your fucking prisoner."

"There you go using that word again. I'm beginning to think that's just what you want me to do. You want me to fuck you until you are a trembling mess."

She screamed then, fueled by fear and more than a little bit of rage. And Kingston loved it. Loved the primal way she expressed herself in that moment. Loved her loss of control and the way it made his dick hard.

She lunged away, but Kingston wouldn't let her go now. Although he would keep his vow of punishing her at the house, he was too inflamed by his own bloodlust to let her behavior pass without tasting her.

His mouth crashed down upon hers, hard and brutal. Taking what he wanted as she squirmed helplessly, it was a clash of teeth and tongues and need. Fear and desire. Lust and desperation.

Kingston had never tasted anything so sweet. Ava's mouth, her flavor, her scent, it was all addictive. He wanted more.

He wanted everything.

But when her teeth scored his lip, the surprise of it loosened his grip. She spun away in a flash, scrambling to escape.

Kingston quickly hooked her feet with his own, sending her crashing to the ground. But still, she would not stop in her attempt to get away. She crawled on her belly through the clearing's thick grass in a frantic bid for freedom.

Kingston grinned. This was becoming more fun by the minute.

"Naughty lamb. Do you really think you can escape that easily?"

He landed on her, sliding an arm beneath her and lifting her to her knees until she was captured back against his chest once more. Then he captured her wrists in one hand and raised them above her head, carefully encircling them.

"You forgot, Ava. No biting. Remember?" His breath brushed the curve of her neck. His lips trailed over the softly fragrant flesh, his nose nuzzling through her hair until he found the nape of her neck. With an impatient movement, he swept her hair aside and latched his mouth over the tender spot.

He sucked hard, and when she lurched forward, his teeth kept her in place. While she writhed and sobbed, he left his mark. One only he would see. Fuck, it might be worth it to have the impression of his teeth tattooed there, or even better, he'd brand that tender place along the curve of her shoulder where he set his teeth before. Maybe he would. Show the world that she was once his. And when she was no longer his prisoner, her new owner would know she'd been his pretty, little toy and nothing would change that fact.

"Please..." Ava begged, her body straining away from his.

Kingston laved the injury with his tongue, soothing it and licking away the tiny drops of blood.

"Oh, Ava. Can't you feel how hard you've made my dick?" He ground his erection against her lower back, their height difference readily apparent in this position. He could shove her forward, face first into the grass, but that would put pressure on her wrist. As cruel as he was, he could not bring himself to do that.

And he really shouldn't, but he also could not stop from roaming a hand over the front of her body while slowly rotating against her. A groan rumbled in his chest when he cupped each full breast in turn, tweaking her nipples through the gown's fabric.

Ava's sharp intake of breath inflamed him, and for a brief second, Kingston reconsidered pushing her down into the dirt and burying himself inside her. His body throbbed. Demanding fulfillment. Release. Her surrender.

His hand slipped to the hem of the gown, jerking it higher so his fingers could find the space between her thighs. But his touch turned tender as he slid beneath the panties he'd given her to wear. The thin scrap of fabric was hardly an effective barrier.

"You're so frightened, and yet, you are soaked for me. Does the fear excite you, Ava? Do you like me touching you like this? Your body says you do." His index finger glided around her clit then dipped inside her in shallow exploration. "I'm the first man ever to do this. The first to finger-fuck you. The first to make you delirious with lust. Isn't that the truth? Answer me, Ava."

"Yes," she hissed in fierce defiance. "But not the first bastard to take what isn't his to take."

Kingston licked the side of her face, catching her tears with his tongue and savoring every salty drop. "But you *are* mine, Ava. Mine to torment for the moment. Mine to use as I desire. Mine to fuck however I want."

"And risk losing the money my brother owes you? All because you want to... sleep with me?" she gritted out between gasps of pleasure. Kingston knew she was getting close to climaxing. Her body was shaking, the words harder to form. Fear had heightened her senses, leaving her vulnerable to any stimulation. Wanted or unwanted, it didn't matter. *He* controlled her response.

"I'll get every penny he owes out of you. And I don't want to sleep with you, Ava. I want to fuck you. Big difference." He plunged his finger in harder, deeper, certain he was close to breaching her hymen but overcome with the need to mark her inside and out. Stupid, considering his plans for her, but totally necessary in this moment of tears, sweat, and blood.

Ava arched away with a panicked cry, but Kingston pressed his hand hard against her pussy. With just a little exertion, he guided her back until she was flush against his body. His cock was a rod of steel, begging to be unleashed. Begging to plunge into his little captive.

"You're sick," she gasped.

Kingston chuckled. "What does it say about you, Ava, when your pussy is so wet for me? Every time I touch you, your body seeks more. Dripping with want. With need. Squeezing my fingers with that sweet little cunt, begging me to fuck you until you explode."

He gathered up her slickness then brought his index finger to his mouth and sucked it clean. "You taste just as I imagined. Like ripe peaches."

His hand slid back between her legs again, rubbing her clit in soft, teasing circles until a helpless moan escaped her throat and her hips bucked toward his hand.

"Will you scream for me, Ava? Will you scream as I destroy you?" Very quickly, he learned just how hard to press, how softly to glide, and with relentless intensity, he drove her to the brink of climax while she sobbed in protest of her body's betrayal. "Come for me right now. Here in the dirt. Here with my cock hard and weeping for you. Accept your punishment and come now around my fingers, my bloodthirsty lamb."

Kingston's finger hooked inside her, his mouth latching onto the nape of her neck as he drove her to a shaking orgasm.

He nearly came in his own pants when her release rolled over her. The low, trembling cry of shamed satisfaction, the terror lacing the notes as the truth of his words tore away her defenses made his cock swell to impossible proportions. She hated him, feared him. But she also wanted him, and that was almost enough to make Kingston forgive her brother's debt. Fuck if he didn't want to keep her for himself.

Maybe he would.

She panted heavily from the whirlwind he'd created, shaking in his arms. Could it be that was her first ever orgasm? Or had she pleasured herself in the past? His jaw hardened with selfishness. It was irrational, but he wanted to be the source of all her pleasures. He wanted to own her climaxes. Her body. Her soul and her mind.

"There, there, Ava. See? It's not complete torture having my hands on you. You just came for me like a good girl. So sweet. So fucking sweet."

Her arousal dripped down the inside of her thigh, and he smeared his fingers through it before bringing it up to her mouth.

"Taste what I do to you." His breath was hot against her ear, but Ava shook her head in denial. Her lips clamped shut.

She moaned as he tried forcing her mouth open while keeping her bound hands raised high above her head. With a muttered curse, he squeezed her injured wrist just hard enough to elicit a pained gasp and successfully thrust two fingers past the barrier of her teeth.

"Lick my fingers clean, Ava. And if you dare bite me again, I'll fuck you to within an inch of your life. Then give whatever is left of you to my men. All of them. Including my depraved brother."

With a choked sob, Ava did as commanded, her tongue swirling around the digits with the skill of a whore. She licked and sucked until Kingston couldn't take another second of her unwilling compliance.

He rose to his feet, pulling her up and spinning her around in one quick motion. Bringing her hands down, he held them captive between their bodies, pressing them against the slabs of his abdomen. Her fingers flexed, digging through his dress shirt as she grabbed him for balance.

"Do you like the taste of yourself, Ava?" He smirked, moving his free hand to her throat and squeezing gently. In the dim light, he saw the flush on her cheeks and the tears staining her creamy skin. She was goddamn gorgeous in the aftermath of her orgasm. "I think next time, I'll make you lick yourself off my cock. I'll spread your juices all over me and enjoy you cleaning up the mess."

Ava's green eyes blazed with hate and rage. "Try it and I'll bite it off. I won't care what you do to me afterward because I'll have the satisfaction of knowing you are nothing more than a dickless monster."

Kingston actually laughed at that. Pulling three zip ties from his back pocket, he quickly fastened one each around her wrists before linking them with the third. He did not remove the makeshift binding of the torn strap from her nightgown. Those stayed in place as a cushion against the hard plastic straps. "I do admire your spirit, Ava. It's misplaced and stupid, but you really do amuse me more than I thought possible. It's going to be difficult letting you go when the time comes."

Your name is written
On my soul.
My heart.
Across my skin.

THE TREK back to the main house was undertaken in silence. Ava stumbled behind Kingston as he led her like a pack mule through the brush and around trees. When it was necessary to climb over rocky formations, he either took her arms and helped guide her, or he simply lifted her and carried her.

She did not bother fighting when he did that. She didn't have it in her... not when her feet ached and stung with various cuts and bruises. Between that and the superficial cut on her knee, she was utterly exhausted.

She'd been through so much over the last few days. The worst being the moment Kingston swept his hand between her legs and sent her tumbling into insanity. Remembering how easily she succumbed to his cruelty made her lips form a hard, straight line. The man was the very Devil himself.

And she hated him with every thread of her being.

"Whatever you hoped to accomplish by undertaking this little afternoon jaunt was a wasted effort," Kingston finally said, breaking the silence. It was dark now, although the light of a bright, full moon penetrated the canopy of trees. He had a pen-sized flashlight in his back pocket that supplemented the moonlight. "The whole of the estate is almost twenty-five thousand acres, and the direction you were headed dead ends in a huge lake. I won't even mention the security fence around the property. Your escape attempt was dangerous and stupid. Especially dressed as you are and with your injury."

"How did you find me so quickly?" Ava asked sullenly. She knew her actions were foolish. She didn't need the man gloating over her failures.

He pointed at an oak tree, and for the first time, Ava saw the blinking, red light of a tiny camera high in the branches. Her heart sank.

"They are all over the estate, including the main house."

"I suppose they are in the cell, too. So you can spy on your prisoners like the pervert you are." Ava's voice was bitter as she stared at his back. The scathing accusation was ruined by the chattering of her teeth.

"There are no cameras in the bathroom, if that's what has you worried." He did not address her statement directly, however.

"This whole nightmare worries me!" she cried out, digging her feet in and coming to an abrupt halt.

"I've neither the time nor the patience for your hysterics, little lamb," Kingston muttered, whirling around and scooping her up into his arms. "While true wolves in these woods are unlikely, there are bears and coyotes. And you are near freezing, as it is."

Ava could not deny that. She hated herself for snuggling closer to the comforting heat of his body. It wasn't because she *wanted* to. It was a necessary evil. Besides, she had no choice. His arms were like steel bands, and there was no escaping his hold.

"Hold on tight." The directive carried a note of mocking amusement and Ava's irritation grew.

"Untie my hands," she snapped, then clamped her teeth together to control the chattering.

"And repeat my mistake in granting you too much freedom? Too much comfort? No. You'll stay bound just as you are. Loop your arms around my neck if you are worried about falling out of my arms."

"Go to hell."

He stopped suddenly with a heavy sigh, and Ava's heart pounded. It was really stupid to keep antagonizing him, but she'd apparently lost all control over her own mouth.

Setting Ava on her feet, Kingston quickly stripped off his shirt, wrapping it around her. It billowed like a blanket, gloriously warm from his skin, but Ava was struck speechless by something else. The sight of inky black tattoos, intricate tendrils and elaborate lines swirling across Kingston's flesh had her eyes widening.

The design was both savage and beautiful. A crooked crown sat upon a snarling lion's head with ears pinned back. Sharp fangs dripped with blood and were situated directly over his heart. One fang gleamed more brightly than the other. Thorny vines twirled and crept over bulky muscles and smooth planes, entwined around and through the crown, lion, and even around one coppery brown nipple before creeping down to flirt with the indentations of his ribs. Something was inscribed along his left flank, but in the moonlight, it was too dark to read.

Ava's fingers itched with the desire to trace every line and swirl. To discover the meaning behind each mark. A man like Kingston did not brand himself with frivolous decoration. There was a purpose behind the tattoo covering only the left side of his body, and God help her, Ava wanted to know every detail.

"Do you want to put your arms around my neck now, or maybe continue staring at me like I'm your next meal?" The mockery in his voice snapped Ava back to awareness.

"You arrogant ass, I'm not staring at you." She glared up at him. "And for your information, I'd rather put my arms around a snake."

The devilish glint in his dark blue eyes competed with the moonlight. "I can arrange that." He pressed closer, reminding Ava how hard and unyielding he was. How big his cock was. When she shuddered, it had nothing to do with the chilly air.

Lifting her bound hands, Kingston unceremoniously placed them over his neck, then slipped an arm beneath her knees, hefting her back up against his chest. "You know, eventually, I'll do something about that smart mouth of yours. And if you don't start calling me 'Sir' as previously instructed, it will only get worse for you."

Despite her best intentions, Ava snuggled closer, enjoying his warmth and angry that she found comfort in his steady heartbeat beneath her cheek. But she was so very tired and her feet were so sore that any thoughts of resistance melted away.

"Haven't you done enough?" Ava murmured as he resumed his deliberate stalking through the woods. "Sir." The word dripped with all the insolence she could muster.

Ava was certain Kingston's mouth brushed the top of her head in a fleeting caress before he softly replied.

"Not enough, little lamb." His arms tightened around her. "Not nearly enough."

Oliver was waiting on the lower terrace when they arrived back at the house. Five or six other men lingered around him. A couple of them were smoking cigarettes, while the others simply leaned against the terrace wall and watched their approach.

"We were just about to send out a search party," Oliver said jovially as Kingston ascended the stone steps. "But it seems you had no issues retrieving our prized possession."

Ava turned her face further into Kingston's shoulder, letting her hair fall around her face so Oliver was no longer in her line of sight.

As much as Kingston frightened her, his brother was far worse. Hatred boiled beneath the amicable surface, and the evil in the man's stare when his eyes tracked over her made Ava shiver.

"How is Neil?" Kingston asked, brushing past Oliver and continuing toward the house. Maybe it was Ava's imagination, her exhausted state playing tricks, but she thought Kingston squeezed her against his chest just a little bit tighter.

As though he were subconsciously shielding her from his brother.

"He'll live. And lucky for our prisoner, he's not even holding a grudge. Says he understands why she bashed him over the head with a soda pop bottle." Oliver chuckled. "He insists he doesn't want her punished because of this."

"That's my decision. Not his."

Oliver grinned. "I reminded him of that. We all know you don't ignore transgressions of any sort."

Kingston nodded at one of the men, who quickly jumped forward to swing open a set of French doors.

Ava took a quick peek as they entered. This was a different area of the house than the point of her earlier escape. This room was oversized, outfitted with two deep, chocolate-hued leather sofas and several occasional chairs upholstered in a soothing design of taupe and cream. A warm fire crackled in an enormous stone fireplace, and the walls were decorated with works of art. Valuable works of art, Ava realized. Degas on one wall. Monet on another.

The space was opulent yet understated, and every inch of it screamed of wealth and privilege.

But Ava was unable to fully appreciate the beauty of it all. Kingston did not linger. He continued through until he reached an open set of double carved-oak doors on the far side of the room. He strode through those then turned down a wide, high-ceilinged corridor lined with floor-to-ceiling windows. Nothing could be seen through those windows other than the blackness of the night beyond.

"I can walk," Ava said in a low voice, wishing he would set her down on her feet and yet dreading that moment. "Sir," she added in hopes of appeasing his anger.

"Not just yet, lamb," he murmured, then called over his shoulder, "Oliver. I want all the men assembled in the conference room. Five minutes."

Peeking over Kingston's shoulder, Ava made eye contact with Oliver, who trailed in their wake. The man smirked at her.

"Sure thing, brother."

"Including Doctor Abbott."

A chill snaked its way through Ava. Would Kingston return her to the cell first before addressing his men? She hoped so, but he continued winding down various corridors, past various rooms, some with the doors closed, some open and revealing lavish furniture and trappings. She began to suspect this meeting had something to do with her.

And her thwarted escape attempt.

Her teeth were chattering again by the time Kingston reached what must be the conference room.

It wasn't a conference room like one might expect. It certainly wasn't one you would find in a corporate building for a Fortune 500 company. No, this was in keeping with the rest of the mansion's décor. It was dark. Masculine. Opulent and yet sleek. It was a room where life and death decisions were made and all by a savage king hellbent on keeping power and control over his subjects. Including herself.

Without speaking, he set her down on a gleaming table which appeared to have been stolen straight out of a vampire's lair. The heavy mahogany rectangle dominated the room. Eleven matching chairs carved from the same wood were assembled around it.

There was only one chair situated at one head of the table. The opposite end was conspicuously empty.

Kingston lifted Ava's bound hands over his head and let them settle in her lap.

When she tried sliding off the table, he gripped her waist and easily pushed her back. "No," he murmured. "Stay where I place you."

Ava frowned as he resettled his shirt around her shoulders. Running his forefinger under her chin, he lifted it until she met his eyes.

Hungry determination lit the blackish-blue depths. And it was crazy, but Ava thought the tattooed lion on his chest snarled with even greater ferocity.

Now that she could see it in the light, she realized the artwork really did serve a purpose. It covered a scar of some sort. The thin, jagged white line about five inches in length over his heart made up one of the lion's fangs. And she could read the words tattooed across his ribs now.

Crush~Conquer~Protect

The words made no sense in Ava's jumbled state of mind. Dragging her gaze back up, she witnessed a grim expression as it crossed Kingston's features. She shivered with belated fear and awareness. This man was capable of doing such terrible things to her, and there was no one who would dare stop him.

"What is happening? Why haven't you returned me to the cell?"

"So eager for its protection now, Miss Blue?" A reluctant smile tugged at his lips.

She did not answer, instead turning her head away as men began filing into the room. Kingston's tone confused her; it was soft but resolute. Like something horrible and wonderful all the same time was about to happen.

There were about fifteen men in all, and at Kingston's nod, they filled the seats. The overflow of men stood lined up along the walls.

Ava recognized only a few of the men. Oliver, of course. Doctor Abbot, sporting a white bandage on his forehead. Paulie, who was scowling fiercely. And Jack, the giant of a man who helped hold her down on Kingston's desk the day she arrived.

The other men regarded her with varying degrees of interest. Some did not bother hiding the lust in their gazes. They stared without shame at her sitting in the center of this medieval table like a prized kill from a hunt.

"Ava."

Kingston's voice swung her gaze back to him. His jaw was tight as he regarded her, and Ava's chin lifted in defiance.

"Sir," she spat in response.

"Are you ready to accept your punishment?"

Ava's heart stuttered in its beat, fear curling inside her belly. "Punishment? But the woods. That was my punishment. You said…"

"I said if you could escape the clearing, I would punish you there when I caught you again," he interrupted with a cruel laugh. "You did not escape the clearing, remember?"

Ava clenched her teeth, the events in those woods a tangled mess of words and actions in her mind. "But what you did to me. It was enough…"

"Fuck, King. What *did* you do out there in the woods with Miss Blue?" Oliver laughed, his light blue eyes raking over Ava's form with rampant lust. "Something dirty and depraved, I'm sure. Something our father taught you, perhaps? She's pretty bruised and banged up. Just like we like them, right?"

"Quiet, Oliver," Kingston snapped before reaching out and pulling his shirt away from Ava's shoulders. Tossing it aside, his gaze drank in every aspect of her tattered state. "What happened there, Ava, had nothing to do with your escape. That was for me because I wanted it. *You* wanted it."

Ava sat up straighter, despite the torn nightgown falling so far off one shoulder that her breasts were nearly exposed. She glared at Kingston. "You're a monster."

Kingston smiled, taking a seat in the one chair at the head of the table. He pushed back far enough that there was space for a person to stand between his outstretched legs.

"So you've repeatedly said." His gaze flicked over his men, his tone turning cold and hard. "All of you, join the others along the wall and face it. Except you, Neil. You have the right to take part in the punishment. Once I'm done with her, you may have a turn."

There was the scraping of chairs pushing back, and the men who were seated now rose as a group. Turning their backs to the table, they lined up against the wall like children forced to stand in the corner for punishment. Even Oliver did as commanded, his mouth a tight line of petulant obedience.

Neil remained in his chair, his eyes trained on Kingston. Ava did not know if she should be grateful for the fact the other men would not witness her disgrace or not. Her hands began shaking as she worried about Kingston's intentions.

"Ava, come here." Kingston's voice was the voice of a conqueror and one she did not dare refuse. How could she when he stood as the only barrier between her and the lust of fifteen men?

This wasn't just retaliation for her daring escape. This was a demonstration of Kingston's power. His rule. His dominion over those he commanded. And it enforced the fact she was safe only with him and even that was a capricious benefit. He could throw her to his wolves at any time.

She slipped off the table with as much dignity as she could muster with bound hands and moved until she stood before him, captured between the table and his chair. Standing between his outstretched legs like a sacrifice to a pagan god.

"Kingston..." Neil muttered, his gaze remaining on Kingston only. "I don't want her punished. She did what any other normal person would do. Of course, she ran. She's in survival mode. Don't you understand that?"

"Oh, I understand. And I understand Ava Blue better than she does herself. But you see, this... this is a necessity." Kingston's gaze flickered back to Ava. "On your knees. Now." He unbuckled his belt. It slid free from the pants' loops with a quick snap.

Ava stood transfixed, staring at the leather strap now doubled over in Kingston's hand.

He wouldn't dare... not here. Not like this. Not with these men in the room. Watching. Panting. Licking their lips like animals hungry for blood.

My blood.

The air thickened, heavy with anticipation. Dripping with the combined lusts of men. Soaked in the desire of a king and those he commanded.

"Knees, Ava. Now." Kingston's voice lowered. "Or shall I instruct them all to turn around?"

There was no disobeying that voice. That cruel, cold voice held no hint of amusement or indulgence. Ava trembled but slowly sank to her knees in front of him. A bewildering cocktail of rage, curiosity, and disbelief swirled inside her.

Kingston unbuttoned his pants with one hand, his gaze locked on hers, his mouth a thin line of need.

Neil stood so quickly his chair nearly toppled over.

"You're wrong for doing this, Kingston," he snarled before joining the others against the wall. "I want no part in it."

"Suit yourself," Kingston drawled in response, giving the doctor a cursory scowl at his defection before his attention swung back to Ava. "Come closer, lamb."

A sob bubbled in Ava's throat, but she shuffled between his legs until his knees could close in on either side and keep her trapped if he wanted.

"Closer," he whispered. She obediently inched forward until her shoulders were even with the inside of his thighs. "Keep your hands in your lap. Now, I'm going to give you a choice in this matter. You'll receive your punishment from either myself or one man in this room. Do you understand?"

"This can't be happening..." Ava whispered beneath her breath. "This can't be real."

Kingston laughed softly. "Make your choice, Ava. We can't expect my men to remain staring at the wall all night. Who will it be? Me or one of them?"

It was cruel to throw such a choice in her lap. One was just as bad as the other.

"I don't want to choose. It's sick. Depraved." Her voice trembled.

"Ah, but you must." His head tilted. "Unless you'd rather pleasure all of us?"

Ava stared at him in horror. He actually meant that. The reality of her situation was abruptly smothering. She couldn't breathe, and yet there was no avoiding what was about to happen.

"You," she choked out in a rush. "I choose you."

How could she make any other choice? Kingston knew she would select him—he only gave her the semblance of control as a way of mocking her.

Kingston nodded, a pleased expression crossing his features. "Very smart of you, Ava. Very smart."

Ava closed her eyes when she heard the unmistakable rasp of a zipper.

"Look at me, Ava."

Her eyes snapped open. Morbid fascination crept over her delicate features when Kingston withdrew his cock from his trousers. He roughly stroked a hand down its enormous length.

"Do you know what I'm going to do now?" His voice was deadly soft.

Ava shook her head, her mouth dry with terror and something else... something confusing and dark. This was completely new to her. She'd only seen a man's penis in movies. But never in real life. Never touched one. Or even thought of touching one. How could something that appeared so threatening, something used as a weapon against her, also be so terrifyingly beautiful?

Kingston's cock was long and alarmingly thick. Delicate veins tracked up its underside, and the crown was fat and wide. The skin resembled the softest silk, and the dark hair of his groin area was neatly trimmed.

Ava's eyes rose. Her gaze clashed with his and she shook her head. "I-I can't do this…"

Kingston stroked himself again, squeezing the thick, mushroom-shaped head between his fingers. "You can. And you will."

The breathing in the room increased. Ava realized that even if each man's back was to her and Kingston, they knew what was happening. And they were excited by it. She glanced in their direction, but Kingston's whip-sharp command startled her.

"Do not look at them. Look only at me, little lamb. They will not see what is about to occur, but they can hear. And they won't dare turn around unless I tell them to." Releasing his cock, Kingston suddenly looped the belt around the back of Ava's neck, using the ends to pull her toward him and hold her in place. "This will keep your eyes where I want them. On me."

His eyes were nearly as black as the shadows of the room, the pupils blown wide with lust. Ava found herself lost in their velvety depths, lost in his soft, terrifying words as he explained exactly what he was going to do.

"I'm going to fuck your mouth. That's your punishment, Miss Blue. I'm going to come down that sweet throat of yours, and you will allow it. And if you think of escaping me again, if you dare try it, I'll give every man in this room a chance to experience this same pleasure from you. Do we understand one another?"

She could not find the words for a response. Terror struck her mute until the belt tightened around her neck.

"Do you understand?" Kingston repeated.

"Yes," Ava stuttered as he pulled her closer until her mouth hovered over his cock.

She *must* do this. She must pleasure him as he demanded.

And she would, too, if it ensured his men were not free to abuse her as well.

She forced herself to concentrate only on Kingston and not the beasts lined against the walls listening to this depraved punishment. Kingston's spicy sharp scent of pine and ocean surrounded her, his even breaths drowning out everything else. It was a vacuum of sight, hearing, and aromas, and she melted into it.

Only Kingston existed inside this den of lions.

Kingston.

"Open your mouth." A thumb slid over her bottom lip, rubbing back and forth. "Wider."

When her lips parted, Kingston let out a low groan of approval. Then his cock was sliding between her lips, the belt holding her hostage so she could not back away. Panic overtook her for a brief second. She could not properly breathe, and he stilled completely, allowing her a moment to adjust and evaluate what it meant to have a man filling her mouth.

He tasted like fresh linen and musk. Salt. Flesh. Insanity. Possession.

"Relax your throat and breathe through your nose. That's it. There's a good girl. Just like that," Kingston murmured in a rough voice.

He pumped in shallow motions, slowing when she gagged, giving her a precious few seconds of recovery before resuming with leisurely intent. Rather than thrusting up into her mouth, he used the belt to pull her down onto his cock, releasing slightly so she could withdraw, then forcing her back down.

"I know you've never given head before, Ava. But you are so fucking good at this." He pulled her closer, holding her in place for a long moment, her mouth full of him, her breathing held hostage as he dominated her. He wasn't even all the way inside, but still, the thick girth and length choked her. "Another of your firsts I've claimed."

He let her go and Ava fell back, gulping for air while staring at him over the muscled slabs of his stomach.

"More," he growled, and Ava hated herself. Because that single word and all it implied twisted inside her until *she* was the one who needed more. She did not understand herself. Could not understand why she was allowing him to do this to her.

She bent forward again, her mouth molding around his flesh, her tongue swirling in a tentative motion that wrung a satisfied grunt out of her tormentor.

Kingston's free hand meshed in her tangled hair, and he pushed her head down while also pulling the belt taut.

Too much...

Ava moaned at his roughness. Her teeth raked the head of his cock.

Kingston jerked her head back and half-shoved her off of him, glaring down at her.

"Were you feeling an overwhelming need to bite, little lamb? After all the warnings I've given you?" His fingers wrapped so tight in her hair that she could not move. His voice was a silken web of cruelty and simmering violence. He could snap her neck and not think twice about it.

"Please," Ava gasped in pain and surprise. "It was an accident. I've never done this before. Please... don't hurt me."

I hate myself for begging for his mercy. But what else can I do? Begging means survival in this den of madness.

"Fuck me," Oliver groaned from his place along the wall. "You're killing us, King. Goddamn killing us."

Still staring at Ava, Kingston addressed his brother. "Look this way even once, Oliver, and I will pluck out your eyes."

"Don't want us watching you with a woman like our father

did, Kingston? That was what he enjoyed most, wasn't it? Making us participate while he hurt his women. Women like my mother," Oliver snapped in reply.

"Shut the fuck up, little brother. I'm nothing like him, no matter how many times you accuse me of it."

Oliver chuckled, resting his forehead against the thick plaster wall. "Oh, don't kid yourself, King. We're *just* like him. Both of us. Depraved and damaged. You, because of what he made you do. Me, because I was forced to watch." Oliver may not have liked it, but he heeded Kingston's warning and kept his eyes trained on the wall. "We're sick bastards and you know it. Everyone knows it."

The men lined up did not dare turn around. Their heavy breaths filled the room. There were groans of frustration. The subtle shifting of bodies as erections were adjusted and crotches tugged. Whatever Oliver was talking about, his references to their childhood and the awful things Kingston did at his father's command, was swallowed up by the increasing aggression of the room.

An animalistic tension was growing, and Ava was acutely aware of it. Kingston's men were disintegrating into some sort of feral state, driven by lust and instinct. Hunters in pursuit of prey. Hungry enough to snatch a doe away from a lion and rip her to shreds in a sexual frenzy.

"How long is this punishment gonna go on?" Oliver muttered. "Because I gotta go jerk myself off after this. Me and all the other blue balls pressed against this goddamn wall."

Kingston either did not care what his men were experiencing or he was supremely confident in his ability to control them. He never turned his attention away from Ava while ignoring his brother's complaints.

"An accident?" Kingston breathed, repeating her stammered excuse. Dark blue eyes blazed with molten fire as he stared down at her. Then his lips twisted into a cruel smirk. "All right. Do it again. Slowly." His hand pushed her head back toward his erection, forcing compliance. "Put your hands around the base and tease the tip with your tongue and teeth."

Flushing pink from the dirtiness of the order, Ava wrapped her fingers around him and did as he asked. He groaned heavily, his hips jerking upward.

She hollowed out her cheeks, sucking him deeper.

A guttural, completely animalistic growl escaped him. A loss of his perfect control.

"Squeeze me tighter, goddammit. And suck, little lamb, as if your life depends on it. Because right now, it does."

He began thrusting harder into her mouth, his breaths growing more ragged as his control frayed at the edges. Ava simply held on, a strange, dark need erupting inside her, the space between her thighs throbbing for attention. If only she could touch herself. Rub away and erase this burning ache with her own hand.

Her mind flashed to that moment in the forest. When Kingston made her come on his fingers. The first time that had ever happened for her...

"Fuck yes, Ava. *Fuck...*" His curses reverberated through her body as his muscles tensed. His grip tightened in her hair while, simultaneously, he also pulled the belt until she had no choice but to open wider and accept every inch of him.

She couldn't breathe. Couldn't cry out. Couldn't break free. He was choking her with the thick length of his cock, and she couldn't push him away.

And a dark, hidden part of her didn't want to. Not really.

A second later, Kingston erupted in her mouth. Hot streams of fluid shot down her throat with such force she nearly gagged.

"Fucking hell. Swallow me, Ava." His voice was evidence of

his loss of control. It was harsh. Shattered. Tortured. "Swallow every goddamn drop..."

She whimpered and choked, doing her best to obey, even while she pressed her legs together to stem the shameful trickle of moisture there. Oh, God. Something was wrong with her. Something broken and twisted. Depraved. How could her body find this degradation so arousing?

"Goddamn," Kingston exhaled as his orgasm faded away, leaving behind an indolent, satisfied beast. "You really are a good fucking girl, aren't you? My sweet little lamb. Sucking my cock so thoroughly you damned near drained me."

The belt slid away from her neck, and Kingston's hand released the grip on her hair. Finally, finally, she was permitted to lean back. With bound hands, she tried wiping her hair from her face, but the strands would not cooperate. They stuck to her skin, plastered in place by the silent tears streaming down her cheeks and the salvia that had escaped her mouth while he used it.

"You're gorgeous, Ava. So goddamn gorgeous," Kingston whispered, sweeping her hair behind her ears with gentle fingers before tucking himself back inside his pants.

Then he did the oddest thing.

For reasons Ava could not comprehend, at least not in her current state of dazed, aroused confusion, Kingston abruptly lifted her up from the floor. She was settled into his lap, his arms folding around her, hiding most of her body as she quaked against him in some kind of delayed reaction.

His mouth repeatedly brushed her temple in soft caresses. Her forehead. Her cheeks. Licking up the salt of her tears. And one brutally quick, extremely thorough kiss was pressed against her mouth, stealing her breath. His hand was gently threatening as his fingers splayed across her throat, ensuring she did not pull away from him as his tongue collided almost angrily with her own.

He must taste himself on my lips...

Then he rested his forehead against her own as though he required a moment of composure before leaning back to search her features.

Ava stared up at Kingston, recognizing the confusion in his dark, fathomless eyes. It mirrored her own internal turmoil.

"Everybody out. Now."

Kingston's quiet command had his men jumping to action. They filed out quickly, silently, and even Oliver said nothing as he exited the room, giving his brother a puzzled glance as he passed.

Once they were alone, Kingston's grip tightened. He pulled her head down until it rested upon his shoulder and his chin grazed the crown of her head. They sat there for the longest time.

Breathing. Processing. Analyzing.

From his pocket, Kingston produced a knife that opened with a flick of his thumb. Slicing easily through both the zip ties and the strips of fabric, he released her from her bonds. Then, he broke the strange truce which had fallen between them.

"You know what I think? I think, beneath that good girl façade is a bad girl dying to come out and play. Behind those wide, innocent green eyes is someone tired of the illusion of safety and ready to be wicked. Someone who hated being held down while her brother's friends tasted her breasts but finds what I do to her exciting. Arousing."

Ava sucked in a horrified breath and pushed at his broad chest as she struggled to sit up. "You're wrong. I-I'm not like that."

His blackish-blue gaze, the color of the darkest depths of the sea during a fierce storm, searched her face. "Am I wrong that when I shot down your throat, you moaned for it like a thirsty little whore? Am I wrong knowing that you wanted to push your own fingers into your sweet pussy? I know how badly you wanted to come. I know you would shatter in an instant if I touched the slickness of your hot little cunt right now. Admit it, lamb. You liked sucking my cock as much as I liked making you do it. And you looked so fucking beautiful choking on me. Oh, what a pair we are, Ava. Goddamn if we aren't made for each other."

TEN

*F*eather *soft and beloved*
Sunshine bright and warm
Tenderly destroying me

Ava languished in her enforced prison for days.

Kingston did not visit her. Not after what happened in the woods and then in the conference room. Despite his best attempt at indifference, he recognized a growing obsession and it terrified him.

He did not want to be attracted to her. Did not want this going anywhere other than the conclusion he envisioned. He wanted payment of the debt her brother owed and then he would wash his hands of the dangerously addictive Ava Blue.

That should be his priority. The objective. The end game.

But things were changing. His plans were not so concrete anymore. She'd been under his control for twelve days and already she'd thrown his life and everything in it into a whirl-wind. And it was stupid and irrational, but there could be no ignoring one simple truth. Ava wasn't safe out in the world on her own. She wasn't safe with her brother. She was hardly safe at The Den.

And she damn sure wasn't safe with him.

Since there'd been no word from Carson, Kingston wondered if the man would actually sacrifice Ava for the opportunity of wiping his debt clean. It wouldn't be surprising, considering the depths Carson had sunk to over the last few years. The man would do anything, including murder, to maintain his current lifestyle.

Sitting in his private control room, Kingston watched Ava on the wall of screens. She'd taken the books delivered a day earlier and was now methodically stacking them until they resembled a game of dominoes.

There were at least a hundred books, which resulted in a long, undulating row. After carefully positioning the last one, Ava knocked it over, setting off a chain reaction.

She studied the fall of each individual book as though fascinated by its role in the makeshift game. Kingston's head tilted when she stood up after the last one toppled over. She then listlessly climbed onto the cot and stared off into space, twirling a lock of hair around one finger. When she released the curl, she began chewing one fingernail again. Void of expression, her face was a blank mask.

I'm going to break her of that habit... one way or another.

Kingston's jaw clenched. He couldn't leave the girl in there much longer, not in this state anyway. She'd shut down on him that evening in the conference room, slipping into a distant world where only she existed. It was possible she teetered on the brink of madness.

And he was going mad keeping himself away.

What if he released Ava from the confines of the cell?

Maybe he could allow her the illusion of freedom inside The Den until her brother made a decision.

But could he trust his men not to touch her? That was an unanswered question, especially after what he'd done in that conference room. He'd worked them into a fevered pitch with that little exercise in depravity. There could be repercussions from that night. A price to pay for his own selfish actions.

Oliver was Kingston's biggest concern, but there were others who might think it was acceptable to take from their prisoner what he had taken. The only men he trusted not to betray him were Paulie, Jack, and Neil. And although they shared the other key to the cell between them, even their loyalty wasn't a guarantee in this murky world of greed and lust.

Kingston's hands clenched. He'd kill a motherfucker if anyone touched Ava without his permission. Murder a man with no remorse or pity. After Neil rejected the offer to punish Ava, Kingston reached a surprising decision. There would be no sharing of his prisoner before he sold her off. Because in this newfound, selfish obsession, he sure as fuck did not want anyone seeing Ava after an orgasm.

Running his fingers through his hair, Kingston sighed heavily. Stealing Ava seemed the best solution at the time, but now, he wasn't sure.

She was becoming a liability. A possession he didn't want to lose. A weakness he couldn't afford. A woman he thought about constantly. Especially in the dark of night when he had only the palm of his hand for solace.

Kingston studied the camera's live feed again, then abruptly shut the system down. He would go to her. Feed his lust before letting her out of her cage. It would only require the exertion of a bit of dominance to ensure she wouldn't run from him again.

Kingston passed Neil on his way out of the cell.

"She's fine," the doctor said with a wave of his hand. "The wrist has healed much quicker than I expected. Possibly due to her lack of activity. I'd prefer she refrain from using it for another few days and let me check it again."

"I'm glad to hear it." Kingston's reply was purposefully bland.

Neil frowned. "She needs out of that cell, King. You can't keep her locked away like this and not face some consequences. It isn't healthy."

"I know." Kingston's jaw tightened. "My hope is she will not be my problem much longer. Thank you for seeing to her welfare."

"Just remember, King, how you hated being a prisoner yourself. When your father ruled everything in your life."

Kingston waved the man away like a king irritated by a wayward subject. He fit the key into the cell's lock and turned it. "How can I forget?"

Ava's gaze was glued to the door when Kingston swung it open. The instant she saw him, she averted her eyes. Plucking at the comforter, she refused to meet his stare.

Kingston's jaw clenched. He did not care for this version of Ava. In fact, he preferred his prisoner's tendency toward feistiness intertwined with her fear. This defeated attitude was something he didn't like at all.

"Ava," he said softly, setting down the bundle he carried.

"Sir Jailer," she responded in a flat voice while cradling her wrist in her lap. The metal splint was gone, but somehow, she appeared even more frail without it.

His brow furrowed with annoyance.

"Come to me."

Her chin tilted in a show of rebellion as she ignored the command.

Kingston cursed beneath his breath, then approached as if he possessed all the time in the world. Grabbing her by the arm, he hauled her up onto her feet.

She sagged against him, eyes blazing with undisguised hatred.

"Do not provoke me, Ava. Unless you wish to spend God knows how long in here alone."

"What difference does it make? Either here or in another cell, I am still your prisoner."

"Yes. My prisoner." He tugged her closer and swept the hair away from her face, tucking the strands behind her delicate ears. "And I'm giving you a choice, lamb."

"Your choices are never to my benefit. You realize this, right?"

"Regardless, I'm giving you one now. Either stay here in this cell with your disobedience for company or take my offer."

"What offer?" Ava's voice was tight with suspicion.

"I will give you freedom in certain areas of The Den. With a guard, of course."

Ava's lips tightened. "Guard? Who would be given the task? Your brother?"

Kingston shook his head. "No. I cannot trust him with you. Even with his healthy fear of me, he would take what he wants and damn the consequences. When I am not with you, Paulie or Jack will accompany you everywhere you go. Until Carson makes a decision, this is the only offer I'll give you."

"And what must I give up in exchange for such generosity?" Ava snarled like a feral little cat. "There's certainly a price to pay. What will it be? Another blowjob with an audience? Or perhaps this time you will fuck me on your damn conference table and give everyone a turn after you've had your fill."

Kingston gave her a little shake, growling with frustration at the harsh accusation. "I'll slice the throat of any man who touches you, Ava."

"Then I expect a short list of applicants lining up to purchase me," she snapped in return.

"You will not be required to do anything for this taste of freedom other than obey me," he bit out. "Be a good girl and you'll get out of this cell. If you'd rather not accept my generosity, then you shall remain here indefinitely."

"Your generosity comes with strings," Ava replied stonily. "I don't trust you not to strangle me with them."

"Of course, you don't trust me. Why should you?"

Ava glared at him, unaware that Kingston was beginning to truly relish these interactions.

It'd been so long since he'd been with a woman who did not immediately follow his every command. And while he certainly preferred his women submissive, Ava's defiance was an alluring departure from the mundane.

"I did not come just to offer you this opportunity for liberation."

"Then why did you come?"

"To help you shave."

"Shave?" Ava shook her head in disbelief. "I don't care if the hair on my legs is long enough to braid. I'm not prettying myself up for you. Or anyone else."

Kingston grinned, truly amused by her sweet innocence. "I'm not talking about shaving your legs, lamb." His gaze drifted down her body, lingering at the juncture of her thighs.

Ava blushed, her jaw clamping tight with revulsion. "I'm not shaving *there,* either. Why should I?"

Kingston brushed his nose alongside hers and said with a murmur, "Because I want nothing else in my mouth other than the taste of you. If you don't do as I request, I shall do it myself."

She twisted in his grip. "And just how will you manage that?"

"You've seen the manacles in this cell. The ones embedded in the wall. I'll use them to get what I want. Spread you. Shackle you. Shave you. Now, either you obey me, or I will do it for you."

For a long moment, Ava simply glared at him, in a standoff of sorts. Then she gave a short, jerky nod of her head. "Fine. Where is the razor? I'll do it later when I take my bath."

"You will do it now, lamb." Kingston pressed his forefinger against her plump lips. "No arguments and no negotiations. I will supervise to make sure you, ah, don't miss a spot. And to make sure that blade is not used as a weapon against me."

The mutinous tilt of Ava's chin told Kingston she'd been planning exactly that.

"I should expect nothing less than your perversion, Mister Winter. Of course, you want to watch me."

He lifted her injured hand and pressed a mocking kiss to the back of it. "That's not all I intend to do, Ava."

The implications of his words sunk in, and Ava blushed an even deeper pink. "Let's get this over with."

Kingston released her and gathered up the bundle he'd carried in. It contained a change of clothing similar to the lounge suit she wore now, a women's disposable razor, and a straight razor—the type found in a gentleman's traditional shave kit.

Grabbing her by the hand, he led her to the bathroom.

"Here we are again," Ava muttered in a voice filled with bitterness. "You forcing me to take a bath for your pleasure. There's a word for that, you know. Pervert."

Kingston put the disposable razor in the huge shower and began unbuttoning his shirt. "No bath this time."

Stunned silence filled the room as Ava's eyes widened. She backed away from him. "Y-you aren't... You seriously don't intend on getting in there with me, do you?"

"Of course. How else will I ensure it's done properly? And also make sure you don't injure yourself?"

Ava hit the wall, her back flush against the marble. She looked terrified. And maybe even a little intrigued at the thought of him being in the shower with her.

"You realize you don't have a choice?" Kingston threw his dress shirt aside, his eyebrow raised as she continued standing there as if frozen. Her gaze locked onto the tattoo etched across his chest as he softly instructed, "Remove your clothes."

When he kicked off his shoes and unzipped his trousers, Ava closed her eyes and took a deep breath.

Shaking his head at her stubbornness, Kingston reached into the shower and turned on the faucets before returning to her.

"Ava." Kingston advanced slowly as if tracking a wild animal. Then he caged her with his hands braced on either side of her head, palms flat against the wall. "There's no escaping this. I will have my way. Disobey me and I will call a couple of my men to assist in holding you down."

Ava nodded, eyes still closed as Kingston's hand dipped beneath her shirt and splayed across her trembling stomach. Very slowly, he ran his fingers along the hem and began lifting it up. She did not struggle as he drew the shirt over her head.

Within seconds, they were both naked, and Ava's eyes locked on his as he led her to the shower. He stepped in first, pulling her alongside him.

This is a really bad idea. Really bad. Seeing her like this... Naked. Glistening. Vulnerable. I just want to bury myself inside her and own her. Keep her captive forever. Forget the two-point-six million she's worth to me.

He stood her under the rainfall showerhead, lathering up her hair with honeysuckle-scented shampoo. With gentle hands, he worked it into the tresses until, with a tiny sigh, her head fell back, giving him better access. After rinsing the shampoo clean, he leisurely soaped her body, his groan internal while his hands lingered over her curves.

She trembled but did not try to stop him as he explored her. Her gaze remained averted, darting everywhere but directly at him until he finally handed her the razor.

Ava took it and, after a moment's hesitation, placed a foot on the built-in bench and began the task of shaving her legs. The strokes were slow and careful, completed with only the rush of water breaking the silence. When she finished there, her attention turned to under her arms. A few quick strokes and she was done.

There was only one area left…

Then she stopped. Crossing her arms over her chest, Ava pivoted away from him. The disposable razor was gripped so tight that her knuckles shone white.

"I can't. I can't do… this… not in front of you." She swallowed hard, her voice trembling. "If you leave me alone for five minutes. If you just get out of this shower, I will do what you want. But don't make me do this in front of you."

Kingston slicked his hair back out of his eyes, the water sluicing over his face and across his shoulders. His gaze raked over the perfect heart-shaped form of Ava's ass and the mouthwatering flare of her hips.

She was fucking perfect, and he had a fucking hard-on despite his intentions to remain fucking unaffected.

"That's not the deal we made, Ava," Kingston admonished softly, reaching around her so he could shut off the water.

"You made the deal. I have no bargaining power. Remember?"

Glancing back over her shoulder, Ava bit her bottom lip in an effort to hold back tears. Her gaze fell to his cock and she choked on a sob.

Kingston enfolded her in an embrace, his jaw hard at the defeat in her tone. She was as stiff as a sail in a hurricane, and it angered him more than it should have.

His mouth pressed against her ear, and his cock, oh, hell, his cock was hard as iron against her ass. It throbbed painfully for her. "Come with me now, Ava. Don't fight me. There's little point in it."

She had no choice when he roughly gripped her by the wrist and pulled her out of the shower. With brisk, efficient motions, he toweled her off and then himself. He did allow her to keep that towel though. She quickly wrapped it tight around her body while he tugged his trousers back on.

Then he wordlessly dragged her to the wall where the chains dangled. The towel was yanked away. A rueful laugh escaped him as she tried shielding her body from the lust in his eyes.

"You should have obeyed me, Ava. Now, you have no control over what happens next." Kingston closed the shackles over her wrists, careful not to overtighten the metal enclosures.

When it became apparent he would do the same to her legs, Ava lashed out like a wild animal, kicking and sobbing with adrenaline-fueled fear. Her foot caught him in the knee.

Grabbing a handful of her hair, he jerked her head back.

"Kick me again and I'll break your leg. Do you understand?"

He pulled her hair harder until she cried out, "Yes!"

"Yes, what?" he crooned, rubbing his nose along her neck.

She smelled so fucking delectable; he was sorely tempted to give in and take what he wanted. To hell with two-point-six million. "Yes, *what?*" he prodded again.

"Yes, sir," Ava whimpered.

Bending on one knee, he calmly shackled her ankles while Ava sobbed in frustration at her own helplessness.

"If you are frightened, you should be. I don't like being disobeyed," he murmured.

"I know that. But I can't let you—"

"It's not about what you can and will not do, Ava. It's about what I want you to do."

He left her chained to the wall, her nakedness a shiny beacon in the cell's shadowed dimness. A second later, a flick of a hidden switch flooded her with a creamy pool of light. Disappearing into the bathroom, Kingston reemerged with several items necessary for the task at hand. Towels, shaving cream, and most importantly, his own personal shaving kit.

Pulling out the straight razor, Kingston caught a glimpse of the sheer terror in Ava's eyes.

"Kingston," she whispered, forgetting to use the title he'd demanded. "Please... don't."

Kingston stepped closer, appreciating the lovely picture she created. Naked, bound, her damp hair streaming like dark ribbons over her shoulders, her nipples contracting into hardened points he wanted to roll between his teeth. God help him, but the fact she was afraid of him and what he might do made his body ache even more for her.

"I won't hurt you unless you make me hurt you." He buried his hand in her damp hair, tilting her face so he could stare into her dark green eyes. He was gentler than he'd been moments before, recognizing the need to ease her fear.

His little lamb was scared, but at the same time, she could not hide her fascination. He recognized that glimmer of aroused fear in her gaze. She desired him, but shame kept her from enjoying anything he would do to her.

Kingston pressed a soft kiss to her mouth. "Be very still and this will be over soon."

"You're sick." Her whisper was anguished.

"Yes. We've established that." His lips moved to her cheek, kissing away the tears that dampened the tender skin. "We're all mad here. Isn't that the saying?"

She closed his eyes to his taunting.

Dragging a chair before her, Kingston sank into it and reached for the shaving cream. Ava's legs shook with finely wrought quivers as he slowly spread the cream over her pussy. His fingers speared through the tidy curls with thorough attention.

A gasp escaped her throat, her eyes flying to meet his as he moved closer between her legs. She was spread wide for him, the length of the chains affording little movement. Her hands curled into fists, and every now and then, she convulsively jerked at the restraints as if she could free herself.

"Did you know a shave with a straight razor is the closest you can get? I'd prefer having you waxed, but I doubt you'd lay still for that. It's somewhat painful the first time, or so I hear. Besides, I'm terribly possessive. I don't want anyone else to see you in such an intimate manner. Only I have that privilege."

He spoke in a low, conversational tone while opening the straight razor from its folded position. The handle was honed from ebony wood, and a gleaming blade crafted of inlaid Damascus steel gave the instrument a perfectly balanced weight.

He showed it to Ava, her face reflecting in the silver metal, then with a careful glide of his hand, whisked it through the cream. It barely skimmed the plump flesh, but the shiny blade was so incredibly sharp that it cut the soft curls down to bare skin with just a flick of his wrist.

While he worked, Ava held her breath, remaining as still as could be expected under the circumstances. Kingston exercised extreme care, wiping her with a hot washcloth as he went about the task.

Finally, he leaned back with a satisfied grin, passing his fingers over the newly shaven flesh. He couldn't resist the urge. She was so damned soft. So smooth and silky.

"There. All done, lamb. You were such a good, brave girl for me. So good and so brave, I believe you deserve a reward."

"You'll let me go?" Her question was laced with disbelieving hope. A tremble of something else rippled beneath the surface of her words as he continued stroking her flesh.

"No," he murmured. "But answer me honestly, Ava. Do you really want to be set free?"

"You cannot keep me forever."

"Can't I?"

Wiping away the last of the cream from her skin, he cleaned the blade on the cloth and then snapped it shut. He leaned back and stared up at Ava. With her cheeks flushed pink, eyes hazy with dawning need, she did not look away.

Kingston's gaze traveled her body. He saw soft, pink nipples budded into tight rosettes, the flat planes of her stomach quivering with anticipation. Evidence of her arousal glistened between her thighs. Heady and intoxicating, her scent filled the room, sinking into his bones.

Honeysuckle and dampness and want.

He inhaled deeply, and she mimicked him without conscious thought.

Fuck, she's as turned on by this as I am.

His fingers tightened on the straight blade and Ava's breath hitched.

"I'll ask again. Do you want to be free, little lamb?"

He saw very plainly the internal war waging in Ava's head. And the moment her resistance fluttered away in defeated tatters, reeking of confusion.

She shook her head slowly, licking her lips while staring hungrily at his mouth.

"I want you to say the words, Ava. Tell me what you want."

She hesitated, then sank into the manacles, gorgeous in her surrender, her eyes so dark green they were nearly black. Her breath came in soft pants for air as he turned the blade over in his hands. When her gaze drifted over the tattooed words scripted along his flank, the air between them shifted. Sizzled. Hummed with the energy of a lightning storm.

Crush. Conquer. Protect.

She had no idea how fiercely he lived by that motto.

He crushed his enemies. Conquered and took what they once held dear. Protected what he gained. It would be the same with Ava. If he allowed her to get close.

But that was something he could never allow, so he must content himself with little tastes of her and nothing more.

Unfortunately for them both, her words had a way of ensnaring him. Her capitulation to his desires and her own would be their mutual downfall. Kingston recognized this. He must resist her even as he took her.

"Here in this cell, I am yours." Ava's eyes glittered with the hard, uncompromising beauty of malachite. "Yours."

CHAPTER

ELEVEN

This body of mine
Aches for your touch
And the way you lash me
With words and deeds

A SENSE of relief overcame Ava as she placed herself in Kingston's hands.

But why was that? She couldn't say for certain. The man was dangerous. Unpredictable. And more than likely psychotic. She should fight him with every fiber of her being—especially after his vile threat of sharing her with his men. But outwitting Kingston Winter was exhausting.

And honestly? She could not deny the way her heartbeat jumped when he touched her. The way her blood sang in her veins. A strange blend of fear and lust drained any willpower to resist this man. She *wanted* him to touch her. Ached for it. Dreamed of it. Was restless for it.

Despite the insanity of it.

He would hurt her. Ruin her. Destroy and conquer her. She might not survive, but there was no eluding him. Her fate lay in his hands and, like a helpless peasant, Ava threw herself at the mercy of a king.

Kingston's gaze burned like fire, and Ava wondered if her capitulation shocked him. She'd fought him every step of the way during her captivity, and now, he appeared indecisive.

Then his lip twitched upward with a sinful smirk.

"My little lamb wants to play."

Ava steeled herself. "I believe your idea of what that means is completely opposite to mine."

"Is it? Let's see if that's true." He ran the straight blade down the valley between her breasts. It was closed so no harm would come to her, but the thought of that razor-sharp instrument slicing skin sent a shiver through Ava.

"I will not cut you, Ava. You are too perfect for that. But I will hack through those walls you have up and leave you defenseless." The blade continued, marking an invisible path down her body until it reached her aching center. "Does this frighten you?"

"Yes." Her chin tilted. "I don't like being helpless."

Another smile ghosted across Kingston's firmly molded lips. "But I like seeing you vulnerable. Too much, I'm afraid."

"I know." Ava's stomach muscles contracted as he drew an imaginary line from hip to hip with the end of the blade's handle. She bit her bottom lip, her brow furrowed. "I-I don't understand that."

Kingston's eyes crinkled at the corners. "You don't need to understand it."

"Do you... Do you bring many women in here? Chain them to your wall?" She should bite her own tongue off for asking such a stupid question, but the burning curiosity in the pit of her stomach demanded an answer.

Kingston shrugged. "Sometimes. Technically, you're my first unwilling prisoner. Of the female sort, anyway."

"And do you keep the cameras on while—"

He gripped her hip, fingers pressing into her flesh. "No more questions, Ava. Now, be quiet. Unless you want your panties used as a gag."

Ava's lips tightened but she nodded obediently.

"And while I would enjoy that visceral image, I much prefer hearing the sweet sounds you make when you come. I've dreamed about it since that day in the woods." Kingston's words curled around her in a deadly web of silk. "Have you dreamed of it, too, Ava? Thought about me touching you?"

Ava's eyes closed, terrified to admit the truth to him and to herself.

The edge of the straight blade's wood handle slid into the crevice of her pussy. A gasp bubbled in her throat when Kingston growled, "Open your eyes. I want to see all of you when you come for me. I want to see your soul acknowledge that I am the one making your body soar."

Her eyes flew open at that, meeting Kingston's fierce gaze as he laid the flat side of the handle snugly against her clitoris.

Ava bit back a whimper of pure, helpless lust.

"Look at you, Ava. Dripping for me. So wet and needy," he murmured, moving the handle back and forth with devilish intent, drenching it with her arousal. "Do you want to come? Do you?"

Ava trembled, straining against the manacles, reaching the limits of the chain's length. Her hips bucked toward the instrument he wielded with such deadly precision. Her wrist began throbbing with pain, but she didn't care.

He laughed softly, pressing harder. "Words, little lamb. Say the fucking words and I'll give you what you need."

But Ava stubbornly remained silent, her heart racing, the blood drumming in her veins like war drums. Kingston was driving her to the point of madness. A mindless, violent state of desire where she was a stranger even to herself.

"Say the words, Ava, damn you."

Her orgasm loomed, driven by his husky voice and the insanity of his possession, but she could not say aloud what he wanted to hear. Those words, once uttered aloud, would hurl her to a place she would never come back from.

"Should I stop?" Kingston's question was cruelly sly. He would, too, if she did not acknowledge what she wanted. What she needed more than the air pulsing in her lungs.

"Last chance," he mocked.

With a moan, she gave in.

"Please. Sir, please. I need... you."

Now that she'd experienced an orgasm at his hands, she was feverish for more. Crazy for it. Mindlessly stupid for it.

She wasn't sure who she hated more at that moment. Herself, for wanting this man and every filthy thing he was doing. Or Kingston, for forcing the catalyst.

"Fuck yes," Kingston snarled.

Standing up, he impatiently kicked the chair aside, sending it skittering across the cell.

Then he sank to the cold stone floor. A savage king on his knees in worship of his prisoner. The switchblade's handle moved to the opening of Ava's body, entering and withdrawing in shallow thrusts and ratcheting her desire to unimaginable heights.

She wanted it deeper. Filling the emptiness inside her. She wanted *him* inside her, pounding her into oblivion.

A heartbeat later, his mouth closed over her pussy, the

scruffy stubble of his chin leaving abrasions on the insides of her thighs. The chains and his warm, broad shoulders kept her legs spread, but he held her pussy open with one hand, seeking out her dark truths with his cruel mouth, twisting the handle of the straight razor within her channel. Never deep enough to fully take her virginity, but enough that she knew what the instrument represented. It was an extension of Kingston and his desires. Sharp. Invasive. Deadly.

His wicked mouth, lips, and tongue drove Ava over the edge. Fierce and hungry, sucking her into the depths of hell, and twisting everything that was right and wrong. This violent claiming of her body. This wild possession of her soul and heart. This was everything, and yet, Ava knew it meant nothing to a man like him.

Heated pleasure flooded her, her body convulsing as Kingston drank from her as though she were the finest of bourbons. He continued fucking her with the blade's handle, his mouth keeping an unrelenting rhythm on her clit as she shook in the chains and cried out his name.

When the shaking of the universe was complete and Ava's world was completely upside down, Kingston leaned away from her body.

His mouth and chin glistened with her surrender. His eyes were dark with fathomless emotion as he glared at her as if he hated her and everything she provoked within him.

"At this rate, little lamb, it won't be long before I've taken all of your firsts. And that will be the day you become fucking useless to me." He slowly withdrew the razor as her inner channel clenched desperately to keep it in place.

Kingston examined it and the evidence of her arousal coating it before tossing it aside. The instrument clattered on the floor as, with a groan, he leaned back into her.

With a long, slow lap of his tongue, Kingston cleaned the

juices away from Ava's sensitive flesh, then muttered in rueful admission, "But your sweet cunt is like heroin, and damned if I can stay away. Every time I close my eyes, I see you on your knees in my conference room. Your eyes so wide and green. Your pretty mouth full of my cock. And it's wrong and goddamn stupid of me, but I just want to fuck you until the world crashes down around us."

CHAPTER

TWELVE

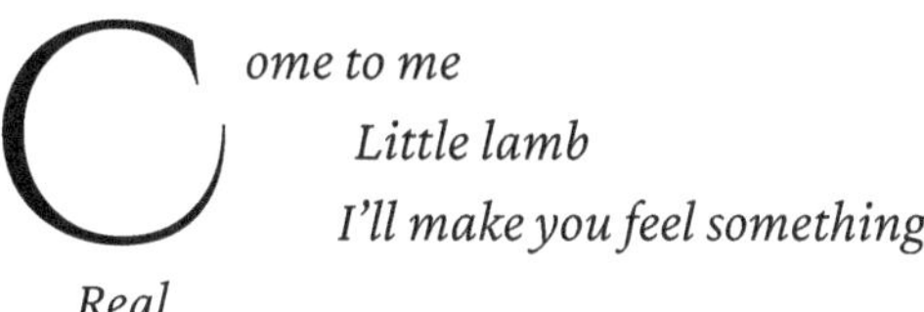

KINGSTON CAREFULLY DRESSED Ava in clean clothes before tucking her back into bed as though she were an invalid. Then, with his conquest of her body complete, he left the cell without a backward glance.

Ava did not even have the energy to protest, nor did she try reminding him of his promise of freedom. After a long night tossing and turning, she woke the next morning with a sense of dread and readied herself for yet another mind-numbing day inside her cell.

The clicking of the lock was not unusual, so she paid it little heed. Breakfast was delivered promptly at seven by Paulie. The man was obviously one of Kingston's most trusted confidants, and Ava liked him despite the circumstances. He was quick with a smile and inquiries about her well-being. He had personally delivered the hundred books meant to occupy her time and her mind. But even while depositing the books inside her cell, Paulie had smiled sadly and shook his head.

"Sorry, miss. I know they can't replace your freedom, but maybe you'll find some enjoyment in them. Kingston says you read a lot."

At the time, Ava only nodded and turned her head as the books were stacked on the floor around her cot.

Today, however, Paulie came accompanied by Jack. The two men entered the room, their demeanors respectful and non-threatening.

"We're to bring you upstairs, miss. To the terrace for breakfast," Paulie said with an encouraging smile.

"Am I to be served breakfast? Or serve *as* breakfast?" Ava asked, brow rising high.

"I believe eggs and ham are on the menu this morning." Jack chuckled at her sarcastic inquiry. "Hurry now, he's waiting for you."

"Heaven forbid the King is inconvenienced by my tardiness," Ava muttered.

Real clothes had been provided since that disastrous night when she'd been given only a flimsy nightgown. She was already dressed for the day in a pair of jeans and an expensive, lightweight sweater in a pretty cream color. There were no shoes to complete her outfit, but Ava knew that was intentional. Being without footwear put her at a disadvantage, a mental one maybe, but Kingston had picked up on that little tidbit of her psyche on the first day of her captivity.

Pulling her hair into a quick braid, Ava padded to the door on her bare feet. "I'm ready. Take me to him."

She was led through the same corridor used in her escape days before. Passing through the main opening to the upper floors of the mansion, the trio took a right instead of a left. Ava vaguely recognized the twisting hallways as those she'd seen when Kingston returned her to the cell once he'd captured her in the woods.

After the incident in the conference room.

That memory made her hands clench tight and left her stomach roiling with nausea. And it was foolish because she should be memorizing escape routes, but instead, she blanked out as she followed his two men. Allowing them to take her without protest to the very man set on destroying her.

Finally, they reached a set of glass-paned doors leading to a wide, covered terrace. The sun was just reaching above the treetops on this side of the house, and it illuminated the terrace and the walled garden below.

It was a scene straight from a fairytale. Blooming roses and honeysuckles twined around several terrace columns. Birds twittered and flew about from plant to plant in the lushness of the garden, and the air was sweet and crisp.

A round antique table of dark walnut sat in a covered section, and waiting there was the Beast in Ava's personal nightmare.

Distress mingled with desire sent unwelcome stabs of awareness through Ava's body. Kingston took a sip of coffee with those perfectly molded lips which had ravished the place between her legs just the night before. The image of this man kneeling before her, lapping at her body while she hung helplessly in his chains was seared into her brain.

She thought she might be sick.

Setting the cup down, Kingston rose from the chair and greeted Ava with a devastating smile. He had removed the bandaging from his cheek, and the cut was still in the process of healing. The bruising was fading, leaving behind the half-moon crescent that was now a dark shade of pink. Soon, it would be a sliver of white. Something he would carry forever. A visible reminder of her own fierceness.

"Good morning, lamb." His gaze traveled her body, a smile twitching at his lips when he noticed her bare feet and how her toes curled in protest against the cold floor of the stone terrace. He waved a hand at his men. "I'll let you know when I need you."

He pulled out a chair for Ava as Paulie and Jack departed.

"Come sit down, Ava," he murmured softly. "I thought you might enjoy breakfast and your first taste of freedom here in the sunshine."

Ava approached cautiously, sliding into the chair as if it were made of thorns. The table was gorgeously set with an overflowing centerpiece of lilies and pink roses. The dishes were an antique Havilland bone china embellished with rosebuds. The pieces appeared far too fragile to withstand Kingston's large hands.

Strange choice for such a brutal man.

"Chef has prepared all your favorites. Apple cinnamon pancakes. Eggs over easy. Country ham. French press coffee." Kingston rattled the items off, and Ava's stomach clenched even tighter with the reminder of his knowledge. He had ferreted out practically everything there was to know about her. Every tidbit of her existence was now part of his own personal database.

It wasn't fair, considering she hardly knew the first thing about him.

"Thank you. This is lovely."

Somehow, she managed to sound normal when every nerve and blood vessel screamed that she should leap over the terrace wall and try escaping a second time. Even with her bare feet.

Kingston's head cocked as he sat down beside her. He

poured coffee into her cup, added the appropriate amount of sugar and cream, and then sipped his own, watching her intently with those dark blue eyes.

Ava picked up a butter knife, running the tip of her index finger over the blade's edge. "Real silverware?"

Kingston's mouth twitched with barely concealed amusement. "Will you make me regret it?"

Ava took a deep breath to steady herself. "No. I won't. Not today, anyway."

He relaxed in his chair despite her words. "I'm glad to hear that. I hope we can have a pleasant breakfast, and afterward, I will show you the areas of the house where you may freely go."

"Okay."

That seemed to satisfy him, and he smiled as an older man emerged from the house carrying silver-covered dishes. These were set down on the gleaming table and the lids removed with a flourish.

"Good morning, Antony," Kingston said to the chef.

"Good morning, sir. Miss Blue?" The elderly man addressed her, obviously nervous at seeing her in person. "I hope you have enjoyed the meals I've prepared during your stay here at The Den. If you would like anything special, you only need to ask. I studied in France at the top culinary school in the world, which is where Mister Winter found me. I can prepare any dish you might like."

"Thank you," Ava replied. "The food has been amazing." How did one react around the servants of a kidnapper? Like nothing was wrong? Or should one send secret signals, begging for assistance in getting away?

Antony grinned ear to ear and set about preparing their plates. Ava sat stiff and silent, hyperaware of Kingston's brooding gaze.

The food was steaming hot, the eggs prepared just as Ava

liked them. She poured a small amount of syrup over the pancakes and began cutting them into small pieces. Despite the twists and knots in her stomach, she was suddenly ravenous.

Kingston's own food remained untouched as he sipped his coffee. A couple of times, he consulted his wristwatch, but his attention remained focused on her.

"Aren't you going to eat?" Ava finally asked, her fork stacked with miniature pancake squares.

Kingston cut into the ham on his own plate and took a bite. "You are so transparent, Ava. I don't think you realize how much so."

Ava chewed slowly before swallowing. "What do you mean?" She held the butter knife casually in one hand. But it pointed his way in a subtle reminder she now held a real weapon in her hand. A butter knife to be sure, but a weapon, nonetheless.

"I know you are still dreaming of escape. But for your own sake, you must abandon that idea. You'll not get far, and you know I'll punish you. And how I will do it."

Ava's heart thumped rapidly as she met his unrelenting gaze. She lowered the butter knife. "I've no intention of attempting it again. Your threats... what you said you would do to me... are enough to keep me from trying something so stupid a second time."

Kingston's eyes flared with unmistakable heat. "I almost wish you would do something foolish. It would give me an excuse to punish you, and I would enjoy that immensely."

Before Ava could reply to that terrifying revelation, the French doors flung open and Oliver strolled onto the terrace.

Wearing a lopsided grin, he plopped down in one of the empty chairs closest to Ava. Now, she was sandwiched between the two brothers, and uneasiness turned the pancakes she'd just swallowed to dust in her mouth.

Oliver gave Ava a deceptively friendly nudge of his shoulder.

"Why wasn't I invited?"

Kingston's lips tightened as he regarded his brother. "You don't eat breakfast."

Oliver winked at Ava. "Maybe I'd like to just admire the scenery." He glanced around the table, lips curving into an even wider grin. "At least offer me a cup of coffee."

Kingston snapped his fingers, and Antony was immediately beside the table. "A cup for Oliver, please."

Oliver leaned toward Ava. "Now, aren't you special? You are eating off a dead woman's china. Not everyone gets that honor."

Ava laid her fork on the plate's edge, folding her hands in her lap. She didn't fully understand the dynamics of the relationship between these two men, but it was quite obvious neither man trusted or even liked the other.

"Shut up, Oliver," Kingston said in a calm voice.

"What?" Oliver's eyes widened innocently. "It's true, isn't it? You don't eat off this china every day. It's reserved for special occasions. And special people."

Kingston did not reply as Ava's gaze bounced between the two men. He simply watched Oliver with detached curiosity as Antony set a cup and saucer before the man. After pouring the coffee, the chef scurried away as if recognizing a dangerous situation and the need to distance himself.

Oliver once again nudged Ava with his shoulder, and said in a loud whisper, "It's his mother's china, if you haven't guessed yet. Hell, I can hardly believe he's allowing me to drink from one of these hallowed cups."

Kingston's glare was brimstone. It should have ignited

Oliver right on the spot, but the younger man ignored him and continued.

"Kingston didn't really know his mother, Ava, so this china is *very* precious to him. It's one of the few things he has to remember her by," Oliver confided with a smile. "Did you know that when he was only four years old, our father killed her? Oh, everyone said it was an accident, but still."

Ava did not dare move, hands clutched tight in her lap. While aware Kingston's parents died years ago, she had no knowledge of the details. That was not important back when Kingston first drifted into her life.

Stealing a glance at him now, she saw his mouth was a hard line. A subtle air of restrained violence emanated from him, and Ava wondered how easily he controlled his reactions when needled by Oliver's taunts.

"Do you want to know how she died?" Oliver smirked. "It's quite heartbreaking, really. And really does explain how our dear King became such a monster."

Still, Kingston said not a word. Just sipped his coffee and listened to the tale his half-brother spewed.

"I think, if he wanted me to know, he would tell me himself," Ava said in a low voice. How strange it was to have this morbid conversation while sitting in the warmth of the morning sun, birds trilling happily in the garden below.

Oliver nodded in approval. "A sensible way of looking at it, Miss Blue. But if you are to fully understand your kidnapper, you should be aware of his background."

Ava slanted Oliver a suspicious glance. "What does any of this have to do with my abduction? With my brother's debt?"

"Sins of the father, you know? Our father was a real bastard when it came to his women. Kingston and I... well, let's just say these two apples did not fall far from that diseased tree." Oliver grinned, shaking a finger at Ava. "Now, pay attention,

Ava. This is the story of how Kingston Vaughn Winter was molded into the man who abducted you for a handful of money. You've already had a taste of his brutality. You might as well know how and why the seeds were planted. So, as I was saying, our father was a real bastard. Four years after Kingston was born, his mother became pregnant again. The doctors advised against a second pregnancy, but Alan Winter forced himself upon her until she finally had another baby in her belly."

"I don't want to hear any more..." Ava said in a shaky voice, but Oliver waved her objection aside.

"Our father was dangerously obsessed with Elena Winter. He wanted her so desperately. So much so that he raped her again and again. One day, after a particularly brutal episode, she began hemorrhaging. He didn't care, of course, brutal man that he was. He fucked her in spite of her screams, left her lying in a pool of blood, and a few hours later, Kingston discovered his mother. She was already dead at that point, but Kingston did not realize it. He was just four years old, after all. And do you know what the really tragic part is? That afternoon, he sat and held his mother's hand for hours before the nanny found him."

Ava swallowed hard, fighting back nausea when it rose high in her throat. Stealing a glance at Kingston, she was frightened by the lack of emotion on his face. He still sipped his coffee, seemingly unmoved by Oliver's tale.

"How was that an accident?" She hated herself for even asking the question, but the idea of a child holding the hand of his dead mother was something straight out of a nightmare. She imagined Kingston at that age. All big, dark blue eyes and ebony black hair. A solemn-faced little boy whose joy was stolen from him by his father's hands.

Had his father really been that much of a monster?

"It's what Alan Winter said it was. And so it was," Oliver shrugged. "The same may have happened with my own mother had she not shot him first. She did us both a favor, isn't that right, King? Although it came too late to change who we are. And *what* we are." His eyes turned even harder and crueler. "I mean, we haven't even addressed the subject of my own mother and how much she meant to Kingston."

Dizziness swamped Ava, the contents of her stomach threatening to spill across the antique tables and the pretty, delicate plates.

Vaguely, she was aware of Oliver sliding an arm around her waist. He stood while dragging her up along with him, and she helplessly followed him.

"Aww, poor darling," he crooned in her ear. "Do you need to lie down somewhere? Let me help you—"

One minute, Oliver was clutching her close; the next, he was forcibly ripped from her side. Kingston's fist connected with Oliver's mouth in a solid thud. It sent the man stumbling back until he finally landed on his backside a few feet away.

Kingston snatched Ava's arm, jerking her to him with a snarl directed at his brother. "I warned you, didn't I? Must I beat it into your thick skull? Keep your fucking hands off her, Oliver." Anger rolled off him in waves, although outwardly, he was the image of composure.

Ava was shocked by the quickness of his attack. His strength. He wasn't even breathing heavily after manhandling Oliver, who now watched them from a spot on the terrace floor.

Brushing away a spot of blood from his lip where Kingston's fist landed, Oliver simply laughed as he got back up on his feet.

"Point taken, dear brother. Forgive me. I was overcome

with emotion in telling your story and seeing how deeply it affected Ava. I was only thinking of her welfare."

"I won't warn you again," Kingston growled. "A bullet between your eyes may help with your memory."

"I'll try to remember that." Oliver inclined his head in a mocking show of respect, then as if remembering something important, he snapped his fingers. "Oh, I nearly forgot to tell you the news."

Kingston glared at Oliver. "What news?"

Oliver grinned. He seemed completely unconcerned his brother had just punched him in the face and threatened his life. "There's been word from Carson. He's interested in negotiating a deal for the safe return of his dear sister."

THIRTEEN

Come to me
Lion of mine
Erase my sorrow
Use your wickedness
Ruin me.

KINGSTON GRIT HIS TEETH.

"Why didn't you say so immediately?"

Oliver slid back into his chair, smiling up at Kingston and Ava. He dabbed the blood at the corner of his mouth with one of the fine, linen napkins. "I didn't want to ruin Ava's breakfast by mentioning her brother."

"You fucking psycho," Kingston muttered under his breath, then louder, he barked, "What is there to negotiate? He either pays the debt or he doesn't."

"Carson wants a meeting. Not here, of course. Somewhere neutral." Oliver picked up a piece of ham from Ava's plate and popped it into his mouth. Chewing thoroughly and grimacing because of the cut to his lip, he squinted at Kingston. "He's afraid of what you might do to him. And it goes without saying he's asking for proof your prisoner is still alive and in one piece. Is she still in one piece, brother? Or is she no longer worth the debt?"

Kingston didn't answer, but he tugged Ava closer, noting she trembled like a leaf caught in a whirlwind. Whether her reaction was due to the fight, Oliver's story, or the news her brother might actually pay for her freedom was unknown.

Or maybe it was from being held so tightly against his body and the memory of what he'd done to her the night before.

He shouldn't have been so quick in promising her freedom. It was a mistake to think she could go anywhere on his estate without first dealing with the issue of his brother. He wished he could go back on his word but feared the damage he might cause her if he tried.

As if aware of his inner turmoil, Ava caught the lapels of his suit jacket, fingers tightly clutching the fine material. "Please don't put me back in that cell." Staring up at him, her eyes were so wide and so green they mimicked the leaves of the roses in the table's centerpiece. "I'll be good. And I won't cause any trouble. I promise." She seemed to grit her teeth when adding the requisite title, "Sir."

"How can you resist when she begs so prettily, King? It's like music to the ears," Oliver interjected, licking blood off his knuckles. He'd scraped them on the terrace stone. "If it's me you're worried about, I'll keep my distance from the prisoner. It's been difficult, but I've managed so far."

"You won't be around to worry about," Kingston responded in a neutral voice. "You'll meet with Carson on my behalf. See what the offer is."

"Shit," Oliver swore, throwing up his hands in exasperation. "I was hoping you wouldn't say that. I've no desire to visit Bitter Springs."

Kingston maneuvered Ava toward the French doors, throwing orders over his shoulder at his petulant brother. "Be in my office in an hour. We'll go over the details."

Walking swiftly down the interior corridor, he forced Ava into a trot beside him or risk losing her arm.

"Where are you taking me?" she asked breathlessly.

"To the room I've designated as yours."

"But not the cell?"

"No. Not the cell. But remember, lamb. Only the walls and the view are different."

Ava did not respond to that, but her lips tightened as she continued following him.

"Have you always owned this house?" she dared asking as they ascended a set of beautifully carved stairs in the grand foyer. The double front doors were massive—a symphony of leaded glass, dark oak, and swirling steel. It was something one might see in a European castle. Decadence and luxury swirled together beneath a façade of civility.

Kingston paused on the stair landing. "No. I purchased The Den once my father's estate was cleared for disbursal and the DA's office dropped their investigation into his misdeeds."

"And my dad helped with that, right?" Ava's eyes were wide and guileless. "I mean, he was an amazing estate attorney, after all. Isn't that why you hired him after your father passed away? He did what you requested, and you monitored everything he did on your behalf."

"How clever you are, figuring that out." Kingston smiled. "It wasn't a difficult choice, hiring your father. The DA's charges were falling apart one by one, but with all the money and assets held in limbo, I needed his expertise. Especially since I was barely surviving on the pitiful allowance the previous attorney allotted."

He continued up the stairs, still gripping her elbow tight. "Turning eighteen my senior year of high school meant I was an adult and would not be placed in foster care like Oliver. And that first year of college was pretty rough—even with the stipend. Your parents invited me to be a part of your home while your father worked his ass off to settle the estate. He saved me from years of chasing my inheritance."

"Do you think he or my mother would approve of what you are doing now?" Ava's voice hardened. "After their kindness to you?"

Kingston chuckled without amusement, irritated by the prick of guilt her words produced. "I highly doubt it. But I'm not the same person your father and mother knew then. Things are different now."

"You aren't so different, Kingston Winter. I'm sure you were the same then as you are in this moment. Cold. Calculating. And heartless."

Kingston didn't respond, although his lips pressed tight. Ava couldn't possibly know how true her accusations were. What would she do if she found out he'd killed his first man on his father's orders when he was just sixteen? How would she react if she knew his father demanded he and Oliver participate while he forced women into sexual acts? Alan Winter called it sex education, but it was nothing more than a fucked-up way of desensitizing his sons to violence and a woman's screams.

Sometimes, he even commanded his boys to join in.

The last woman his father terrorized was Oliver's mother. Kingston still sometimes woke drenched in cold sweat, hearing his stepmother's screams even in his sleep. And the dual gunshots from that fateful night haunted him still.

When he slipped Rebecca that pistol for her own protection, Kingston never imagined she would turn the gun on herself after killing his father. Or that Oliver would witness the entire incident and blame Kingston for her death. He only wanted to help the woman he'd grown to love. Once he realized Rebecca's intentions, it was too late. She'd easily manipulated him while carefully planning his father's murder and her own suicide.

Kingston pushed his thoughts aside when they finally reached a room on the third floor. Ava entered ahead of him and cautiously examined the space.

It was close to his own suite of rooms, occupying the opposite end of the same wing. The large, airy space was impeccably appointed in shades of green and grey with a lovely view of the distant mountain range. But there was nothing remotely personal about it or the décor. The attached bath was also perfectly bland and perfectly perfect. No one had ever actually slept in this room, now that Kingston thought about it. It was just one of several unused spaces in this huge, lonely mansion.

Ava walked over to the windows and peeked past the thick drapes. When she turned and gave him an unfathomable stare, Kingston gestured about the room.

"There is a double lock on the door, as you can see. I expect you to utilize it whenever you are in here. Paulie or Jack will guard you when I'm not physically with you. You can pick up practically any channel you desire on the television, but access to the internet has been disabled."

"Are there cameras in this room, too?" Ava demanded, her brow knitted with concern.

Kingston considered telling her the truth but decided against it. "No."

She scoffed. "I don't believe you."

His shoulders lifted in a shrug. "I really don't care if you do or don't."

Biting her lip, Ava hesitated then asked softly, "Was that story true, then?"

She was referring to everything Oliver said. And the reluctant pity in her gaze infuriated Kingston.

"Most of it," he bit out, burying the pang of guilt he always carried.

She sighed, appearing genuinely distressed by his admission.

"I'm sorry. I had no idea. Everyone knew your dad and stepmom were dead, but there was very little gossip about the details of your mom's passing. At least, as far as I'm aware. But I probably would have listened to rumors anyway. My parents shielded me from a lot of the unpleasantness of the world. And Carson was always so mean, I would have never sought him out for comfort or an explanation of why people did such awful things."

Kingston leaned a shoulder against the door jamb, watching the play of emotions cross her face. Seeing how her eyes softened. He didn't like it. Didn't like how her sympathy made him weaker. Nor did he like the fact her brother wished to bargain for her release.

"Who shielded you when you learned of your own parents' deaths?" he asked rather brusquely.

She was startled by the question, which wasn't surprising. Ava Blue was so incredibly innocent. She had no idea of the crimes committed by her own flesh and blood.

"I don't understand..." she stammered. "I didn't need shielding. The accident was unexpected, but still, it was an—"

"Accident," Kingston finished for her with a sardonic smile. "One day, I'll enlighten you on what that word means in certain instances."

"Enlighten me now." Ava's chin tilted high. "Because you're speaking in circles. Are you suggesting my parents' deaths were caused by something other than a tragic car crash?"

Stalking toward her, Kingston was gratified when she retreated a few steps. She was still frightened of him, and that was a good thing. It was best she remain terrified of his intentions. "Now is not the time for such in-depth discussions."

Her eyes narrowed when he reached out, tucking a bit of silky blonde hair behind her ear. "You are avoiding the subject," she accused.

"Yes." He continued advancing until she finally retreated far enough to hit the bedroom's far wall. "One that is off the table for the moment."

"Then I'll ask another which should be easier to answer. Why did you punch Oliver?" The question was so softly spoken, Kingston was forced to lean closer to hear it. The fragrant scent of delicate honeysuckles drifted up from her hair and surrounded him.

"Because you are not his."

"I'm not yours, either," she reminded him, even though tiny quivers rippled beneath her skin. "Why do you care if another man touches me? Hurts me?"

He laughed at that and it was as cruel as his words.

"I *don't* care, lamb. This isn't a goddamn fairytale, and I'm not the hero in the story. In fact, I'm more of a villain than you can possibly imagine. But make no mistake; you *are* mine until I recover my money, and like it or not, your value is based on your purity. And my own *dear* brother would happily fuck you, destroy you, and delight in my losses." Kingston cupped Ava's chin in the palm of his hand, forcing her to meet his gaze when she would have jerked free. "He'll dance on my grave given the first opportunity."

"Then you probably need to stop assaulting me, Kingston Winter. I've had your fingers inside me, your—" she hesitated before saying the word with an enchanting blush— "cock in my mouth, and your tongue between my legs." Her eyes flashed with a bold, green fire. "How long will I keep my innocence if you continue doing these things?"

Something akin to insanity overtook Kingston with her accusation. His mouth actually watered as he remembered the sweetness of her taste. And his cock hardened almost painfully as he recalled erupting down her throat and the exquisitely helpless way she choked on him while he thrust with ruthless intent.

"Assault?" His eyebrows raised.

A furious cry hung up in Ava's throat. "My body may not realize it, but it does not change what you've done to an unwilling woman."

"Unwilling?" Kingston grinned as he repeated the word. "Right."

Ava stomped her foot. "You coaxed arousal from me. It's not unusual for a woman to respond in such a manner, even if realistically she's aware of the danger. You forced my body to accept these things."

"You drenched my fingers. Flooded my mouth with your sweetness." Kingston's head tilted. "Maybe you'd like another go 'round. Is that it, Ava?"

Her gaze fell to his mouth, and Kingston wondered if she even realized she licked her lips while staring at his.

"I-I just want you to be honest with me," she finally managed.

Kingston brushed her mouth with his, delighting in its softness and the little gasp she couldn't quite conceal.

"All right," he said. "I honestly want to kiss you."

Her eyes became hazy. "You do whatever you want. Whenever you want. You're king here. So, what's stopping you now?"

He gently nibbled the corner of her lush mouth and curled his fingers around her throat, holding her in place. "Because I want to fuck you, too," was his icy cold reply. "And that would only complicate matters by costing me money."

Ava tugged at his hand with a cry, pushing him back when his fingers loosened. Dismay stretched her mouth tight. "Stop reminding me that I'm nothing but a commodity."

Kingston let her slip past him and make her way to the bedroom suite's entrance. It was best he let her go at that moment. His body was irrationally demanding he throw her onto that king-sized bed. Reacquaint his mouth with her pussy. His fingers with her silky wetness.

Bad idea. Bad, bad idea.

Kingston hardened his heart, ignoring the pounding insistence in his brain that he do exactly what he wanted with her.

"Come with me if you wish to see the other areas in the house you may make use of." He took her by the elbow and led her out into the corridor. "And remember, lock that door whenever you are inside this room."

Ava peered up at him, her eyes flashing with a defiance Kingston longed to explore and crush. "Should I barricade it even against you?"

"No." Kingston's grip tightened, his mouth quirking with reluctant appreciation for her foolish feistiness. "Don't you fucking try it, either. My tolerance for that type of insubordination is non-existent. I'll spank you until your ass is red and you won't sit for a week."

"Barbarian," she muttered under her breath.

Kingston let her comment slide. Taking her downstairs, he made sure she knew the route with its twists and turns before showing her the kitchens and a bright sunroom overlooking the west side of the mansion. Next was a huge, den-like sitting room filled with leather couches, overstuffed chairs, and a large fireplace. Kingston noticed how her toes curled into the expensive wool rug in the sitting room, seeking some warmth. He must provide her shoes now that she understood the consequences of running away.

Occasionally, they came across Kingston's men. They appeared indolent, but each man was responsible for keeping the estate secure and protected. Those duties were taken very seriously. With the amount of money paid for their services, a level of loyalty was expected and demanded. Failure to live up to Kingston's exacting rules and expectations meant swift consequences.

The men simply nodded as Kingston and Ava passed. They'd already been apprised of Ava's limited freedom and what was expected of them. Their demeanor was respect mixed with a healthy bit of fear should anything disappoint their boss.

Kingston purposefully avoided both the conference room and his office. Along with his own personal suite of rooms, those areas were off-limits unless he decided to take Ava there himself.

When they finally entered the last room of the mansion she was allowed to use, Jack had caught up with them.

"I'm leaving you here now," Kingston said as Ava trailed her fingertips over the spines of the numerous books lining the library's shelves. "Jack will look after you while I take care of this meeting with your brother."

Ava cast a questioning glare over her shoulder. "I thought you needed proof of life? Carson will want to see I'm still in one piece. Relatively speaking."

"Later. Right now, this is between Oliver, myself, and the message I want conveyed. Stay out of trouble and don't give Jack any reason to report something bad back to me."

CHAPTER

FOURTEEN

AVA KNEW BETTER than to be romanced by the luxurious surroundings. Like the man holding her prisoner, wicked savagery existed beneath all of the breathtaking beauty. She could not let herself be swayed by any of it.

But the vastness of the library was astounding, and it was difficult remaining unimpressed by its grandeur.

It was something straight out of a fairy tale. Bookshelves reached from floor to ceiling, every inch occupied by a wide variety of subjects. A few were first-edition classics, so rare they should have been placed behind glass and protected from dirty fingertips.

Jack waited outside the library's double doors, giving her privacy to do as she wished. While she knew it was foolish, Ava found herself searching the room's contents in an effort to gain some insight into her captor.

But the library was decorated like the rest of the house. Impersonal and coldly perfect. Tasteful decorations interspersed with valuable antiques. The only room containing a hint of Kingston himself was his office. Brutal and stark yet decadently lavish—steel draped in silk.

Cracking open one of the library's double doors, Ava poked her head out. She'd spent almost two hours flipping through books, examining artifacts and various curiosities interspersed between the hardbacks.

Jack was in the hallway slouched in a high back chair, arms crossed over his barrel chest. He wasn't dozing, but he was relaxed enough that his legs stretched before him. They took up most of the corridor and blocked the library's entrance.

"Miss Blue." He nodded, one blond eyebrow cocking high. "May I get you something?"

Ava swallowed hard. The man resembled a Norse god—all muscles and dark blond hair cut in a high fade style with thick waves piled on top of his head. She guessed he was around the age of thirty based on the tiny laugh lines around his bright blue eyes. Built like a giant, he was at least two inches taller than Kingston.

"If it is allowed, I'd like to sit on the terrace where I had breakfast earlier today. It's so lovely outside and I—"

"Of course." Jack unfurled his body. Coming to his feet, he cracked his neck from side to side. The smile he gave her was friendly, and while Ava knew he was there to keep her safe, she wasn't stupid enough to fully trust him.

"Kingston said you were allowed to go there and the walled garden below it if you want."

Ava nodded. "Yes. I would like that very much. Perhaps we could first stop by the kitchen and get something to drink?"

"I think I could whip up some kind of cocktail, if necessary." Jack laughed, sweeping his arm out to indicate she could exit the library.

"Oh, no." Ava blushed. "Just water. Or maybe an iced tea, if it isn't too much trouble."

"I'm sure we can manage to find something."

Upon reaching the kitchen, it was Antony who poured her a specially mixed combination of iced tea and peach juice. The refreshing concoction reminded Ava of Savannah, and for a brief second, thoughts of that stolen life twisted her stomach with resentment. She should be there now. Starting her new job. Buying stuff for her apartment and making it her own safe place.

"Ugh. Too sweet for me." Jack grimaced, pouring his glass of tea out in the double sink.

"I think it's perfect." Ava smiled at Antony. "I never knew how much I loved peach tea until I moved down south. Yours is as good as any I've had."

Antony's scowl for Jack turned to a pleased grin that lit up his plump features. "Thank you, Miss Blue. If you like, I can bring a pitcher out onto the terrace along with some snacks as well. I can whip up some canapés. A few sweets and some fruit and cheese. There's this amazing recipe I've been dying to try—"

"That's very considerate of you, Antony. But I think I'll have just the tea for now. I'm still full from that wonderful breakfast you prepared."

Antony huffed under his breath. "Mister Oliver sure ruined that, didn't he?" Then he brightened. "I'll have the tea ready in a few minutes, miss."

All evidence of the breakfast she'd shared with Kingston on the terrace had been cleared away. Ava sat on a bench overlooking the garden below and absorbed the sunlight with her eyes closed.

"Am I allowed to walk into the garden?" She directed her question to Jack as he took a seat in the shade near the French doors.

"Yes. But you haven't any shoes and the path is made of crushed Bahamian stone. Might be rough on your feet."

Ava glanced down at her feet, frowning. "I wonder how long he intends for me to walk around barefoot? He knows I won't run from him again. Not after..." She broke off, remembering Jack was also in the conference room that night. He knew what Kingston had made her do. What he promised would happen if she attempted to escape again.

"I'm sorry, Miss Blue," Jack said apologetically. He apparently knew where her mind had wandered.

Ava's face flamed hot with mortification.

The man was embarrassed for her. For what she'd done. And because he'd been there to hear it.

Ava did not respond to the apology. When Antony arrived with the iced peach tea, she thanked him and then turned her attention back to the birds flitting back and forth between the garden hedges and rose bushes.

She didn't realize she'd dozed off in the sunshine, warm and drowsy until the scraping of a chair on the terrace stones startled her awake.

"Sorry." Oliver grinned as he dragged the chair closer and positioned it almost in front of the bench where she sat. He plopped down and sprawled across the seat as though it were a throne.

Ava did not respond but quickly cast a glance over her shoulder, ensuring herself that Jack was still on duty.

Her guard still lounged in his chair in the deep shade of the terrace. The two-finger salute he gave let Ava know his watch had not ended. His gaze fixated on Oliver, a frown creasing his brow.

A little sigh of relief escaped Ava, even as Oliver mockingly laughed.

"Don't worry. Your watchdog is still there. I suppose King will have you guarded twenty-four-seven now that he's let you loose from that cell." Oliver's tone turned bitter. "Isn't that so fucking generous of him? Gives you just enough freedom to make you forget the shackle still clamped about your neck."

"What do you want?" Of everyone she'd come across so far in The Den, Oliver was the one she thought the most unpredictable.

"Loaded question, Miss Blue." Oliver smirked. Picking up her glass of tea, he took a sip and made a hum of approval deep in his throat. "Mmm. Fucking delicious. I love peaches. I bet you taste even better than this, though."

"Does Kingston know you are here?" Ava ignored the greedy hunger in his tone and his hot gaze as it traced her features.

She wanted to hide away from it but did not dare show a hint of weakness.

Oliver's light blue eyes glinted. "This is my home, Miss Blue. I go where I please, regardless if you are occupying the same space or not."

Oliver wanted to antagonize her. Goad her into saying or doing something reckless. Maybe he wanted to see her punished again. He seemed the type to enjoy that sort of thing. To relish the pain and humiliation of a woman.

He shifted closer and Ava stiffened, ready to cry out for aid if need be. Jack's hands were big enough to snap Oliver's neck with just a twist. Would he do that if necessary to his employer's own brother?

"We can be friends, Ava. You and I." Oliver's voice was low, reminding Ava of a serpent, iridescent and starkly beautiful but so, so dangerous. Reaching out, he stroked a finger along her knee, fully aware Jack could not see his action. When he smiled, Ava did not return it as he continued. "If you let me get close enough, I can help you."

"I've no need for friends. Not in this place, anyway."

"I don't think that's true." Oliver's brow furrowed. He squeezed her knee. "I've spoken with your brother, and we've devised a solution. One which does not involve you being sold to Kingston's highest bidder. We could avoid that bit of unpleasantness. Handle matters ourselves. Keep it just between the two of us."

Ava stared stonily ahead. "Carson's debt won't be erased unless Kingston agrees. Has he come up with the money then?"

"In a way, yes."

Ava shifted so Oliver could not continue caressing her knee. "What's in it for you, Oliver?"

The cruelty of his smile chilled Ava's blood. "Ample compensation. But you should only concern yourself with this. Kingston would be unable to sell you, your brother's debt would be paid, and you would no longer be a prisoner here."

There was some unknown element missing from Oliver's promises. Everything he stated was too good to be true. Ava knew this, but still, hope flared wildly inside her. The two things working in her favor were Carson's greedy desperation and Oliver's obvious lust. Perhaps it was possible to play one against the other. And use both men against Kingston.

She must be careful though. Oliver was dangerous. And Carson, too, now that he was backed into a corner.

"Kingston would find out."

Oliver's blue eyes regarded her so intently, Ava wondered if he could see her intent to somehow trick him. "Yes, he would. Eventually. But it would be too late to do anything about it.

You would no longer be his prisoner. Let's just say we would both be free of him."

Ava took the glass of tea from his hand and sipped it, her lips delicately skating over the glass rim. Oliver's eyes were practically glued to her mouth, his desire so apparent it was almost comical.

"You expect to betray your brother and come out unscathed?" Her head tilted. "And that I will escape unharmed? I may be naïve, but even I know Kingston won't allow that kind of betrayal to go unpunished."

"If you do as I say, you'll be far out of his reach. Trust me." Oliver stretched out his leg, rubbing his boot over Ava's bare toes.

"Trust you?" Ava snatched her foot out of his reach, quickly folding her legs and tucking her feet under her body. While Oliver chuckled at her aversion to his touch, she turned her gaze back to the gardens and admitted softly, "I'd be very stupid placing my faith with anyone in this house."

L*ittle lamb, save me*
I'm so damaged
And the night is so black
No moon to see you by

AFTER SPENDING the morning exploring all the places she was allowed to go in the huge mansion, Ava inexplicably found herself back in the cell.

"I want to get the shampoo I've been using," she stammered in response to Jack's raised eyebrow when she asked to be taken down below the mansion.

The man did as Ava requested, respectively staying outside the cell as she hurried into the bathroom and grabbed the bottles she wanted.

Coming back out into the cell's main area, she glanced around the room where she'd spent the last ten days.

The books had not yet been moved to her new quarters. They still lay scattered about the room. Ava compulsively set about tidying up the haphazard stacks. She could not examine too closely the real reason she'd come back, but her gaze continually strayed to the wall with its embedded manacles. With every helpless glance, her stomach tightened.

"I've men for that, lamb."

Ava let out a little scream and dropped the small pile of books while also tripping over a stack by her feet. She wound up on the floor, braced on her elbows, wincing at the dull pain in her wrist.

Glaring up at Kingston, she snapped, "Why did you do that?"

"Christ, you're a jumpy little thing," Kingston muttered, hurrying forward. "Your wrist. Have you injured it again?"

"What do you care?" she mumbled as she was hauled to her feet. "And I've good reason to be jumpy. In case it's slipped your mind, I've been abducted by a bunch of psychos."

Kingston's hard hands gripped her elbows. "How can I forget? I upended everything when I took you from your dreary little existence."

"You mean the normal life I was living until you decided I was worth an unpaid debt?"

Kingston's eyes did not soften, but his hold loosened enough that Ava could place some distance between their bodies.

"Why are you down here?" he asked in his usual gruff tone.

"Why are you?" Injecting as much insolence into her tone as she dared, Ava countered, "Don't worry, *sir*. I've not strayed from the approved areas, and Jack never left my side."

"Hmmm. I know."

"Of course, you do." Her chin tilted higher as she met his liquid gaze. "You've been spying on me again, haven't you?"

His mouth twitched with the accusation. "Guilty. I even zoomed in a few times, if you want the terrible truth."

Ava's eyes flared. Why she suddenly found that so damn hot was beyond her comprehension. It should disgust her rather than make her heart thump faster.

"I came to get the shampoo I've been using. I like the scent."

Kingston nodded. "I know. I included it with the toiletries stocked in your bathroom upstairs."

Ava's lips tightened. This small kindness was unexpected. "Oh. I did not know. Thank you."

Kingston nodded in acknowledgment, his thumbs rubbing the skin of her elbows in a stroking motion.

"Is there a reason for coming to find me?" Ava bit out. If only she had the strength to yank free of him. To place some distance between herself and this unhealthy attraction. "What do you want?"

Kingston smiled. "Loaded question."

It was not lost on Ava that his response mirrored Oliver's from just a few hours before. Had Kingston overheard their conversation? Had he listened with the help of the sophisticated network of cameras hidden in every corner of this mansion?

Releasing one of her elbows, Kingston's hand raised until his palm cupped her chin. He held it firmly before his fingers trailed down, his thumb settling in the hollow of her throat. He stroked softly, and his gentleness frightened Ava more than she cared to admit. He gripped her often in this manner with his fingers around her throat. She wondered if it was a compulsion with just her or if this was something ingrained in his psyche. Something he did with all his women.

"Come with me to my office."

Ava quivered. "Why?" Only bad things happened in his office and that awful conference room.

"Because I said so."

"If I say no?"

A sadistic chuckle escaped Kingston's throat. "You do make it hard to resist punishing you. Are you that desperate for what I'd do with you?"

Ava ignored the question and countered with one of her own. "Do you punish all of your women?"

Kingston's fingers tightened over her pulse. "Only the ones who deserve it. And you, wicked lamb, definitely deserve it."

"Is that what you want to do with me in your office? Punish me for defying you?"

"More than that. What I want invades my thoughts constantly." His voice lowered an octave, his eyes glittering like a thousand star-strung galaxies of dark indigo. He leaned closer, his cologne tantalizing her nostrils. "I want to make you cry, little lamb. Scream. Beg. Until every cry and whimper you make is embedded in my brain. I want to pin you over my knee and turn the creamy flesh of your ass pink with the palm of my hand. I want to whip you—for having a smart mouth and the stupidity to not keep it shut. I want to bury my cock so far down your throat that you gag on me. And I want to fuck you until you are nothing but a goddamn, defeated mess of lust and need." There was no remorse in his voice when he finished with, "I want to see you suffering like I am suffering."

Ava's knees nearly buckled beneath his filthy, incinerating words and her own terror.

Then Kingston laughed beneath his breath. "But I'll settle for a video of you holding up today's newspaper. Something I can send to your brother. Proof of life, remember? For what it's worth anyway... considering the circumstances."

Kingston waved Jack away as they exited the cell.

"Please have all of Miss Blue's books and other favored items moved to her new accommodations, Jack."

"Sure thing, boss."

Eyes crinkling, he added, "And you are dismissed for the rest of the day. Paulie can take over this evening."

"Got it." Jack nodded, then inclined his head toward Ava. "Miss Blue."

Ava's brow creased slightly, unsure if she should actually thank the man for serving as her babysitter all morning. "Thank you, Jack." She watched as he moved down the corridor in the opposite direction and wondered where the other exits were located in this twisted network below ground.

Kingston pulled her along until they were ascending the stairs with her being pushed ahead of him.

"Do you like Jack?" His voice was a low murmur in her ear as they reached the door leading to the main house. He didn't open it right away, just pushed closer until she was trapped against it with nowhere to go.

"What do you mean?" Ava took a steadying breath, fighting hard to ignore his warm breath on the back of her neck.

"You know exactly what I mean, Ava. He's good-looking. Big. Strong. Maybe you think he can help you escape. Once you make him fall in love with you, of course, with all those breathy little sighs and the shy way you look at him."

Ava's lips tightened. "You're crazy. I don't want him. Or anyone else in this house. I just want to go home…"

Kingston chuckled darkly. "Back to your sweet, boring boyfriend? The one who hasn't dared pushed his fingers into your pussy? The one who hasn't demanded a blowjob from you?"

Ava turned to face him, her back against the door. Glaring up at him, she snapped, "Maybe. What do you care? Once you get your money, I'll no longer be your concern. And you have no idea what goes on between me and Drake."

"I know he hasn't fucked you. Which is commendable on his part, I admit. But the fact remains that I'll snap the neck of any man who touches you without my permission. I don't care who he is." Kingston trailed his finger over her jawline, then tipped her chin up. "So think carefully before seducing a man with those pretty smiles and fluttering eyelashes."

Ava grit her teeth. "I'm not interested in seducing anyone. And I don't *flutter* my eyelashes. That's a ridiculous thing to accuse me of."

"You're doing it this very moment, lamb." He leaned closer, brushing his nose against hers while breathing her in. "You know, as much as I like you calling me 'sir', I believe I enjoy your resistance just as much. I wonder why that is."

Ava avoided his penetrating gaze. Because as much as she hated calling him "sir", she was beginning to crave the sense of... belonging... the word implied.

And she hated it. Hated the strange link tying her to this man. Hated that, after years of floating through life untethered and alone, this stranger made her feel something wild and fierce. How could she explain an attraction that shouldn't exist? There was no rationalization for it. Not when he was a bloodthirsty, greedy monster who'd stolen her away from the world and locked her in a gilded cage.

An expression of understanding stole over Kingston's features. "Ahh. You're experiencing it, too. This inexplicable magnetism pulling us to one another."

Ava reached behind her and encountered his hand already gripping the knob.

"I don't feel anything where you are concerned," she said. "Unless one counts fear and disgust."

Kingston grinned, brushing her mouth with his. "Quit flirting with me, little lamb."

He tasted of wintergreen and whiskey. Spicy. Brisk. Irresistible. In spite of herself, Ava's lips parted to receive his kiss.

But he merely chuckled and withdrew, leaving her aching for his possession and hating herself for it.

"It'd be so easy to have you on your knees for me, Ava. So easy. And so tempting. But we've other matters to attend to this afternoon. We should see to those now."

CHAPTER

SIXTEEN

No stars to wish upon
Something inside me
Was broken long ago
Shattered on the sea

KINGSTON KEPT a tight grip on Ava's arm while guiding her toward the wing of the mansion containing his office and study.

It was a space useful when it came to intimidation. His enemies were brought there when a reminder of his power was needed. His victims saw the rooms as well when it was necessary. Sometimes, it was the last thing they saw on earth.

He brought Ava to this room on the first day of her abduction, hoping to frighten her into submission. Now, he brought her here for another reason. Other than his own suite of rooms, it was the one place he knew she was utterly safe. And a place he knew no one would interrupt him.

Watching Ava on the camera system earlier while she interacted with his brother had greatly annoyed him. He couldn't hear what Oliver said. The man was clever enough to keep his voice so low it could not be picked up on the audio. But Ava spoke clearly, and hearing the admission she didn't trust anyone stung more than it should have.

Why should he care if she trusted him or not? He wasn't here to play the whole boyfriend/girlfriend with his captive. The money she represented was his focus. Nothing more.

But still...

It was difficult ignoring Ava Blue's appeal. It existed on a level he'd never experienced with a woman, and it infuriated him. He should be able to take what he wanted from her and discard her as he had the others. Only, he couldn't find the willpower to make that happen.

Setting Ava in one of the leather club chairs, Kingston threw a Bitter Springs newspaper in her lap. She snatched it up, hurriedly scanning the front page and soaking in the information.

"If you're looking for news of your disappearance, you won't find it, Ava." Withdrawing a fragrant cigar from a tabletop humidor, Kingston clipped the end of it, moistened it with his mouth, then lit it with the lion head lighter. "No one has missed you. And your brother isn't stupid enough to report your abduction."

Why does that fact annoy me so much? I should be glad no one has missed her instead of this furious sense of outrage on her behalf. Why is no one desperately searching for her? She's a fucking treasure. A goddess.

Ava lowered the paper, glaring at him. "I don't need a reminder of just how invisible I am to the world, Mister Winter. I'm very much aware of that fact. And I've become accustomed to it."

That only made Kingston angrier. To hear her acknowledge

her insignificance made him want to break something. Preferably her bastard of a brother's skull.

Callously burying that emotion, he drew on the cigar until the smoke curled around his head. "Sir," he reminded her with a smirk. "Remember? And I wouldn't say you are invisible, Ava. There are others very much aware of your existence. People who seek to use you for their personal advantage."

"They can't be worse than you," she huffed, snapping the pages of the newspaper and folding it back into order.

Kingston shrugged. "You might regard me as the lesser of all evils before this is over. You may even beg me to keep you. Hearing the words fall from your lips will be something I might even treasure after you've gone."

Ava's laughter was sharp with disbelief. "Your reputation as the cruelest of kings is well deserved. And I'll die before begging you to keep me. I won't be your little pet."

"So stubborn. So stubborn and so stupid," Kingston murmured under his breath. "You've no idea how desperate your brother is. How dangerous. You won't be able to return to your innocuous life after this. There will be a target on you. Right in the center of your chest."

Ava's head cocked. "Carson is interested in paying the debt, right? He wants assurance I am still alive before handing over the money. Tell me how I am in danger with my own brother. You said before he would use me to settle this debt, that he would sell me to the highest bidder, but just because you say it, doesn't make it true."

Kingston set the cigar down and crossed over to where Ava sat in the chair. Bracing his hands on the armrests, he bent over, caging her in. "Carson cannot be trusted."

Ava's eyes glittered like green fire. "Neither can you."

"You are right about that. We're bad men. Both of us. All of us."

"Are you going to record me or not? I'd like to go to the new prison cell you've assigned me when this is done," Ava spat like an angry kitten.

Kingston pushed away with a low growl of frustration. "If you only knew what he's done, what he's capable of doing, you wouldn't be so eager to be free of me."

"Then tell me. Tell me why I would ever, in a thousand years, be safer with you than with my brother. He's only ignored me. While you… you're the stuff of nightmares."

"Far be it for me to shatter your naïve illusions." Kingston pulled his cell phone from his trouser pocket. Pushing a few buttons, he brought up the video program and pointed it at Ava. "Hold the paper in front of you, state today's date and say whatever you want to him." He hit record and nodded his head. "Go."

Ava did as commanded. But before Kingston turned off his phone, she stared straight into the cellphone's lens and whispered, "Carson, if you still possess a shred of decency and any love for our parents, you will do what's right."

The tears in her eyes as she added that final statement were nothing less than individual iron stakes impaling Kingston's heart. It was almost painful to witness Ava's distress and realize how easily it would weaken his resolve if he allowed it.

Returning the phone to his pocket, he took the paper away from her and pulled her to her feet.

"If your brother possessed a heart, he might actually be moved by that sweet performance. But I know him. Know the type of man he has become. And I know his demand for a meeting is simply a ploy to buy more time. It's been ten days already. He has no intention of paying off the debt unless he can make money for himself somehow at the same time."

"Not discounting my brother because we both know what

type of person he is, but not everyone has the same devious, larcenous heart as you."

Kingston's laugh was darkly cynical. "Yes, they do. Some just hide it better than others."

She peered up at him. "Carson's never been an affectionate brother where I am concerned. Other than that one awful incident, where he stopped his friends from going any further for your information, there are worse things he could do."

"He *has* done worse. Although it can't be easily proven. And I know exactly what happened that night. And I know the names and personal details of every man involved."

Ava scowled. "Unless you can list Carson's transgressions plainly as well as prove them, they remain simply accusations."

"So loyal even to those less than deserving," Kingston mocked, but he held back from voicing aloud the worst of his suspicions. "Do not pin your hopes on Carson saving you. Nor should you trust a word that spews out of my own brother's mouth."

"I'll say it again. I don't trust you, him, or anyone else here, for that matter."

Ava returned Kingston's stare, chin tilted in the mutinous angle which both annoyed and intrigued him. She placed him in a unique position. One that left him with a desperate need to shield her from the ugliness in the world while at the same time proving just how much of a fucked-up monster he was beneath the polished, bespoke suit.

"Are you through with this lesson on how shitty our two brothers are?" Now, it was her turn to mock him in a bitterly crisp tone. "Sir?"

Sliding a hand to the base of her neck, Kingston entangled Ava's dark golden hair in his fist, holding her immobilized like a rabbit caught in a snare. "I think a different type of lesson is in order, one focusing on obedience and respect for whomever your future owner might be. I'm sure any efforts on my part in the matter will be greatly appreciated."

Her mossy green eyes narrowed. "You might auction me off, but no one will ever *own* me."

Kingston's smile was grim. "How upset will you be when I disprove that foolish notion?"

"Carson will pay the debt, so it won't be an issue."

"Your faith is admirable. Misplaced but admirable." Kingston untangled his hand from her hair and leaned a hip against his desk. "You better go to your room now."

Ava seemed surprised by his abrupt willingness to allow her to escape. "Bored with me already?" she asked flippantly.

"On the contrary, lamb." Taking a drag of his cigar, he scrutinized her through the haze of smoke. "I want to throw you on my desk and reacquaint myself with your taste. But I've work to do and you're a terrible distraction."

Ava's lips tightened. "I'm happy to go. Ecstatic, in fact. But I've no idea how to get to my room from here. Call for one of my guards or take me there yourself."

"Being a brat doesn't work on me," Kingston calmly replied to the subtle taunt in her challenge.

"Meaning what?"

"Meaning I won't give you what you want."

"What I want?" Ava seemed genuinely confused, then snarled, "Tell me what it is you think I want other than my freedom."

"Oh, Ava. You are so damn transparent and yet so innocent when it comes to how these things truly work. What do you want? I'll enlighten you. You seek punishment. Attention. *My* attention, to be precise. I know we just left there, but shall we revisit the cell for an impromptu demonstration?"

There was that spark in her eyes again. The one that made

Kingston's pulse beat double-time with irrational, possessive hunger. He was quickly becoming addicted to that look of reluctant curiosity mixed with fear she displayed whenever he mentioned punishment.

Her defiant stance did not weaken, but Ava shook her head in response to his question.

"I'd like to go to my room." She gritted out between clenched teeth, "Please, sir."

"That's what I thought." With a smirk, he pressed the button on the phone that would summon Paulie. "I've matters to attend to this evening, so you will remain in your room overnight during my absence. I shall return in two days, and you will join me for dinner. You'll find a black cocktail dress in the closet of your new quarters. Wear it."

"Am I permitted to wear shoes?" A thread of sarcasm wove through the question as she glanced down at her bare feet.

Kingston grinned. "Of course. I expect to see you in a pair of stilettos, dressed to kill."

"If only I could be so lucky," she threw back with a smirk to rival his own.

CHAPTER

SEVENTEEN

R*uin and salvation*
   Aren't enough for me.

Ava spent the next two nights tossing and turning in the lushly appointed but cold and sterile bedroom. At any moment, she expected Kingston to come strolling through the locked doors, but he never did.

During the day, she explored more of the estate grounds as Jack trailed her steps. Late September was a delight in the mountains, with crisp, clear weather and the beauty of the changing leaves all around.

Had it been under different circumstances, Ava would have enjoyed it immensely. But the dark cloud of captivity and possible servitude to the cruelty of an unknown man tempered any pleasure she took in the beauty of her surroundings.

Before she knew it, the evening of Kingston's return had come and she reluctantly prepared herself for dinner.

It was a surreal experience, dressing for the enjoyment and pleasure of a kidnapper. Ava had come to a grim realization during her brief time alone. If there was any hope of escaping this nightmare, she must either flee at the first opportunity—which didn't seem possible—or she must convince Kingston to let her go.

Appeasement meant information. Compliance resulted in greater freedom. And any connection she created between the two of them might result in a personal attachment.

An attachment that could be exploited.

Could she possibly manipulate her jailer into experiencing something for her other than lust? Ava wasn't sure, but every avenue must be explored, even if submitting to the will of the cold, heartless Kingston Winter was the only option.

Checking her reflection, Ava shuddered. The image reflected in the full-length mirror might as well have been someone else. The dress she wore was a black cocktail number and was far from demure. The hemline hit about mid-thigh and the bodice had a low scoop neck. It fit as if made specifically for her body, highlighting her breasts and curves. Even she had to admit she looked amazing in it.

Black lace over thin, nude material created the illusion she wore nothing beneath the lace. Cap sleeves dipped off her shoulders, and the back of the dress plunged nearly to her waist, the material hugging her shoulder blades. There was no appropriate bra included in the dresser drawer full of lingerie —all in her size—so Ava was uncomfortably bare beneath the dress. Bare with the exception of a thin, very skimpy, black lace thong.

Ava's lips tightened as she considered the garments Kingston provided her. All of the choices for underwear were of the thong variety with expensive labels. It was as though she wore nothing at all under the dress. A purposeful move on Kingston's part and honestly not unexpected.

The shoes were the most surprising. There were dozens to choose from—stilettos, kitten heels, boots, tennis shoes, and strappy flat sandals in a myriad of colors. While exploring the house and grounds earlier that day, she'd worn a comfortable pair of English riding-style, knee-high boots. She did not even want to dwell on the fact all the clothes and shoes were her exact size and fit her personal style and taste. It was as though Kingston had always planned on plucking her out of her old life and plugging her into this one.

With a huff, Ava pushed her thoughts aside and selected a pair of black Louboutins. The heels were so high she might as well be tottering around on circus stilts. Sheer, thigh-high stockings completed the ensemble, and from the array of expensive cosmetics in the luxurious bathroom, she applied pale, golden brown eyeshadow and blood-red lipstick. Her hair was twisted into an elegant bun with curling tendrils framing her face in a style she'd seen her mother wear many times in the past.

Ava stared at her reflection, her heart squeezing tight with apprehension. "Oh, Ava. You look like a high-priced call girl," she muttered beneath her breath.

Perhaps that was Kingston's intention. A cruel reminder that she was temporarily his property. A little doll he could dress up as he pleased. A pet to trot about whenever he wished to be entertained.

Ava tugged the hem of the dress down with a scowl. It was much shorter than she would have liked. She was horribly exposed. Bare. Vulnerable.

With a sigh, she sat on the edge of the king-sized bed. No more cold cells and damp stone walls. No more of the tiny cot that barely accommodated the full length of her body. No more staring at wall manacles and reliving every moment that Kingston Winter destroyed her with heartless caresses. Now, instead of being locked in, she could lock people out.

Except him. She could not lock him out.

What punishment would be exacted if she tried? Ava shivered, a chill passing through her at the thought of defying Kingston. The confusing thing was, her body also tingled with something forbidden. Something dark and needy.

But why? Why should she find excitement in his threats of punishment? In his cruel caresses? His savage nature should repel her. Kingston Winter had blood on his hands and a chunk of ice for a heart. And Ava's limited experience with men had her instincts screaming with a warning. He was no different from Carson and his group of friends. Men who squeezed and pinched and took what they wanted despite a woman's cries to stop.

A low knock on the door interrupted Ava's thoughts and sent her heart leaping up into her throat. Her escort had arrived, ready to lead her down to the gladiator's arena.

Opening the door after unclicking the double locks revealed Paulie in the corridor. His eyes widened slightly at seeing her, but a warm smile curved his mouth and immediately put Ava at ease.

"I'm here to take you to Kingston, miss."

Ava nodded. "Yes. I suppose you are."

"Are you ready?"

Ava inclined her head and exited the room, pulling the door shut behind her. "Would it matter if I said no? I'm not ready for whatever your boss has planned for me."

"As far as I'm aware," Paulie turned pink, "it's just dinner."

"I'm sure he has more depraved plans than just sharing a meal."

Paulie's jaw tightened. "I couldn't say, miss."

Ava crossed her arms, staring at the man for a long moment before sighing heavily. "I'm sorry, Paulie. I know this entire ordeal is not of your doing. I shouldn't take my frustration out on you. Or Jack, for that matter."

Paulie extended his arm, indicating she should begin walking. "This is certainly a difficult situation for you, miss. Kingston can be... stubborn... on certain matters. He expects obedience in all things, especially from those of us who work for him."

"I understand. You are just doing what you've been instructed and paid to do," Ava replied. "Even if it isn't right I'm kept as a hostage."

"Yes, miss." Paulie's relief in light of Ava's reluctant understanding was painfully evident. He seemed almost embarrassed by his role in the entire affair. How odd for a man employed by a mysterious king of the underworld and ruler of its miscreants.

"Have you worked for him very long?" It was important to discover just how deep the loyalty ran in these men working for Kingston. Who might be swayed to her side when faced with the choice between right and wrong? Would a single one of them abandon their vow of service to a heartless monster? She wondered if they would have leaped into action had she tried escaping during Kingston's absence.

"Years, miss," Paulie said, giving her an odd look as if realizing the direction of Ava's questions. "And I worked for his father before that."

"I see."

They continued through the dizzying twists and turns of the corridors toward what Ava assumed was the final destination of a dining room.

"Miss?" Paulie's voice was soft with understanding. "It may not seem like it from where you stand, but Kingston is a man of his word—good or bad. A man of principles, regardless of how perverse they may seem to an outsider. If he says he'll release you when the debt is paid, he will."

"I'm afraid of what he'll do when my brother continues ignoring his demands," Ava replied solemnly.

Paulie's weathered features turned equally grim. He scrubbed a hand through short salt and pepper hair. "Like I said, good or bad, he keeps his word.

The dining room was one of the areas Ava was free to utilize inside the house. She'd not paid it much attention when Kingston showed it to her before, but it truly was decadent. It resembled something straight out of a European castle, and under other circumstances, Ava would have delighted in its overwhelming grandeur.

"Here you go, miss." Paulie held one of the double doors open until she passed through, then softly closed it behind her.

Ava took a deep breath, her eyes immediately locking with Kingston's.

He was seated at the head of a table, an imposing piece of furniture that could have come straight from Buckingham Palace. Easily accommodating twenty-five people, it was a long, continuous expanse of gleaming ebony wood. A table like that costs thousands of dollars. Probably more than she'd paid for her car, a used beat-up Toyota purchased with savings from her first job at a local museum.

Slowly, Kingston rose from one of the ornate chairs. Arms crossed behind his back, he waited as she approached. Soft, classical music played in the background, drifting throughout the room from speakers that were as well hidden as the mansion's cameras.

Ava bit her lip then quickly released it, mindful of the lipstick she wore. She hated how fast her blood thumped through her veins. As if her body subconsciously missed him and now rejoiced with his return.

He appeared so stern and foreboding that, for a brief moment, Ava hesitated going to him. Why was she so easily commanded by Kingston Winter? It required just the tiniest gleam in his eye indicating desire and she moved forward as if under his spell. There was no reason behind it. If she possessed even a sliver of self-preservation, she would run screaming in the opposite direction.

But truly, what choice did she have? She must remain committed to this intent of softening his heart. She must somehow change his mind about selling her.

Kingston's lips twisted. How easily he must recognize her inner turmoil. Did he know how badly she wanted to tug her skirt down so her thighs weren't so exposed to his hot gaze? How her brain screamed that she turn and run?

Even the subjects in the various gilt-framed artwork adorning the wood-paneled walls seemed to watch Ava as she made her way further into the dining room.

She recognized some of the pieces. Pastoral scenes of meadows and maidens, surrounded by a flock of lambs. Conversations between elegantly dressed lords and ladies at tables set for a tea party in a lush garden. A meeting between a shy woman standing beside a stone wall smothered in a cascade of lush, pink roses and a dark-haired gentleman doffing his cap on the opposite side of the wall. A winding river with a woman and man sprawled upon its banks. The woman lay tucked between the man's legs with skirts ruched high, her breasts exposed to his mouth and lips. His hands gripped her rounded shoulders, pulling her to him.

And another Ava recognized with a startled jolt of awareness—*The Coward* by Edward Robert Hughes. The girl fled the banks of a placid lake where others swam. With clothes clutched tight in one hand, her bare, pale legs flashed in the pursuit of escape. It was an exquisite piece of art held in a private collection. The curator at the museum where Ava once worked coveted that particular painting. Seeing it now, she understood why.

A strange sense of connection with the girl in the painting settled over Ava. She, too, was a coward. Running from situations and people she found uncomfortable. She'd been closing her eyes to the hard truths in her life for far too long.

Dragging her gaze away from the artwork, Ava concentrated on walking with suddenly wobbly legs. When she was close enough that he could reach out and grab her, Kingston finally spoke.

"You are stunning." His voice was low with approval. Dropping his gaze to her mouth, he almost growled, "And fuck, that lipstick. It's begging to be smeared in places other than your lips."

She wanted to ask where he'd gone during his absence, but the words couldn't form fast enough when he talked like that. Like he was dying to ravish her and might at any second. She focused instead on the lavishly set table.

It was set for three diners. Dark grey china and square-based crystal goblets carved into exquisitely modern sharp facets adorned the table. Gleaming silverware, heavy and expensive, reflected the light cast by three oversized crystal and antique bronze chandeliers.

Mesmerized by the luxuriousness of the room, Ava did not realize the heel of one stiletto had become entangled in the fringe of the plush Aubusson rug.

She tripped, plunging headfirst so quickly that there was no hope of stopping her body's momentum.

In one swift motion, Kingston caught her before she tumbled on her hands and knees in front of him. With his large hands wedged beneath her armpits, he swooped Ava up as though she weighed nothing at all.

Landing so hard against his body sent the air in Ava's lungs whooshing out. Instinctively, her fingers gripped the muscles bulging beneath the material of his expensive tuxedo. A squeak of alarm escaped her throat as he crushed her against him.

"Are you okay?" Kingston's voice rumbled.

Ava's face flushed scarlet red with embarrassment. She was holding him as tightly as he held her. "Yes. I'm sorry…"

He would release her any second, but how she would hate the moment it happened. Something between them shifted as Ava stared up at him. A flash of understanding and mutual need. A mystifying pull drew them closer and closer.

It was madness, of course.

Insanity.

But there was no escaping reality.

She was attracted to her kidnapper. Her captor. Her jailer.

Her tormentor.

Kingston's brow furrowed, his husky voice breaking the odd spell between them. "I believe you are still caught in the rug."

Ava gulped and tried tugging her shoe free. If she pulled harder, it would tear the rug's fringe, and that rug probably cost more than a year's worth of rent for her tiny apartment back in Bitter Springs. "It seems so." She could not ignore the heaviness of the air hanging between them. How it thickened and swirled the longer Kingston retained his grip on her. "I'm not used to wearing such high heels. I'm sorry," she apologized again.

"You should wear such things often," Kingston replied huskily. His dark blue eyes searched hers, then dropped to stare at the outline of her mouth. Ava startled when his thumb brushed lightly across her bottom lip, smudging the scarlet lipstick just enough so that it imprinted onto his skin. "You are gorgeous dressed like this. Wearing these shoes... this dress. Even more so because you are dressed for my pleasure."

Ava held her breath, hating how his attention made her so compliant. His words did something strange to her insides. She was melting into his arms, head swimming with over-whelming desire and awareness. She wanted him as badly as he wanted her, and it was horrifying. "Your decorator likely wouldn't agree, considering my heel is probably ripping the fringe on this expensive rug," she responded with a nervous laugh.

"Let me fix that..."

Then he sank to his knees before her.

His stance was reminiscent of a man proposing, and Ava's hands immediately slid to his shoulders, holding on tightly to retain her balance. In an almost dazed state of consciousness, she stared down at the top of Kingston's head. A dizzying sense of déjà vu overtook her as flashbacks of the cell assaulted her memory.

Memories of this man on his knees before her. Worship-ping her body with his mouth. His tongue. His teeth.

Ava's knees nearly buckled when he spread a large hand over her calf as a way of steadying her balance.

Kingston worked swiftly, untangling the fringe and freeing the shoe within a matter of seconds. But when he was done, he remained kneeling at her feet, gazing up at her from beneath the thick fringe of his eyelashes.

It should be criminal for a man to possess such thick eyelashes, to smell so damn good, and to be so good-looking. All that wickedness hidden beneath such a handsome veneer.

"There. No harm done," he whispered, both hands now cupping her calves. Slowly, he slid them higher until they were at her knees, then higher still until he gripped the back of her thighs. He held her like that for a long moment while Ava's breath lodged in her throat.

His hands were so warm. Hot, actually. Burning through the sheer thigh-high stockings as though she wore nothing but gossamer. His fingers pressed harder, leaving matched divots in her flesh.

Ava shivered with disturbing restlessness.

"Fuck, you are beautiful, Ava Blue. So damned beautiful." His thumbs moved up and down in a caressing manner, his hands moving higher until they slipped beneath the dress's short hem. Those large, rough hands coasted even higher until they cupped the cheeks of her bare behind exposed by the skimpy thong. Ava's face heated with embarrassment.

"Did you miss me while I was away, Ava?" he demanded in a low voice that made her insides clench.

"No. I did not." Ava gasped, digging her fingers into his shoulders. "Kingston. You shouldn't..."

He squeezed her flesh in response, a dark chuckle escaping him when she let out a breathy moan.

"You are a liar. God, I'd love nothing more than to toss you up onto that table and devour my dessert before the first course is served. I'd feast on you until you screamed for mercy. Until you begged me to fuck you. However," Kingston's hands slowly withdrew, sliding away from Ava as he rose to his feet. He towered over her, a wicked grin curving his beautiful mouth as he took her hand. Pressing a hot kiss to the back of it, he held tight when she would have jerked free. "You want that, and this isn't about what *you* want."

EIGHTEEN

ot with a cloudless sky so far
Above
And Hell not so far
Below

AVA'S MOUTH tightened with his words.

He'd angered her. Mostly because what he said was the truth. But Ava couldn't possibly know he found this attraction between them just as perplexing and infuriating as she obviously did.

While away in the city, he'd spent a great deal of time checking the cameras for glimpses of his prisoner as she drifted in and out of the mansion's rooms and explored the grounds of his estate. And he logged in too many times to count during the night just so he could watch her sleep in that king-size bed.

Pulling a chair out from the table, Kingston indicated she

should sit down. Ava hesitated for a brief moment before sliding into the cool wooden seat.

Her eyes darted to the place setting opposite her own as Kingston sat in the chair situated at the head of the table.

"It's not just the two of us for dinner tonight," he murmured. "Doctor Abbott will be joining us. You do like Doctor Abbott, don't you?"

He could see the question made Ava nervous. Was she worried about what he might do if she said yes?

"It's okay if you like Neil, Ava. He's one of my closest confidants. A trusted friend. I *want* you to like him."

Her gaze narrowed. "I think he's a very kind man who has been placed in a difficult situation."

Kingston could not conceal his smile. "And what might that situation be, lamb?"

Ava's breath hitched, but she met his stare defiantly. "He works for you. That can't be easy, considering your reputation."

"My reputation?" Kingston's head tilted as he softly mocked her. "As a businessman, it is above reproach."

Her chin tilted. "I'm referring to your reputation as a murderer and kidnapper."

"Ah. That." Amusement seeped into his tone. "You should know I've never taken a life without prior justification. And I told you I've never abducted a woman before. You are the first and last."

Her hands twisted in her lap, consternation flooding her delicate features. "You think this revelation should please me."

"It doesn't?" Kingston ran a finger along the rim of one of the crystal goblets before him. A faint, melodic note rang out. "At the very least, it should ease your mind."

Ava was prevented from replying when Neil pushed through

the double doors into the dining room. Kingston noted a flash of appreciation in Ava's gaze for the dashing figure the doctor cut in his tuxedo. An air of relief also seemed to wash over her.

"Hello, Miss Blue," Neil said. Ava did not rise from her chair as he came forward and took her hand. He placed a quick kiss on the back of it, mimicking Kingston's own gesture.

His hackles immediately rose.

He hated the shy smile Ava gave his friend in response. Hated the way Neil handled her so gently. Mostly, he hated the instant jealousy roiling through his body at the sight of another man handling his captive.

"Have a seat, Neil," Kingston said in a tight voice.

Neil shot him a curious glance but did as requested. His chair was on Kingston's right side and directly across from Ava.

As if awaiting a magical signal, Antony entered the dining room followed by his kitchen assistant, Cal. The men carried large trays laden with the first course of the meal. Bowls of delicate tomato soup with fresh basil and cream were placed before them.

Ava's mouth drew even further into a thin line, her dismay evident.

"It is your favorite, is it not?" Kingston asked as Antony ceremoniously popped the cork on an expensive bottle of sauvignon blanc. The chef poured wine into Ava's and Neil's goblets while Kingston enjoyed a glass of scotch on the rocks.

"You already know the answer to that," she replied. "Obviously."

Kingston smirked. "Yes. Obviously."

"Your wrist has healed nicely, Miss Blue," Neil interjected with a determined note in his voice. The tension between Kingston and Ava was laughably evident. The atmosphere almost crackled with it. Little wonder the doctor would try diffusing it with banal conversation.

Ava favored Neil with another one of those smiles that had Kingston's stomach clenching with some unknown emotion.

"Yes. It hardly hurts at all now."

From the fierce glint in her eyes, Kingston knew Ava was remembering the moments surrounding that injury. And everything she'd suffered since.

"Do you live here at the estate, Dr. Abbott?" Ava asked, dipping a spoon into the creamy soup.

"I have a room but prefer living in the city. I have an apartment there." Neil's eyes crinkled with friendliness. "And I've asked you to call me by name."

"Only if you call me by mine, Dr. Abbott," was her shy response.

Kingston bristled. Had the two of them become so cozy that first names were now involved?

"Neil likes his privacy too much. He never stays longer than a few days at a time," Kingston muttered around a mouthful of scotch.

Ava and Neil both glanced at him as if surprised by his terse tone.

"That's true. My visits here are usually of a social, nature although I do technically work for our host." Neil's laugh was easy. "I've numerous responsibilities in the city, and I chair several charitable organizations as well."

"So, your main job isn't necessarily tending to victims here at The Den?" Ava asked with deceptively innocent wide eyes.

"Dead people do not require a doctor's care," Kingston growled. "And, Ava?"

"Sir?" Her gaze swung back to clash with his. She practically purred the single word, well aware she'd succeeded in pissing him off. She even mocked him with the use of the title he'd insisted upon.

"Drop the subject." Kingston idly swirled his scotch until it mingled with the ice, gliding up along the sides of the glass. "Unless you'd like a repeat of the night you tried running away from me."

Ava's fingers tightened on the spoon. The glance she gave him was nothing short of murderous.

"Do I make myself clear?" he prodded, an eyebrow arching high. He almost wished she would continue this rash foray into defiance. Having her mouth around his cock again was something he would thoroughly enjoy.

"Crystal clear," she bit out.

Neil cleared his throat in obvious discomfort. He shot Kingston a disapproving glare as he sipped his wine and ate his soup.

Twenty years his senior, the doctor had become one of Kingston's closest friends while in service as a physician to his father. He'd stitched Kingston up the night Alan Winter sliced his chest open during a drunken rage. He tended to Oliver's mother during her bouts of depression and self-harm. He doctored him and Oliver both when his father beat them. Now, he tended the employees at LIST, the exclusive club Kingston operated. The man had knowledge of Kingston's worst transgressions, and yet, he remained fiercely loyal.

"Let us talk of other things," Kingston said. "I've made Neil uncomfortable, reminding him of the night you bashed him in the head with a soda pop bottle."

Ava flushed as she laid her spoon down alongside the bowl. Her gaze flitted to meet Neil's. "I've apologized to the doctor many times for that."

Neil smiled at her across the table. "And I've accepted many times."

It was a friendly exchange, but Kingston hated it.

"Now that we've cleared that up, you can stop eye-fucking each other right in front of me," he bit out, swallowing the remainder of his scotch in one swallow. He slammed the glass down on the table, immediately regretting the words the moment they tumbled from his mouth. He came across jealous and sulky.

Completely unlike his usual dry, cruel self.

Neil leaned back in his chair, giving Kingston an exasperated glare. "Whatever you are imagining, King, it is simply that. Your imagination."

Kingston did not answer as Antony entered the dining room with the next course of the meal. He ignored Ava's gaze trained upon him, the tension in her body plainly conveying her disgust with his behavior.

Antony preened over the dish he set before them, explaining in great detail the preparation of the swordfish and the intricate sauce accompanying it. Ava listened intently, granting the chef a sweet smile that suddenly… irrationally… crazily… Kingston wanted for himself.

What the fuck is wrong with me?

Time spent away from her had only solidified Kingston's growing obsession. The sole purpose of his trip was to determine the level of interest in this prize he'd captured. And yet, discovering how intrigued men were by the prospect of purchasing Ava only left Kingston with a twisted knot in the pit of his stomach.

Carson really did have feelers out for the purpose of selling his own sister. In fact, Ava's brother had already contacted some of the same buyers Kingston extended invitations to. And Oliver was there in the middle of it all, facilitating matters with the inclination to somehow knock Kingston off his throne.

Finally, Antony retreated from the dining room. With soft music echoing in the huge room, there was no conversation between the three diners. Kingston noticed Ava simply pushing the fish around on her plate while drinking more wine than she should have.

Which seemed fitting, as he drank far more scotch than he needed.

Ava finished a third glass of wine, and that, apparently, was the magic number to loosen her tongue. Smiling at Neil across the table, she shook her fork in his direction and squinted her eyes.

"What charitable work do you actually *do*, Doctor?"

"Neil," he reminded her, then with a quick glance in Kingston's direction, he said, "I work with an organization that assists women in getting back on their feet after escaping abusive situations."

"Really?" Ava's eyes widened. "These would be women fleeing a husband or boyfriend who has mistreated them?"

Neil nodded. "It's not always husbands or boyfriends. We also help women whose family life is not ideal. Women and girls who have suffered a tragedy and require a little help. Kingston is the most generous donor we have."

"Shut up, Neil," Kingston growled.

Neil continued with a benign smile. "I'm also the on-call physician at LIST. Have you heard of it?"

Ava's head tilted in confusion. "Some girls were discussing it once at a campus bar. I thought it was something related to the university. When I asked one of them if it was a scholarship opportunity, she looked me up and down and said I should apply. But when I asked the scholarship office about it, they had no idea what I was talking about."

Kingston scowled. This was definitely a subject he wished to avoid. Neil, on the other hand, blithely ignored his irritation.

"It's a club of sorts," Neil explained. "The employees specialize in certain... activities... and I help ensure everyone stays safe and healthy."

Ava's face was blank for a few moments before realization sank in. "It's a sex club." Her gaze swung to Kingston. "You own a sex club?"

"It's an exclusive social club," Kingston replied stoically. "If members engage in sexual relations, there are mutually agreed upon protocols which are strictly followed."

"Do you harvest your employees at LIST from Dr. Abbott's charitable work?"

"No. That would be unethical, of course."

Ava stared at him in disbelief as Kingston huffed out a more thorough explanation. "Many of those women are far too damaged for that type of work. Rest assured, no one at LIST is forced to be there." He refused to acknowledge even the slightest bit of shame for being involved with this particular business venture. A membership in LIST was highly coveted and the opportunity to work there even more so. His employees were handsomely compensated for their time and enjoyed the freedom to work as they willed.

A bit of devilry danced in Ava's mossy green eyes. She was inebriated, her cheeks flushed pink from the warmth of the wine. "How that must annoy you, Kingston Winter. Helping disadvantaged women under the guise of charity while also kidnapping and selling a few here and there for your own personal benefit. Kind of a contradiction, don't you think?"

"I've not yet sold you, lamb. Remember, I might decide keeping you is far more lucrative."

"If you possessed a single thread of decency, you'd let me go," she hissed.

"If I do, your own brother will sell you off before I can snap my fingers. That's his plan, you know. He's already set things in motion. Trust me, Ava, you're safer here at The Den with me as your jailer until I learn more of his plans and intentions.

When Oliver returns, a few of these questions will be answered."

"Will you add me to your stable of prostitutes at this LIST place? Will I be passed around or will I belong to a single man?" She demanded answers, the words flailing Kingston like lashes. Even Neil sat silent, his fork hovering above his plate as Ava fired off questions.

"Those women are not prostitutes, Ava. Positions at LIST are highly coveted. Employees are carefully selected, work of their own free will, make a shit-ton of money, and are pampered and protected until they leave my employment." Kingston fixed Ava with a stony glare. "They want for nothing and make their own choices—regardless of the situation. Or a client's kink."

"Ah, the benevolent pimp." Ava laughed disparagingly. "How refreshing."

"Ava, it isn't like that. I can personally attest to the truth of what King is telling you," Neil assured her.

Kingston winced to hear the level of concern in the other's man's voice. His best friend would like nothing more than to scoop Ava up and comfort her.

Ava's gaze flashed to the doctor. "I will likely be sold to the highest bidder. In the meantime, I'm held here against my will, dressed like a doll, and paraded about this mansion for Kingston Winter's personal enjoyment. I'd say that makes me a whore. And he is nothing but an Armani tuxedo-wearing pimp."

"You've had far too much wine. It's making you overly emotional and irrational," Kingston muttered. "I should have remembered you rarely drink alcohol and limited your consumption."

"I'm not a child. You can't tell me what to drink, nor how much I can drink." Ava's fingers tightened on the wine goblet's stem before she defiantly swallowed down the remains in the glass.

"You're earning a punishment, lamb," Kingston warned. If Neil hadn't been present, he would have already wrapped a hand in Ava's hair and had her body anchored over his lap for a much-needed spanking. Damn if that wasn't the image pounding in his brain now.

Ava's breath caught at that. As if she couldn't believe his audacity in mentioning punishment. Then all the fight seem to rush from her body, her shoulders slumping with dejected weariness.

"I want to go home."

The anguish in her words and the underlying sob were as loud as a nuclear bomb going off. And when her heart-shaped chin wobbled, the tiny movement was a dagger stabbing Kingston's heart.

Then he ruthlessly crushed his reaction to her pain.

"This isn't about what you want, Ava. This is about the repayment of a debt owed. A rather large debt. If I ignore or forgive it, should I fail in making an example of your brother, my enemies will attack from all sides. And Oliver will be leading the charge. Do you think you'll find yourself in better hands if that occurs?" Kingston refilled his scotch and gave a subtle shake of his head at Antony. The chef hovered in the dining room doorway, ready to remove their dishes and bring in the final course of dessert. A frown creased the elderly man's forehead, but he dutifully backed out.

"I don't care. I don't care what you do to my brother. Or what you do to your own. I hope you all kill each other, honestly. Then I can go on with my life," Ava said, wrapping her arms around herself. An almost hysterical laugh escaped her. "I can't believe I must argue the point of how insane and wrong it is to kidnap and sell people. I don't care how much charity work you sponsor. One does not cancel out the other."

"We've had this discussion previously. We won't have it a second time," Kingston replied. "The wrongness of this is a non-issue."

"You drugged me. You kidnapped me. You've held me against my will in a dungeon cell. You watched while your brother mauled me. *You* assaulted me. And you will sell me for money." Ava's voice trembled as she hovered on the verge of tears.

"This discussion is over," Kingston said in his hardest tone yet. The litany of transgressions committed against Ava was not something he wanted to dwell upon. Especially the mention of what his brother had done.

A familiar stubbornness overtook Ava's features. "Talking about your crimes is upsetting? Imagine being the victim of them."

"Ava, don't push him on this. Please. It won't end well," Neil advised.

Ava slanted the doctor a harsh glare. "You... you should be ashamed. You are a doctor. A decent man, I think. You have a duty to take care of others and see to their well-being. And yet, you sit at the right hand of a monster and condone his crimes."

Neil possessed enough decency that Ava's words made his face flush a dull red. "You're absolutely correct, Ava. But like you, I'm a part of something much bigger than myself."

"That's enough, both of you." Kingston's hands clenched into fists.

Ava stood up quickly. "You're right. It is enough. *I've* had enough. Excuse me... I'm ready to return to my room."

Kingston watched impassively as she fled the dining room.

"Will you let her go alone?" Neil threw his napkin down

across his plate. His features were stormy with conflicted emotion.

"No." Kingston picked up his glass, swirling the liquor inside it in a circular motion. "But she needs a few moments so she can calm herself down."

"Before you punish her?" Neil snorted in disgust.

Kingston tilted his head while regarding his friend. He understood Neil's desire to rescue the princess in the tower. But that was an impossibility here. Ava was *his* princess. His to ruin. His to own. *His to save.* "That's not your concern now, is it?"

Neil pushed back from the table. "It became my concern when you brought her here, King."

"Don't suddenly develop a conscience now, Neil. I've done a lot worse over the years, and you know as well as anyone the amount of blood on my hands. I've not harmed her, no matter what she thinks or says to the contrary."

"Yeah. Blood from people who deserved it. That girl doesn't deserve any of this. Let her go and focus your attention on her brother."

Kingston's laughter was harsh. "I can't let her go. Haven't you been listening? She's not safe... not with Carson making his plans and my own brother helping him."

"You know this for a fact? That Oliver has aligned himself with Carson?"

"I had him followed. He reached out to my enemies and offered up Ava." Kingston shook his head. "I always suspected Oliver would betray me one day. He still blames me for Rebecca's death. Seems he's using Carson and this debt as a way of achieving that goal. He returns tomorrow but I haven't decided how I shall deal with him. He is my brother, after all."

Neil shook his head. "I can hardly believe he would go against you like that. But Kingston... make no mistake, you are all using Ava as a pawn. It's wrong and so damned disturbing on all levels. She doesn't belong in this world. And deep down inside, you know this."

Kingston scowled. "I haven't crawled up to where I am by doing the right thing, Neil. She might not belong in this world, but for the moment, she belongs to me."

"Then you must protect Ava by any means necessary. She should not be used by Carson or Oliver." Neil's voice lowered. "Or by you, Kingston. Don't make her a whore for your own personal benefit."

Kingston tossed back the scotch. His fists clenched with the effort it took to keep from punching Neil in the mouth.

His friend's statement hit a raw nerve in the recesses of Kingston's black heart. Realization made everything so much clearer. So much brighter. This obsession with his captive was leading him into unchartered territory. A foreign land where it might be possible to care for another's welfare. And while Ava certainly hated him, it wouldn't stop him from protecting what was his.

Even if he was forced to erase the threats with his own bare hands.

CHAPTER

NINETEEN

or I love you with a wounded heart
For all of time
Across universes and fallen stars

AVA FLED THE ROOM, chest tight with emotion and her head spinning from the wine.

Her destination was not clear-cut. While she'd intended on returning to her room, her feet carried her someplace else. She wasn't even sure where her blind panic led her until she found herself on the pool deck.

Leaning over a low stone wall, she stared out into the ominously dark edge of the forest and heaved in giant gulps of the cold night air.

How foolish she'd been, thinking a man as cruel and heartless as Kingston would show mercy. Her hands shook as the reality of her situation truly and completely sunk in. She gripped the stones of the wall, digging her fingers into the nooks and crannies of the rocks.

She would indeed be sacrificed for Carson's debt. There was no escaping it.

Nausea boiled inside Ava, despair mingling with white-hot rage. Never before in her life had she experienced such raw anger. It was all-consuming and foreign. And she didn't like it. Didn't like the ugliness soaking through her. Didn't like that she could justify hurting someone and likely revel in their pain.

A choked sob escaped the tightness of her throat. She could not become a monster like the man holding her captive. She must escape here before she lost herself in rage and despair and vengeance. Fighting off the urge to bite her nails, she instead dug them into the stones, welcoming how the rough surface was tearing them up.

Waking her up.

She couldn't sleepwalk through life any longer. She had to fight back. Against Carson and his years of cruelty. Against life as it smothered her. Against Kingston Winter and his desire to own her.

That one would be the hardest to fight. Because some twisted, deviant sliver of her darkest soul wanted to belong to the Devil. She'd never wanted anything so badly than to be Kingston's good girl. His wicked lamb. *His.*

God, what is wrong with me?

"Ava."

His voice startled her, but she wasn't surprised by his presence. He stalked her as a lion would its prey. Silent. Merciless. Fatal.

"Get away from me." Ava's hands dropped from the stone wall, curling into fists at her sides. Like a steel rod, her back straightened. Staring out into the night's darkness, she wished for the ability to melt into its stars. Away from him. Away from this ugly world and its array of painful deceptions and betrayals.

Kingston's voice was steely, and yet, somewhere below its surface, just as tormented. "The fuck I will."

Ava took a deep, shuddering breath. She teetered on the high heels, unsteady with emotions and the effects of the wine. "Can't you understand what this is doing to me?"

"I don't care."

She tried another approach. "This is wrong. It's heartless and cruel."

"Playing on my sympathies won't work." Kingston huffed out a laugh. "I have no heart, Ava. Don't bother looking for one."

"Just let me go…" Ava whispered in despair. She didn't mean the words, but her soul depended on him showing mercy. "Please…"

His reply was gruff and instant.

"I cannot. Not when the sound of you begging makes my cock so hard, I think it might burst."

He was on her then, arms wrapping like steel bands around her waist while yanking her back against him. His head dipped to the curve between her neck and shoulder, his mouth marking her with fiercely gentle kisses and tiny bites from sharp teeth. Then he soothed it and the faint bruising from his previous bite with soft, persuasive lips.

"The reality is you are only safe within the walls of The Den, Ava. Here with me. At my side."

"Where you will eventually tear me apart?" Ava demanded, digging her fingernails into Kingston's forearm to no avail. "I'll take my chances out in the real world."

"Fuck me, lamb. I'm trying to protect you—"

"But who will protect me from you, Kingston Winter?" Ava cried out. "Who will stand between me and what you have planned for my fate?"

"Your fate," he scoffed, "it appears, is tied to my own." His words were clipped and brutally direct. "I won't forgo the claim to my pound of flesh. Any mercy I show comes with a price."

"When my brother pays up, will you let me go unharmed?"

"Perhaps. If I believe it's safe, yes. Although it will be a mistake of a magnitude you obviously cannot comprehend. Carson will place you in this same situation again." Kingston released her until there was just enough room that she could rotate within the circle of his arms. "And the next man who takes you as payment for your brother's debts might be far worse than me."

"I doubt such a man exists."

Kingston smiled, the gesture failing to reach his eyes. "You'd be surprised at the depth of depravity existing in the real world, Ava. For the moment, I'm the only barrier between your sheltered sensibilities and everything wicked."

"You don't have to be the bad guy, Kingston," Ava flung at him, her voice trembling and low-pitched. "You can do the right thing and find reward in being a decent person."

Kingston laughed under his breath, the dark chuckle sending a tremor of fire-sparked awareness through Ava.

"But I enjoy being the bad guy, Ava. I like it when people are afraid of me. I like not having others get too close. You should give it a try. Less of a chance of you getting yourself hurt. Or worse, letting someone down after they placed their faith in you."

Ava peered up at him, surprised by the bitterness of that unprovoked confession.

As though aware he'd revealed too much, Kingston's mouth twisted into a cold grimace of a smile.

"I don't want to damage you to the point of brokenness, but if it becomes necessary, I will not hesitate. When Carson fails to pay, you will accept your fate. You will become mine in full. And whatever manifestation that takes, you will submit." His dark blue eyes scrutinized her. "Are we agreed on this, Ava?"

Ava shivered at the implications of being his until the day he eventually tired of her. What would become of her then? A bullet to the head or a miserable existence spent on her back as a sex slave? "It's not fair I should pay the price for my brother's greed."

Kingston inclined his head. "We've established how unfair and wrong this situation is. It's also unavoidable. I don't forgive debts, lamb. Someone must pay."

"Lucky me," Ava muttered as another shiver racked her body.

"Come back inside the house now," Kingston commanded in his usual calm, collected manner. "You aren't dressed for this kind of weather."

With his long strides and the grip of her wrist, Ava was left with no choice but to totter after him. As they entered the mansion, she cursed herself for being so stubborn. The effects of that last glass of wine left her woefully unprepared to protest Kingston's handling. Even though fury boiled inside her, she still followed her captor.

By the time they reached Ava's luxurious prison on the third floor, she was definitely lightheaded and disgusted with her own weakness.

The wine had her head spinning, her brain struggling to make sense of Kingston's actions and words as well as her own. Why did she keep swaying between acceptance and desire and heated resistance to this man's intentions?

"Here you are," Kingston muttered as he swung open the door and tugged her inside.

Ava practically fell into the room. She caught herself just

enough to land on the edge of the bed instead of ending up sprawled across the floor.

"Careful now." Kingston quickly helped steady her before stepping back. But in a telling gesture, his hand moved from gripping her shoulder and slid along her jaw. And Ava nuzzled into the warm cradle of his palm before snapping back to awareness.

With a shake of her head, Ava pushed him away, then bent with the intention of removing her shoes. Her fingers fumbled with the tiny straps wrapped about her ankles. Angry tears formed but she blinked them away.

Kingston stopped her, gently pushing her upright. Those blue-black eyes glittered as he stared down at her. His jaw tightened in recognition of her inner turmoil.

"Let me, Ava."

Before she knew what he was doing, he sank down on a knee. Lifting one of her feet, he placed it on his thigh, not seeming to care when the stiletto heel dug into his flesh.

He unfastened the delicate buckle on the thin strap. When his fingers brushed her ankle through the thin barrier of the silk stockings, an involuntary moan fluttered in Ava's chest. Kingston's hand was a flame against her skin, and there was no defense against it.

A tiny smile lifted the corners of Kingston's lips as he slipped the shoe from her foot. He admired the expensive bit of footwear for a moment before setting it aside. Placing her now bare foot on the floor, he lifted the other and made quick work of the remaining shoe's strap and buckle.

"Do you do this for all of your women?" Ava whispered, dreading his answer and yet unable to keep the words from spilling out of her mouth. Jealousy consumed her. Stupid, foolish envy she had no business entertaining. He was her enemy. Her captor. And she should be fighting tooth and nail to free herself rather than staring at him in simpering adoration.

Kingston glanced up from beneath a sweep of dark lashes. "Only the ones I've taken captive."

Ava fell silent, her tongue twisted with both longing and disgust that she felt anything at all for this man.

Slipping the shoe from her foot, Kingston sighed. "You intrigue me, Ava, if you must know the truth. I should not have this compulsion to keep you. Or even to help you. And yet, I cannot stop thinking about you. How sweet you taste. How gorgeous you are in your defiance."

Ava's mouth tightened. She wasn't quite sure how one responded to an admission of obsession.

Kingston still did not rise from his kneeling position. Instead, he fixed her with a probing stare while his hands moved up between her thighs. His palms slid over the silk stockings until they finally reached the lace banding which kept them in place.

"I find myself kneeling before you frequently, lamb." He tugged the stockings down her legs, carefully slipping them past her knees and ankles until the flimsy pieces fluttered away like rose petals. "Too often for my own peace of mind. Too often for my liking. I don't like it. A king does not kneel to his slave."

Ava's eyes closed with the reminder of her status. She had no rights in The Den. No status or privilege. Everything she was given was dependent upon this man's capricious, cruel whim. "I've not asked it of you, Sir."

Kingston's fingers coasted over her skin, charting a path toward the inner softness of her thighs. His lips pulled into a slight frown upon hearing the voluntary use of the title he'd demanded of her.

"Say my name, Ava." The request was a low growl.

Ava met his gaze, an unfamiliar warmth curling through her. The intensity of emotions in Kingston's fiery black-blue eyes stole her breath.

This was dangerous. Heady. Frightening and foolish. The burgeoning need and desire to belong to a beast like Kingston would ultimately be her downfall. Because he could not be trusted. He could *never* be trusted. He would rip her to shreds at any second and laugh while doing it.

Yet, the danger called to Ava, and she was helpless against its lure.

Hesitantly, her hand stretched out toward him. Then her fingers were tunneling through the thickness of his dark hair, the strands sliding like the most luxurious silk. The ends curled ever so slightly, and it was almost endearing how the waves of his hair coiled around her fingertips.

"Kingston." Her voice was barely audible, the wine softening her tone. Lowering her defenses. Leaving her vulnerable to a villain's attention.

With shaky fingers, she traced the silver-pink scar on his left cheek.

Kingston's eyes closed, and for a brief moment, his shoulders relaxed. With its faint etchings of worry and cruelty, his face smoothed into something almost peaceful. He sank into her reluctant caress like a massive cat hungry for attention.

Ava trembled, realizing with abrupt clarity that she was not completely helpless and at this man's mercy.

I do hold some power here; I only need to harness it. Use it. Give him reason to become infatuated with me. Because I must ensnare him as easily as he captured me. Because if he grows to care for me, even if it is only sexual, maybe... maybe he won't hurt me.

As if capable of hearing Ava's innermost thoughts, Kingston's eyes snapped open. The blazing intensity in the swirling sapphire depths was mesmerizing.

"Do you think to tame me, lamb?"

Ava shook her head, even as her heart leaped in her throat hearing the silky note of violence in his question. "No, of course not. How could I even accomplish such a thing? It would be impossible."

His eyes narrowed. "But you aren't above trying, are you?" His fingers drifted higher until they disappeared beneath the hem of her dress. "You'd like nothing more than to bring me to my knees and keep me there, wouldn't you?"

Pushing her immediate response aside, Ava calmly returned his questioning stare. "I'm of the impression no one can make you do anything you don't want to do, Mister Winter."

The small smile curving his pillowy-soft lips was dangerously benign. Ava sucked in a breath because his fingers were now tracing the minuscule lacy triangle of her underwear.

"That's true enough." His fingers pressed a bit harder as if attempting to breach the fabric. Ava wanted badly to close her legs, but something dark and wicked deep inside her soul stopped her. She inched them apart a little further.

"Please..." The words slipped out, and Ava's cheeks flushed hot pink. Why was she begging him? She'd promised herself she would never...

"I like hearing you like this," Kingston said in a low voice. One large finger threatened to nudge past the thong's gusset until it brushed over bare flesh. "All breathless and needy."

Ava swallowed hard as desire swelled inside her with his words.

"Do you like me touching you like this, Ava?" His eyes were trained on her as his finger moved over her panties in a rhythmic glide. "You will answer me, lamb. Do you like this?"

"Y-yes," she groaned in surrender, struggling to stay upright on the bed.

Kingston's laugh was darkly knowing. "Lie back, Ava. Let me make you feel good."

A sliver of pride floated to the surface. *No.* No, she would not let him use her like this. He could not just decide when and how to play with her and her emotions. God, everything inside her ran hot and cold when it came to this man.

How could she hate him so much but want him so terribly?

"I can't," she choked out, pushing his hand away and scrambling back on the bed. "This isn't right. *You* have no right."

Kingston sat back on his haunches; his eyes darkened with lust. "Your brother's debt says otherwise."

Ava's chin lifted. "I want to negotiate terms. I've a right to make demands when it comes to what happens with my body."

Kingston rose to his feet, raking a hand through his dark mane of hair. "*You* want to negotiate?" Rocking back on his heels, devilishly handsome in his black tuxedo, he gave her an indulgent smile. "All right. Let's hear it."

Ava pushed the hem of her dress back down, well aware of Kington's gaze following her movements. The tension between them was almost palatable. It hung so heavy in the room Ava could barely breathe.

"You will not touch me until there is an answer from my brother." She purposefully hardened her tone. "And the moment he pays, you will release me. In the same condition that I came to you."

"I don't care for those terms," Kingston replied in a languid tone. "We both know your brother will not honor this debt. For all intents and purposes, you are already mine." He leaned a shoulder against one of the bed's columns, his manner casual and relaxed. But Ava knew better. She recognized the tension in his hands as he crossed his arms. A muscle ticked along his jawline as he contemplated her. "Denying me only makes me angry." His smile turned mocking. "And you don't want to see me angry, little lamb. It isn't very pleasant."

"You've promised my freedom," Ava stubbornly pressed. "You wouldn't go back on that. You *wouldn't*. Honor among thieves... isn't that the saying?"

"But you're not a thief, Ava."

"Perhaps I'll change my ways," she retorted. "A life of crime may suit me just fine. After all, look how well you've done with it."

The silence stretched and popped until, finally, Kingston muttered beneath his breath, "Fine."

His jaw was clenched so tight, Ava thought it might shatter like glass. But Kingston simply nodded his head, his mouth stretching into a grim line.

"I already agreed to release you if Carson pays what he owes. And if he doesn't, you will be mine in every sense of the word. To do with as I wish. Sell you or keep you, it's my decision, and you will surrender yourself to that reality." He turned to leave the room but then paused by the door. Throwing her a scorching hot glare, he added, "A word of advice, Ava. Even thieves will honor an honest debt. So, you better prepare yourself for the moment I collect mine."

CHAPTER

TWENTY

I am mystified by you
And this aching need.

THE HIGH-PITCHED, muffled scream woke Kingston from a dead sleep.

At first, he thought he must be dreaming. Reliving a nightmare from his youth. A flashback to those days when his father abused women simply for the pleasure of it. Those women were usually willing at first, but the intensity of his father's punishments often meant a quick reversal of their complete submission.

The scream echoed again, and Kingston's heart clenched with unreasonable dread. He rolled from the bed, grabbing his pistol and then reaching for the solitary key resting on the nightstand.

Ava...

Racing down the hall, Kingston's blood pounded in his

veins. He was already mentally prepared to annihilate the person harming her, his hands automatically preparing the weapon for use.

He drew up short at seeing Jack pounding the door to Ava's room. The man struck the thick wood over and over while intermittently calling her name.

"She's not answering, Kingston. Just keeps sobbing. You heard her screaming? You've got the key, right?" Jack rammed his shoulder into the door in an attempt at forcing it open. "Goddamn this thick-ass door."

"Move over," Kingston ordered, pulling the key from the pocket of his sleep pants. Within seconds, he had both locks undone and was shoving his way into the room with pistol drawn.

The room was not completely dark. Light from the bathroom crept in, throwing little slivers that arced across the floor. There was just enough illumination to reveal Ava sitting in the middle of the bed.

She was alone. Her hands gripped the covers, and even in the shadowy dimness, Kingston could see the terror etched on her face. Sharp cries interspersed with her heavy breathing filled the room.

Kingston rushed to the bed, gathering her against his bare chest and holding her tight. She shook within his embrace and continued whimpering.

"Check everything," he said to Jack, who was already pushing open the door to the bathroom with his own gun drawn.

"Clear," Jack announced before moving onto the only hidden space in the room, the closet. That done, he moved to the windows, yanking the drapes aside and checking the locks.

Kingston smoothed a hand over Ava's hair. It was a tangle of blonde curls, and when he gripped a handful of it, the essence of honeysuckles and wild roses drifted to his nostrils.

"Shh, Ava. Shh..." The attempts at soothing her hardly made a dent, but at least she was no longer screaming. She huddled against Kingston, trembling and still making those awful sounds. Muffled, agonizing cries that seemed as though they'd hung up in her throat but would break free at any moment. She seemed unaware of Kingston's presence, and Jack's as well.

"Closet's clear. No one is in this room, King." Jack's face was a study of confusion as Kingston cradled Ava closer. "And no one got past me and that door. The windows are secured as well with no sign of being opened or closed. They are securely locked."

Kingston shifted on the bed, moving until he could peer down into Ava's face. She stared back at him with unseeing eyes, sobbing with such heartbreaking pain that Kingston couldn't help but wince.

"I think she's having a nightmare or something. She doesn't seem to realize we're even here," Kingston muttered as he rubbed a hand over Ava's bare arms. She wore a silky night-gown of deep blue silk and one strap had slipped off her shoulder.

"Might be a night terror. My sister had them a lot when she was young," Jack said, leaning over to peer into Ava's face. "They say you shouldn't try waking a person up from a night terror. They might hurt themselves or you."

"Night terror?" Kingston frowned.

"Yeah." Jack straightened, returning his gun to its holster. "It's like a nightmare but the person never remembers what happened. She'll come out of it eventually. My sister always did, and she wouldn't remember a damn thing about the commotion she'd caused." He chuckled. "Gotta admit, I just about shit myself hearing Miss Blue scream that first time."

Ava was finally quieting down within the circle of Kingston's arms. Realizing his own pistol was ready to fire, he flicked the safety and laid it on the bed.

The matching robe to her gown lay across the end of the mattress. Snatching it up in his free hand, he settled it over her quaking shoulders.

"I think I might have lost a few years myself," Kingston said in a low voice. "It would be an impossible feat in this house with all safety measures in place, but I thought someone had gotten to her. Oliver... her brother... one of my enemies."

Jack did not say anything, but he moved to the bedroom door and hesitated in the opening. "My sister outgrew her night terrors, although she still has them when she's stressed out. She almost always has a migraine prior to an episode. But there's no rhyme or reason to these things. Sometimes they can be from prior trauma, but more often than not, it's just one of those weird things some people suffer from. Doctors told my parents it was no cause for alarm and they were right."

Kingston's jaw clenched tight at the mention of trauma.

Had he done this to Ava with his own actions? Had he terrorized her enough that she had nightmares about him?

"She probably shouldn't be left alone, King," Jack commented with just enough concern in his voice to set Kingston's teeth into a firm clench. "Want me to stay in here with her?"

Fuck no, I don't want you in here with her like this. I don't want any other man around her.

Kingston barely kept from blurting out something completely out of character for him. Shaking his head instead, he tucked the robe tighter around Ava's body before rising from the bed with her slight weight nestled in his arms. His gun rested in the same hand he curled around her shoulders. Big and ugly in comparison to Ava's delicate beauty.

She settled against him with a low sigh, a small frown creasing her brow, even as she continued sleeping as though she'd been drugged.

Seeing Kingston's confusion, Jack offered, "Night terrors are exhausting. She probably won't wake up until morning."

"I'll take her back to my room." Kingston wasn't sure how he remained so calm. Every instinct he possessed and every fiber of his being was firing off with the explosive need to hold and protect this girl. It left him slightly woozy. "You're off duty, Jack. I've got her for the rest of tonight."

Jack gave his signature two-finger salute and exited the room to wait in the hallway. Once Kingston passed through the doorway, Jack pulled the door shut and made sure it was secure.

Once inside his own suite of rooms, Kingston deposited Ava on the bed and removed the robe from her shoulders. His weapon was replaced in its specialized hidden space on the headboard, and with a sigh of consternation, he slid under the covers beside her.

Laying on his back, he tucked an arm beneath his head and stared up at the ceiling. He'd never had a woman share his bed. Never slept with one for an entire night. This was totally new to him.

Would Ava be angry once she woke and discovered where she was? Would she scream and fight? Try to get away? All unknown factors. And Kingston hated unknown factors.

Beside him, Ava moaned and rolled closer. Kingston held his breath as her lithe body snuggled beside him. Her sweet scent drifted over him, and he found himself relaxing. What a strange thing this was. To be so disturbed and yet calmed by another human being.

"Hmmm," Ava mumbled, and in the next instant, she was fully against him, one arm thrown across his chest as though he were nothing more than a huge body pillow. She burrowed in so close, her breath feathered his neck.

"Shit." Kingston sighed. His body was instinctively reacting to hers. He grew harder, his cock swelling in response to her soft warmth.

He positioned his arm so she used his shoulder as a pillow, then shifted so she naturally moved closer. Damn. He wanted her badly. Badly enough to disregard how utterly wrong it would be to fuck an unconscious woman.

Which reminded him of this apparent issue with night terrors. Why did he not know of this condition? How was it possible this slipped his investigation into every aspect of this girl's life and background? He knew *everything* about her. It was unacceptable that he was just now learning about this.

The most pressing question was how long she'd suffered from the condition. When did it start? What was the catalyst? Did it have anything to do with her asshole of a brother? Was it possible this was a result of her parents' untimely death?

Or was this her first episode?

Could it be that he was responsible for such a violent occurrence?

A spearing of guilt twisted Kingston's insides. Maybe he was to blame. After everything he'd done to this girl since her arrival at The Den, he wouldn't be surprised.

After all, she was innocent in all of this. This ruthless mission to make her brother pay. This punishment of others who dared cross or cheat him. While his terrifying reputation dictated such actions, Kingston reluctantly acknowledged that dragging Ava into the middle of it was wrong.

Wrong. Wrong. Wrong.

It was a concept he'd not concerned himself with for many years. He did what was best for himself and his interests.

Kingston scowled.

He'd conceded this girl would be set free if her brother paid the amount he owed. He'd conceded he would not take her virginity until her brother made his decision. Yes, he'd agreed to Ava's foolish demands, but would he actually honor them?

He wasn't sure. This growing possessiveness was adversely affecting his decision-making. He'd thought he'd get what he wanted—either the money or her virginity—and then toss her aside at the end of her usefulness.

But that was not happening.

Invisible threads were being woven, meshing the two of them together. He'd made far too many concessions already. Had overplayed his hand by claiming this girl as his. These lapses in judgment would broadcast his weakness to his enemies, including his own brother.

Ava Bella Blue had become a dangerous liability Kingston could not afford.

But letting her go was not an option.

TWENTY-ONE

*T*o belong.
To possess.
To stay.

KINGSTON KNEW the moment Ava woke. He knew because he'd lain in a suspended state of agonized arousal for most of the night.

Earlier, he'd breathed a sigh of relief when Ava rolled away from him. The new position meant those firm, perfect breasts of hers were no longer pressed like hot irons against his ribs.

But the relief was short-lived. No sooner did Kingston exhale, a groan of disbelief escaped him when her rounded ass settled against his hip.

As a result of that, he remained on his back until apparently dozing off. But now, as he came awake, he realized he too was on his side. One arm was wrapped around her slender waist, holding her firmly in place.

Which meant her ass was lodged in his groin. As close as

close could be. Only the thin, blue silk of her nightgown and the sleep pants he wore separated their flesh from bare contact.

Kingston wanted to rip away the barriers when Ava mumbled in sleepy confusion. Her eyes fluttered open.

Like a band of iron, his arm tightened around her waist while his mouth hovered above her ear.

"Good morning, lamb. Or maybe it's still night. I'm not sure."

To her credit, Ava did not react in the hysterics he expected. She lay completely still, assessing this unforeseen situation and how she might have landed in it.

"Did you steal me from my bed?" she finally whispered.

"No. But it was necessary I bring you here."

"Necessary?" Ava sighed. "The Devil thinks it's his right to steal souls. I'm not surprised that you believe you can do what you want. Take what you want."

"Maybe that's true. Maybe I am the Devil himself, but I've not yet taken what I truly want." Kingston's lips brushed along her neck. Goosebumps immediately sprinkled her bare arms and shoulders. He smiled at seeing evidence of how he affected her.

"Why am I in your bed, Kingston?"

He nibbled the lobe of her ear. "Are you so certain this is my bed?"

Ava was quiet for a moment, then said, "It smells like you."

"And how do I smell, lamb?"

Her calm acceptance of her situation amused him. Did she always wake up so complacent after a night terror episode?

He knew she chewed her bottom lip before she murmured, "Like Christmas trees and salty air. And Earl Grey tea. But I'm waking up in your bed, Kingston, when I fell asleep in my own. I want to know why. I hardly drank enough wine to pass out."

Kingston's arm tightened again, effectively moving her closer. When his hand splayed across the flat plane of her stomach, Ava inhaled a sharp breath. With her free hand, she gripped his wrist, preventing any further movement.

"You promised you wouldn't until there was word from Carson one way or another."

He *tsked-tsked* in mock disappointment.

"I never promised anything of the sort. I said I would let you go if he paid. Does my touch worry you, Ava? It shouldn't. I won't do anything you don't like," he growled in her ear, his body settling more firmly against her until there was no mistaking his arousal. "Let loose of my hand. Now."

"No. You're twisting what we agreed to last night..."

An annoyed grunt escaped Kingston. Fuck, she was persistent in these attempts at making him behave. And she was partially correct in her accusations. He purposefully manipulated their negotiations to his satisfaction. Ava was insane if she thought he would agree to those conditions. There was just no way that was going to happen. Not when he was already addicted to her smooth skin under his fingertips. Not when he needed it, needed *her,* like the air in his lungs.

His hand moved lower and Ava trembled. Her fingernails dug into his skin, leaving little half-moon indentations behind.

"I won't fuck you, but I will touch you as I please," he said. "Now, let go of my hand before I decide punishment is in order."

"Y-you tricked me. This isn't fair."

"I'm a bad man, remember? You can't expect someone like me to play by the rules when it comes to something I want."

Ava slowly loosened her grip as the truth of his statement and what she'd negotiated sank in. "Will you at least answer my question? How I ended up here?"

Kingston stroked her belly through the silk of her nightgown, ignoring her hum of distress. "You don't remember, obviously, but you suffered a nightmare of some sort. The screaming woke me up. When I entered your room, you were hysterical but also still asleep."

"Oh." Her tone held no surprise at hearing this. Just a sort of sad resignation.

"You nearly scared Jack half to death. I've never seen the man turn so white."

"I'm sorry. For Jack's sake, anyway."

"You've had this happen before?" Kingston frowned, his hand stilling in its sensual caresses. "This wasn't the first time?"

Her body, already tense, tightened even more until she was a slab of unyielding marble lying beside him. "Being your prisoner does not give you unlimited access to everything that makes me who I am," she argued. "It's really none of your business, Mister Winter."

"Everything about you is my business, Ava."

The words murmured into her hair made her soften for the briefest moment before she regained her composure.

"Your concern is unnecessary and unwanted. *I* don't want it."

"That smart mouth of yours is going to get you into trouble," Kingston calmly replied, his hand resuming its subtle caressing through the silk gown. "I answered your question, lamb. Now, you will answer mine. You've had these incidents in the past?"

Ava hesitated as if considering how to respond before she grudgingly replied, "Yes. It's happened before."

"When did it start?"

"The year my parents died." Her voice quivered. She went to chew her fingernails, but with his free hand, Kingston stopped her.

"I'm gonna break you of that habit, Ava. Maybe give you something else to put in your mouth every time you feel the need."

The intention behind the threat was clear enough. Ava immediately lowered her hand with a defeated sigh.

"Does this stem from the night Carson's friends assaulted you," Kingston probed.

"Maybe. I don't know," she snapped, frustrated by the interrogation. "Does it even matter?"

Kingston was already making plans to eliminate those men from the face of the earth. A necessary thing that should have taken place years ago. "It matters to me."

"Why?" Ava's incredulous laugh rang out. "Nothing they did compares to what you've done."

"You're right about that. There is no comparison, lamb. Shall I list the differences between their sordid behavior and my own depravity? *They* didn't make you wet. They didn't leave you panting with lust or limp with satisfaction." Kingston's hand inched up the hem of her nightgown, tugging it higher until his fingers gained access to bare skin. "They didn't make you come like I make you come. *They* didn't even try."

"What are you doing?" The desperation in the question made Kingston smile.

"Pleasing us both," he replied, his hand slipping closer to the tiny scrap of her thong. "Have you kept yourself shaved for me?"

She made a frustrated noise in her throat and squirmed against him. "I'm not answering that!"

Ignoring her indignation, he nipped her ear. "Tell me, Ava. Have you?"

He knew the question both embarrassed and angered her. When it became apparent he expected an answer and would have it regardless, she finally snarled, "Yes," in an almost inaudible voice.

"Good girl," he praised, and damned if she didn't subtly arch against him with a reluctant purr.

Kingston's fingers danced closer to the gusset of her underwear. "You like being my good girl, don't you, Ava?"

"No," she choked out angrily while writhing her ass against his crotch.

"Liar." His chuckle drifted over her neck, followed by his lips as he pressed a warm kiss there. Her sweet innocence intrigued him. It softened him in ways he didn't quite understand. He shouldn't care whether he had her approval or surrender, but for some inexplicable, *insane* reason, he asked, "May I touch you, Ava? Will you let me make you feel good?"

The request for permission didn't startle Ava nearly as much as it did Kingston himself. Because he *never* asked for permission. He just took what he wanted, when he wanted it.

Why he deviated from his usual MO now was shocking, but the words, once spoken, could not be retracted.

Ava was still for a long moment, then her body relaxed in slight degrees against his.

Something intangible shifted between them. A meeting of mutual desires of some sort. Silent acknowledgment and acceptance of the attraction between them and the inevitability of the course it would take.

"Would you stop if I said no?" Her question was a whisper.

Kingston frowned, but still, his lips moved over her neck once more. "I don't know. Maybe. But I guarantee I'll not ask permission a second time." He nipped the spot where her pulse beat just below her jawline. "I suppose this is an unforeseen opportunity for you. You may deny me this once."

She seemed to think it over, and Kingston swore the heat of her body increased with every passing second. His fingers twitched, waiting for her response. Whichever she chose—surrender or rejection—would destroy him.

"Will you hurt me?" Ava finally asked in a murmur so low he could barely make out her words.

"Probably, lamb. But I think you'll like it."

"Yes," she agreed in a strangled voice that held all the tortured confusion of the moment. Disappointment, desire, and anger at her own weakness laced the words. "Yes, I want this. Whatever this is. It's wrong and dangerous, but I'm tired of resisting. Tired of pretending it's not extraordinary when your hands are on me. Please touch me, Kingston. Please."

CHAPTER
TWENTY-TWO

G*ossamer threads bind us*
Blind us
Intention and reason
Delicately ripped away.

Ava knew it was madness.

She'd just invited the lion to rip her apart. To feast on her at his leisure. To devour her until nothing remained of her soul.

This man would take and take until there was nothing left for her to defend.

But still, she nearly wept with pleasure when he growled against her neck and his hand delved fully between her thighs, pushing past the silk of her underwear as though it did not exist.

Cupping her mound, the heat of his large palm branded bare skin. His hum of approval vibrated her body.

Some crazy part of her wanted to please him. To gain his

approval. She wanted his eyes burning with the same lust capable of incinerating her feeble defenses.

God help her, but she wanted Kingston's surrender as badly as he wanted hers.

She tried turning in his arms, her hands moving so she could explore his body. But his gently snarled command stopped her.

"Be still, Ava. If you must grab something, then reach above you and grip the bars of the headboard." He chuckled darkly, pressing his palm against her until she gasped. "In fact, I want you to do just that and remain as you are on your side."

Ava quickly obeyed, her fingers wrapping around the headboard's thick iron bars with distressing eagerness.

"What a good, fucking girl you are," Kingston crooned, and those wicked words sent a lightning bolt of electricity straight to Ava's center. "And how soft and slick you are here. So wet. Drenching my hand with your lust. You've no idea how much it pleases me to know you kept yourself shaved, anticipating this moment when I would see you like this again."

Lifting his hand slightly, he smoothed an index finger over her tender flesh with such delicate intensity, Ava could not stop her hips from bucking forward, melting inside from his words of praise.

What is wrong with me? Why am I craving this of all things from this man? He's a monster. A liar. A criminal and user of women... I should not...

"Shh, lamb." Kingston shifted his own body until his other arm cradled her head and his free hand was anchored around her throat. "Shh. Don't you trust me?"

It was as though he knew the path of her most secret thoughts. Could hear the inner turmoil rattling around her psyche. How could she defend herself against such deviousness? It was impossible.

"No," Ava moaned. "But I don't want you to stop either."

"Clever girl. You should never trust the Devil." His one hand tightened around her throat while his fingers slid over her pussy, parting her flesh and spreading her arousal. "This makes you wet, doesn't it, Ava? Touching you like this excites you, but at the same time, you're wondering if I might squeeze just a little too hard. And you're wondering how you can even like this." His fingers flexed slightly, and Ava choked back a whimper of fear, even as her body quickened with a staggering burst of lust.

Kingston chuckled, his finger moving in a steady pace against her pussy. Slow, steady, and maddeningly insistent. He flirted with the sensitive nub there, never quite touching it as he glided everywhere else.

"My hand holding your breath hostage makes you even wetter. Hotter. Maybe that's the key to unlocking you. The hint of danger. Oh, my good girl really is bad, after all." His thumb brushed over her clit, and Ava whimpered in helpless, greedy supplication. Her legs parted to give him better access, and without letting loose of the headboard, she writhed against Kingston's muscular body.

Every part of her burned like fire. Her breasts ached, her nipples hard against the silk nightgown. Her inner channel clenched with need, and blood sang through her veins as though she'd ingested the purest drug on the planet.

And Kingston... Oh God, *Kingston.* His erection was hard and heavy against the cheeks of her ass. She could not stop herself from rocking against it as his fingers parted the folds of her pussy and his thumb pressed harder against her clit.

She was delving into madness, but she didn't care. This insanity was too good. Too right. Too perfect.

"You keep grinding on my cock like that, and I'm gonna end up fucking you, Ava," Kingston's calm warning rasped in her ear. He'd not moved at all, except for his hands, and Ava marveled at his restraint as she pushed back harder against him.

Desire left her dizzy with recklessness. She *wanted* him to fuck her. To make her come. To obliterate her quiet, sane, *boring* life. To claim her so she belonged *somewhere*.

To someone.

"Please," was the single word she managed as the crescendo inside her rose higher and higher.

"Please what, Ava?" Kingston taunted. His voice was rough with need, and yet, at the same time, he was so perfectly in control that it was frightening. "Please fuck you as hard as I want to? Or please make you come on my hand while you ride my fingers?"

Two fingers slid inside her channel as his thumb pressed harder on her clit. The hand around her throat tightened just a bit, and with deliberate slowness, Kingston pumped the digits he'd inserted inside her. When they curled against the inner wall of her vagina, stroking in the most maddening way, she nearly screamed at the intense sensation.

"Oh *God...*"

"You're so tight. Goddamn, Ava. I'm gonna love stretching your pussy until you are a custom fit for my cock. And I can't wait to hear you scream when I finally fuck you. From pleasure. From pain. From the need to get more of what I can give you. I want to push in another finger, but I doubt you can handle three. And I don't want you to bleed. Not yet, anyway."

Pressing harder on her clit, Kingston rotated his thumb a certain way, and all the blood rushed from Ava's head to where his fingers invaded her body.

Her vision blurred, the shadows of the room darkening as her climax came roaring upon her, and Kingston whispered dark, dirty things in her ear.

"Come for me, Ava. Just for me and no one else. Come for me because you are mine. Because your body, your soul, this pussy gripping my fingers so tight, they're all mine. All of you, every fucking inch. *Mine*. And fuck me, I don't care what I promised in a moment of weakness. I'm *not* letting you go."

Her head turned toward him, her mouth seeking his. Their lips fused and melted together, their tongues tangling and twisting in a frantic searching of souls.

Ava shattered into a million, broken, desperate shards with those words. Release, sweet and heady, cascaded through her body along with a terrible, sobering realization.

She was his. *His*. And she could hate Kingston Vaughn Winter, despise him, try escaping him, or even attempt to murder him, but nothing could or would ever change this simple truth.

She belonged to him.

No. That wasn't right. That just made her a possession. A nameless, faceless body Kingston desired and coveted for the moment. He wanted her like he would a new car. Or maybe an expensive watch.

She was more than that. She would *become* more than that to this man.

I belong with *him*.

Whether she wanted the lunacy of it all or not, that was the godawful truth of the matter.

"Christ, Ava," Kingston muttered along the curve of her neck when he finally stopped kissing her.

Loosening the hold of her throat, he stroked the skin below her jawline—soothing away any residual evidence of his mastery. "I've never seen or felt anything more goddamn gorgeous than you coming in the palm of my hand. The way you cry out. The sounds you make. The way your sweet, greedy pussy squeezes my fingers. I'm addicted to it."

Ava did not respond. She couldn't, not really. She was too exhausted. Too languid to think straight while drifting away on a sea of endorphins. She lay in a complacent state of pleasure and smiled slowly when Kingston untangled her fingers from the headboard.

"You can let go now." Pulling her closer, he cradled her against his body until they could have been matching spoons.

"If I do, I might fall over the cliff," Ava mumbled around a yawn, linking her fingers with his where his hand nestled in the valley of her breasts. She still wore her nightgown, and through it, the heat of his flesh warmed her. Against the swell of her bottom, his cock strained for entrance.

Kingston made no move to rectify his condition. The realization put Ava at ease more than it should have. She was so drowsy. And tired of thinking. Tired of strategizing. Tired of fighting.

"Why would you fall off of a cliff, Ava?" A hint of amusement lurked in his voice. Didn't he realize she was speaking metaphorically?

"When this is all over. When I'm back in the real world," she explained in a sleepy mumble. "Don't worry. Even if I fall, I can take care of myself. I always do…"

"You won't fall, Ava. I won't allow it."

"So domineering," Ava grumbled as she snuggled deeper into the pillows and his embrace. Her eyes fluttered shut although she really wanted to stay awake. His odd statement demanded further exploration, but she was already drifting off to sleep. "You can't control everything, Kingston Winter."

His arms tightened around her, and his mouth was surprisingly gentle when he brushed a kiss over her temple. "If you say so, lamb."

TWENTY-THREE

All that remains
        Is the heartbeat
                Of something wild and untamed.

WHEN AVA WOKE the second time, the room was still murky with shadows, but slivers of greyish daylight penetrated past the heavy drapes.

It was morning, but just barely.

She lay very still for a long time, her breathing even and measured, before slowly turning her head toward the second set of pillows.

Kingston was not there. She was alone in his bed.

Sitting up, Ava pulled one of the pillows to her chest, taking a quick assessment of the room. It was very spacious. Impeccably decorated in black and grey tones. Contemporary artwork adorned the walls, and the furniture was heavy, dark wood. Behind the bed, the entire wall was constructed of a single slab of slate-colored stone. It must have been hewn straight from the mountains surrounding The Den and secured on-site. It was rough. Rugged. And it was a stark contrast to the modern sleekness of the room's furnishings.

Had Kingston purposefully left her there alone? Had he been called away? Would he come back...?

Ava's breath caught in her throat at that thought. And the next made her heart thump even faster.

Will he touch me again? Will I try stopping him if he does?

She hugged the pillow, eyes squeezing tight while her body strummed with trepidation. The flesh between her legs was sore and tender. A harsh reminder of Kingston's invading fingers.

Remembering how easily he destroyed her defenses was disturbing on so many levels. How could she want him like that? Why had she begged him when she'd sworn so many times she would never plead for mercy?

Taking a deep breath, Ava pushed back the silk comforter and tugged at her nightgown until it covered the tops of her thighs. The matching robe lay in a discarded heap on the edge of the bed, and she snatched it up. Once it settled over her shoulders, she swung her legs to the edge of the bed and sat up. Her body sagged with the familiar exhaustion she usually experienced after an episode of night terrors.

Then she simply listened.

Within the quiet stillness came the faint rush of running water. In the gloomy darkness, Ava located the door leading to what must be the bathroom. A thin sliver of light illuminated through a crack at the bottom of it.

Kingston was in there. Probably taking a shower. Maybe even scraping away the shadow of his beard with that custom-made straight razor he'd recently used on her own body.

Ava tugged her bottom lip between her teeth. She worried it while wondering what she should do. Laying down and going back to sleep was out of the question. Escape was a possibility. In fact, she could return to her own room before Kingston emerged from that bathroom. She wouldn't have to face him.

Coward.

Her lips twisted in acknowledgment. She was certainly that. A weak coward subject to the rule of one man.

But she didn't have to be. She could stand straighter. Stand up for herself.

"Remember what you told him," she murmured. "You don't have to be his puppet. You don't have to be his good girl. You don't have to listen when he tells you what to do. But to survive, you will."

She hopped out of bed, tying the sash of the robe tighter around her waist with sharp, business-like movements. Stomping to the bedroom door, her hand was actually on the knob when a strange groan came from the bathroom. It reverberated beneath the running water. Ava stopped in her tracks, ears pricking up.

A low grunt this time. A muttered curse.

Her name… hissed as if the person who uttered it was in excruciating pain.

Hesitating, Ava contemplated following through with her plan. She should escape Kingston's lair before he realized her actions and stopped her. But when the noise came again, she leaned her forehead against the door and took a deep breath.

What if he was hurt? Maybe he'd fallen and required medical attention. Was she the type of person who could turn her back on an injured person?

"Damnit," she whispered.

Padding silently to the bathroom door, Ava pressed her ear against the thick wood. She could not bring herself to just burst into that room. Something told her to move a bit more stealthily than the situation perhaps called for, but that was her nature. To think and react methodically. Consider options and solutions.

She almost started to chew a fingernail in her usual method of dealing with stress but stopped herself. Kingston didn't like it when she bit her nails. He wanted her to stop, and she wanted that, too. There was a sense of accomplishment when she resisted the urge by taking a deep breath.

Ava turned the doorknob carefully, slowly. Taking another inhaled breath of courage, she leaned her head around the door's edge and peeked into the bathroom while standing just outside the door.

The room was constructed entirely of white, creamy marble. The walls and floor glistened with the expensive material. Along one wall, a freestanding tub sat framed by a huge arched window, and an enormous antique chandelier dripping with crystals was suspended above it. The window's glass was dark, but Ava could see the forest beyond it. There was a switch on the wall enabling one to operate the glass's opacity.

Tearing her gaze from that, her attention went to the shower area. It was an enormous space built of marble and glass. Through the swirling steam, Ava saw double rain shower heads, multiple jets, and matching handheld shower wands on opposite sides. The shower took up a huge portion of the bathroom, and its luxuriousness was magnificent.

But it was what Ava saw inside the shower that was responsible for the immediate flames of fire licking through her body. She stared in rapt fascination at the man standing beneath the water's onslaught.

Kingston leaned forward with one hand braced against the marble wall. Water sluiced down his form. Because the other three walls of the shower were clear glass, Ava viewed him in all his heart-pounding, chiseled glory. Every muscle, every slab of sinewy flesh, every contour was on full display. As she stared in dazed appreciation, she slowly realized that while Kingston steadied himself with that one hand, the other was between his own legs. And he was slowly stroking a massive erection.

Ava could not look away. She gripped the edge of the door until her fingernails ached, and within the pit of her belly, a shameful craving erupted. Kingston Vaughn Winter was beautiful. A man hewn from granite and muscle. And she knew how his cock felt when it pressed against her trembling body. Knew what his flesh tasted like because he'd pushed himself into her mouth and forced her to savor him once before.

No. She could not look away as her enemy pleasured himself, all the while muttering her name as though it were a curse.

For a heartbeat of absolute insanity, Ava considered slipping out of her nightgown and into the shower with him. Her hands flexed in a convulsive grip on the door, her throat dry as she watched in avid curiosity. Kingston's large hands stroked with rough urgency. His cock expanded within the circle created by his capable palms, and still, to Ava's utter damnation, she could not tear her eyes away from the magnificent spectacle before her.

"Ava."

The low growling of her name had her gaze flying to clash with his. A gasp pushed past her lips as Kingston pinned her with a glare. Even through the steam, Ava could see his eyes. Dark, stormy blue blazing with furious lust. Burning through her. Incinerating her embarrassment and quickly disintegrating the last shreds of any modesty she still possessed.

She returned his stare. Embarrassed. Stubborn. Curious.

And worst of all, aroused.

Kingston's fingers tightened around his cock. He groaned, never breaking eye contact.

He *knew* she watched him. And he enjoyed it. Relished shocking her. Reveled in knowing she desperately wanted what he held so tight within his own hands. His mouth quirked with recognition of their mutual lust.

Sanity flashed through Ava. She was losing herself in this man. Drowning in his twisted world of sex and power and domination. He was changing her into someone she did not recognize. Someone desperate for his attention. And willing to take anything he deemed she could have.

Fumbling with the door, she tried retreating, but Kingston's sharp command froze her in place.

"Don't you fucking dare run now, lamb. I'm two seconds from coming in my own goddamn hand instead of filling you with my cum. And you are to blame for *that*. So, don't you fucking move. You... you stand right there. Right where you are..." Another long stroke, faster this time, elicited a guttural groan from deep within him. "And you watch me, Ava Blue. You watch what you've made me do. And if you don't like standing on the sidelines, then get your sweet little ass into this shower and get down onto your knees. I want to fill that pretty mouth of yours up until you choke on me."

Ava could not move even if she wanted to. His words... his filthy, degrading words sent a flood of moisture to the aching flesh between her legs.

It was quickly followed by a wave of shame so intense it left her reeling.

Because for a heart-stopping moment, she seriously considered following his orders. She *wanted* to sink to her knees before him. Suck him off until tears ran down her cheeks and he exploded in her mouth. She wanted everything he could give her—no matter the loss of her own soul. She was prepared to sell that useless bit of nothing to the very Devil himself. Which could only mean one thing.

She was as sick as he was. Just as twisted and depraved. After all, what normal, *sane* woman wanted to be treated in such a manner?

Oh, God. What had Kingston done to her during the short time she'd been his captive?

"Fuck, Ava... The things I'm imagining right now. All the dirty, amazing, terrible things I'm gonna do to you..."

His movement stilled, his hand gripping his cock as though he could stop the inevitable. But there was no stopping the freight train of his climax, nor the resulting tremors shaking through Ava when she witnessed the visible evidence of his satisfaction. It was as though *she* experienced his orgasm along with him.

Kingston groaned louder; the hand braced on the wall clenching into a tight, white-knuckled fist. Semen splattered on the marble, his release painting the creamy white surface before washing away in pale rivulets.

His head hung low, his wide chest heaving from the exertion of jacking himself off. The rain shower fixture drenched his sculpted body, and the steam of the bathroom increased by the second. Ava could see it rolling in filmy waves over his wide shoulders and down his muscular back.

None of it seemed real. This was a scene torn from a dirty fairytale, a sensual nightmare that just couldn't be real. She'd stood like an imbecile and watched a man masturbate himself to completion. This wasn't reality. It couldn't be... and yet...

"Get in here and lick me clean, Ava. I want to feel your mouth on me..."

Kingston's eyes burned into hers with smoldering intensity. When his mouth tilted upward in a smirk, Ava knew he intended the words to both shock her and assert his dominance.

If she obeyed that depraved order, she was truly doomed.

"No. No…"

Was she saying the words aloud, or did they only echo inside her head? Was the refusal directed at Kingston and his command, or at herself for wanting exactly what *he* wanted?

Ava quickly backed out of the bathroom, bumping the door jamb with her shoulder before slamming it with a forceful bang. Kingston's amused laughter echoed in the room as the water was shut off. There was the click of the shower door opening and then closing with a muted thump.

I can't stay… I can't stay here…

Frantically, Ava searched for something that would effectively barricade the door. There were few precious seconds to act. A little bit of time could be gained while he leisurely toweled himself off, but it wouldn't be much.

Instinct told Ava he was in no hurry to come after her— arrogantly secure in the belief she would never run from him again. But eventually, he would emerge from that bathroom and find her trembling for him. Her panties soaked. Breath coming in gasps. Nipples hard and aching for the pinch of his cruel fingers. He would bend her over the bed, slide inside her, and she would let him.

A whimper of frantic despair rattled inside her throat. She couldn't stay in this room. Couldn't be near him.

Because she had no control over herself or the situation.

Ahhh—there!

An occasional chair sculpted into clean, modern lines of iron and leather strapping occupied one corner. It might do the trick. Dragging it to the bathroom door, Ava jammed its rounded back under the doorknob. She'd seen that done in a movie once. Hopefully, the makeshift wedge would work in real life, although she would not stick around to see if it did.

Her fingers shook as she exited the bedroom. She relocked the door behind her, giving her a few more seconds to flee.

A heavy wood and iron bench sat directly across from Kingston's bedroom door. Thinking quickly, Ava untied the sash of her robe and knotted one end around the door handle and the other through the bench's fretwork. When Kingston opened the door, there would be the extra resistance of the bench's weight. Even more time in which she could make her escape.

With only a vague memory of her own bedroom's location, she sprinted to the suite's main door and entered a dimly lit corridor. Her heart pounded like wild horses within her chest, thumping against the cage of her ribs as she turned in what she hoped was the right direction.

There was no illusion of escaping the mansion itself. Dressed as she was, it would be insane to attempt it again. The mansion was surrounded by dense woods, and cameras were everywhere. And ringing in Ava's ears was Kingston's terrifying threat of what he would do if she dared try it a second time.

No, she would not run from the mansion, but for her own sanity, she must escape this man. Even if the safety of her room was a temporary and fragile shelter, she must take it.

TWENTY-FOUR

rush
   Conquer
   Protect

ONCE PAST THOSE secondary doors protecting the entry into Kingston's wing of the house, Ava ran down the corridors in a blind panic. She constantly glanced over her shoulder in case Kingston chased her. If he caught her now, there was no hope.

With attention focused on who might be chasing her, Ava was unprepared when she rounded a corner and collided with the solid, muscled form of a man. The impact knocked her backward, slamming her to the floor on her rear end. Bracing herself with her hands was a mistake, the sharp stab of pain a reminder that her wrist was still tender.

"Son-of-a-bitch..." an unfamiliar voice exclaimed before large hands reached down and jerked her back onto her feet.

Ava stared up at the man. She did not recognize him as being one of the men under Kingston's command, but obviously, he had the freedom to roam throughout The Den. Swarthy skin and dark eyes were her first impression, followed by the realization this man was holding her aloft in a grip bordering on painful.

"Well, what do we have here?" The man grinned, his teeth flashing white. "Are you lost, sweetheart? Or maybe you're a welcome back present."

"O-Oh, I j-just—" Ava stuttered, acutely aware of the provocative nature of her clothing. She wore only the silky blue nightgown and the matching robe which fluttered open without the sash. "Yes, I do seem to be somewhat lost. This place is enormous, and I guess I, uh, took a wrong turn."

"Boss doesn't usually let his girls up here. He always secures them down in the cells until he's done using them." His gaze flickered over Ava's body. "Guess I can see why he made an exception for you."

Ava shuddered, although she quickly hid the involuntary reaction. The man still held her by the arms, his gaze hotly assessing. He was younger than Kingston. Mean looking with a low forehead and a burly mass of muscles encased in the same understated suit worn by the other men here.

The plan to escape popped into her head. Hopefully, her response came across as nonchalant. "Yes, ah, Mister Winter's done with me. I thought it best I should just go... since he's done with me and sleeping now. Said I could ask that a car be brought around for me so I can get back to the city. You know, since he's done. With me, that is."

Would the man notice how she bumbled through that or would lust blind him?

"Done with you, huh?" His head tilted in question while a larcenous gleam illuminated his dark brown eyes. "I can't imagine he's okay with letting you leave. Sweet little thing like you... I bet you fucked him all night long."

Ava shrugged. The window for escape was closing with every second that she endured this unexpected interrogation. Why was this man roaming the halls at this time of the morning anyway? "Yeah, I guess. So, can you get a car for me? I came to The Den dressed like this... special request and all."

She was certain the bluff was working until the man's cruel lips quirked upward.

"What will you give me in exchange?" He backed Ava up until her shoulder blades hit the wall, her wrists transferred into one of his meaty hands. The other slid her robe open. His eyes darkened with appreciation at the sight of her curves accentuated by the silky nightgown.

He palmed her breast through the material, rubbing her nipple. "No need to rush off so quickly when I just got back. Been in Mexico, doing a job. Didn't even have time to get my dick wet. So, I'm thinking a quick fuck right here will suit me just fine. Don't worry about how you just left his bed. I don't mind sloppy seconds one bit."

Ava's heart seized with nauseating fear, although she managed a calm response to his vulgar suggestion. "Mister Winter won't like that. He, ah, doesn't like sharing, you know?"

"Do you think I give a damn what the boss likes and don't like? Because I don't. Besides, most of my orders come from his half-brother." He brushed his mouth across hers, and Ava tasted sour beer like he'd been out all night drinking with buddies. "This job has few perks, so when one runs right into me, I'd be stupid not to take advantage of it. Tell you what, after I get a taste of what the boss man's had, I'll get you a car. Hell, I might even drive you myself. Anywhere you want to go."

Ava trembled. She must remain focused on this unexpected opportunity to escape and play it out as best she could. He obviously thought she was one of Kingston's whores. The ones shackled down in the cells who were used until it was time to toss them aside. And he'd just returned from out of the country. He must have no idea who she was. Was it surprising the man believed she was fair game and he had every right to assault her? No. Nothing about The Den and the brutal men inside it surprised her.

"Look, dude." She sighed as if greatly inconvenienced by his persistence. "I gotta get back to List. It's long past time for me to get out of here. Otherwise, someone's gonna have to pay extra for my services…"

Would this brute fall for the continued attempt at this charade? Maybe she shouldn't use List as a detail of authenticity.

"Looks like you don't listen so well." He cuffed her with the broadside of his hand before Ava had a chance to even blink. "Shut the fuck up."

She cried out, slumping in his grip with her ears ringing. The man's tone was guttural as her head lolled back until she was staring up into his coarse features. "I haven't had any pussy in three weeks, and I'm getting a fuck out of this. Whether you like it or not. Now, my name is Malcolm, sweet thing. And I wanna hear you crying it out loud while I'm fucking you. Understand me?"

He pawed at her, ripping her robe down off her shoulders. His mouth was suddenly everywhere. Hot. Wet. Disgusting. Ava whimpered in terror, bucking in a useless effort to move his body away from hers. There was an unmistakable bulge in his pants when he rubbed against her. She fought harder. Although dazed by the blow he'd delivered, she still clenched her teeth when he tried forcing his thick tongue into her mouth.

"Goddamn whore… I'm gonna rip you in two. Bet you've never had a cock as big as mine inside that little cunt of yours," Malcolm muttered in frustration as she struggled. His free hand dove between their bodies. "I like a little fight in my women, so keep doing what you're doing. Damn, I'm gonna fuck you until you bleed."

"Stop. Please, stop. You don't understand who I am. Why I'm here." The words tumbled from her lips, a scream close behind them. She strangled it instead with a babbling explanation. "Carson Blue is my brother."

Malcolm paused and Ava almost wailed in relief. Kingston's very name was enough to curtail rape. Was that enlightening bit of information horrifying or a diabolical form of salvation?

"No fucking way…" Malcolm grinned. "Blue's little sister? The one Oliver grabbed? I heard about that. Before I cut off contact, he told me all about snatching you in that hotel. A true-blue virgin, am I right? Well, this might just screw everyone's grand plans, but I'm still gonna get what I want from you. I don't even care if it pisses Oliver off." He trailed a finger across her lips, his eyes almost black with sadistic pleasure. When he suddenly slapped her, he also violently shoved two fingers into her mouth until she gagged in pained surprise.

With a laugh, he mimicked the motion of a blowjob. "Hell, you might even like getting fucked by me. And don't worry," he bent closer and whispered in her ear, his breath moist and oily, "Winter won't be the boss much longer. He won't ever have a chance to miss the money you would have made him."

Ava hardly understood what he was saying. She could think of nothing other than the fact he was choking her. Her teeth clamped down on the thick digits jammed into her mouth. She bit so hard that tangy, metallic fluid welled and pooled under her tongue.

Malcolm yelped, snatching his fingers free. He glared at Ava. "Fucking bitch."

Ava spat in his face, knowing it would mean another blow from the hands holding her with such cruelty.

"When my dick is painted red with your blood, I'm gonna take a photo of it so I've got something to remember you by." Malcolm's vow was guttural. Brutal. "And then you're gonna lick away the mess left behind."

He kissed her again, harder this time. Crushing her with the weight of his body, leaving her with no hope of escape. She tried kneeing him in the groin, but he simply laughed, blocking the futile attempt by wedging his knee between her legs and forcing her to widen her stance.

He slapped her again, and as if from a distance, Ava heard the jingle of his belt buckle. The rasp of a zipper. And an unfamiliar roar that must have been a freight train bearing down on them both.

One moment, she was pinned against the wall, and the next, there was empty space where Malcolm once stood.

Something sticky and dark red splattered across her chest. Ava stared at it, then looked up, puzzled by the abrupt disappearance of her attacker.

Grunts. The *thwack* of fists slamming into skin. Bones crunching. Two bodies grappled before her, and with terrified clarity, Ava understood what she was seeing.

Kingston, clad only in a pair of sleeping pants, had the other man down on the floor. He straddled Malcolm, repeatedly punching him in the face. Without mercy. Without thought. Without hesitation.

Malcolm fought back, but even as large as he was, he was no match for Kingston.

Because Kingston fought like a tornado of fury, his fists unrelenting. Every strike sent droplets of blood spraying through the air in a fine mist. It was soon smeared across his bare chest like war paint, dripping from the lion tattoo's fangs as though inked into his skin. His knuckles were coated in dark red, and Ava stared in transfixed horror as Kingston eliminated the threat to her safety.

"You dare touch what's mine?" Kingston roared, the words punctuated with fierce blows to Malcolm's face. "You *fucking* dare? I'll slice you open from end to end and use your entrails to hang you by your worthless neck."

After a while, Malcolm no longer fought back. Gurgling whimpers issued from swollen lips and misshapen features. Ava stood in numb silence, frozen in her spot against the wall until Kingston finally stopped pummeling the man.

Cold, starlit, dark blue eyes lifted to hers. His hair was still damp from the shower, the strands curling around his ears. Sweat glistened on his brow.

It took some effort to beat Malcolm to a pulp.

Ava shrank away, melting as best she could into the wall. That possessive light in Kingston's eyes was terrifying. The rage on his face solidified her belief that he was nothing more than a monster. He'd just beaten a man to the point of death right in front of her.

But simmering below all of it, emanating from Kingston's entire body, oozing from his very pores was something entirely unexpected. It swirled between them, curling and binding the two of them until Ava could barely breathe from the pressure.

Fear.

For her.

Kingston slowly rose from Malcolm's body, his intense gaze never leaving Ava's. He was splattered with blood, bare chest heaving with exertion as he stepped over the man he'd just crushed. The lion tattoo emblazoned upon his chest seemed to roar with victorious satisfaction. Real blood dripped from the fangs, mingling with ink until Ava thought the beast was truly breathing. A living thing. Ready to tear her apart, too.

Like a conquering savage, Kingston reached a bloodied hand toward Ava and cupped her chin.

"Did he hurt you?"

Instead of shrinking away from this man, instead of hiding from the husky growl of concerned violence in Kingston's voice, Ava inexplicably leaned into the warmth of his palm. Her own hand slid up and clasped his wrist while he held her immobile beneath the weight of his dark blue eyes.

"A little," she whispered. "But you... you stopped him before..."

Her words faltered as she realized what would have occurred had Kingston not rescued her. What she risked with her own foolish, headstrong actions.

He had saved her.

Saved her.

"I fucking warned you about this. About the danger of roaming the halls without protection." His words were harsh snarls punctuated by intense fury, but that little spark of fear still bloomed bright in his eyes. It could not be concealed. "Now do you understand why, Ava? Why you aren't safe anywhere? Even from my own men?"

She did not answer as Jack and Paulie came racing down the corridor.

"Oh, shit," Paulie breathed when he saw Malcolm in a non-responsive heap. "I think you might have killed him, Kingston.

"He attacked Ava." Kingston turned back to Malcolm with an ice-cold sneer on his lips. A swift, well-placed kick to the man's ribs resulted in an agonized groan. "And as you can see, the bastard is still alive."

His attention returned to Ava, his gaze darkening like a gathering storm on the horizon. Roughly gentle fingertips skated over a tender spot high on Ava's cheek. A bruise was already blooming there, and Malcolm's blood trickled from the corner of her mouth.

A muscle ticked in Kingston's jaw.

"He struck you."

There was no hiding the evidence of Malcolm's actions. But a feather of pride unfurled in the pit of Ava's stomach. She'd inflicted a bit of damage all on her own against her attacker.

"I bit him." She spat again, desperate to remove the phantom memory of the other man's fingers in her mouth. His tongue. His blood.

Kingston pulled her into a tight embrace. His large, warm body shielded hers from the other men's gazes. With blood-streaked hands, he pulled the robe around her shoulders and closed it over her breasts.

She was shaking. Reality was catching up with her, and Kingston's grip was one of steel. Ava knew he hovered on the edge of violence. Would he unleash it upon her next?

She shivered harder at the thought. Maybe she deserved his brand of punishment.

Jack knelt beside Malcom, checking his pulse with two fingers. "Should I call Neil to come back? I know he left for the city after dinner last night."

"Neil's presence is unnecessary."

Paulie peered at Kingston, his lined face grim with awareness. "What do you want done with him?"

"North cell." Kingston's voice was cold, unattached. Like a bored king dealing with unruly subjects. "I'll pay him a visit once I've taken care of Ava."

CHAPTER
TWENTY-FIVE

Kington raked a hand through his damp hair as he hustled Ava back down the hallway toward his suite of rooms.

He felt nothing for the man he'd nearly beaten to death. If anything, the blood in his veins surged and roared, demanding he waste no time in finishing the job.

Fucking Malcolm.

The man was ensconced in Oliver's camp of supporters, always had been, and Kingston could only imagine the riches his brother had promised. He employed those men at his brother's sullen insistence, but Kingston never trusted any of them.

Of course, there were very few he did trust. Malcolm definitely resided at the bottom of that list.

The bastard would pay for his actions. If he didn't die

before Kingston visited him down in the cells, his demise was imminent, regardless.

Striding down the corridors, their bare feet silent on the gleaming wood floors, Kingston reflected on the moment he realized Ava had imprisoned him inside his own bathroom. Once he'd broken through the flimsy barricade wedged against the bathroom door, Kingston immediately entered his private office.

Located in a separate, secured room inside the suite, the wall of cameras there provided the quickest way of locating his wayward little lamb. He knew precisely where she was in the maze of corridors and just who had cornered her.

He'd even listened for a minute or two as Ava made a desperate play for escape. Her acting skills had his lips tweaking with reluctant amusement. For a brief moment, he even believed Malcolm would simply bring her sweet little ass right back to him.

But that didn't happen. Kingston could not shut out the image of Malcolm looming over Ava. How his thick hands grabbed and yanked at her clothes, roaming over places she should never be touched. How small and delicate she was compared to that bear of a man. Her cries of pain had ignited a fear within him that bloomed past obsession.

And Kingston discovered the rage overwhelming him was directed not only at his employee, but at himself for failing to keep Ava safe.

A gasp of surprise slipped past Ava's lips as they entered Kingston's suite of rooms.

The bench sat haphazardly in two jagged pieces now, one half of a tattered silk sash fluttering from its curved arm while the other dangled from the doorknob.

"Did you think that flimsy barricade would keep me contained? I'd go through a thousand brick walls to get to you,

Ava. Through hell, if necessary." Kingston shoved the wood bench aside as he guided Ava into his room.

The damage was even worse inside the bedroom. The chair once wedged under the bathroom door knob was upside down and splintered. It had landed several feet away when Kingston kicked his way out. The door itself hung crooked and haphazard, the ornately carved framing cracked and in pieces.

Ava inhaled a breath of alarm at seeing the damage, and Kingston allowed himself a satisfied smirk.

He hoped she was sufficiently frightened. Maybe now she understood the way things would go between them.

At first, Kingston found himself amused by Ava's daring cleverness in barricading him inside the bathroom. As he forcibly shouldered his way through the door, a sliver of admiration for her resourcefulness had warmed him. But witnessing the aftermath of her decision to flee from him and the dangerous situation she'd encountered had the blood pounding like a raging river inside his veins.

His little lamb must be taught a valuable lesson. And once he took care of Malcolm, that particular issue would be addressed accordingly.

With his hand across her backside.

Pushing her onto the bed, he grabbed his cell phone. It had been ringing incessantly since they entered the room.

"Yeah?" His voice was a gruff bark, and hearing it had Ava nervously wrapping her arms around herself. Like him, spatters of blood covered her arms and chest. She swiped her mouth with the back of a hand that trembled. Tentatively, she touched the apple of her cheek with the tips of her fingers and winced.

The neck of the robe had slipped off her delicate shoulders, and now, he could see the bruising on her upper arms. She would be black and blue soon.

Something primitive, a pang of emotion that was wild and vicious, surged through Kingston. Never had he been so excited at the prospect of killing a man with his bare hands. He was going to take his time with Malcolm. Make sure the piece of shit waiting in the cells below died slowly and with as much pain as possible.

"Hey," Oliver said on the other end of the line. "What's up? You sound majorly pissed. Well, you always sound pissed but more than usual."

"There's a problem."

"With what? Or more precisely, with whom? Our little visitor?" Oliver's tone was puzzled. "She giving you trouble? How very brave of her. I think she might just be a girl after my own heart."

"It's Malcolm," Kingston sneered. He *hated* the idea of his brother even being near Ava, much less giving her his heart. That was never going to happen as long as he drew breath. "Gotta cut him loose."

"Didn't he just get back from that job in Mexico?" Oliver asked, perplexed. "Don't tell me he screwed all that up. Fucking idiot. I gave him the details myself."

"It's not Mexico," Kingston replied, gritting his teeth. "He put his hands on something he shouldn't have."

"Well... was he aware this thing was off limits? You know he goes dark when he's out on jobs. He probably didn't know."

"Oh, he fucking knew. He just didn't care."

There was silence for a long moment, then Oliver said in a hardened voice, "I won't stand in the way. Gotta do what you think best, King."

"Don't worry. I will." Kingston scrubbed a hand over his jaw, abruptly realizing that Ava's dark green eyes tracked his movements. She stared at his hand, and with a grimace, he realized it was the same hand that had smashed in Malcolm's nose. The blood coating his knuckles, a mix of his own and the other man's, was now smeared across his own face.

"Why did you call?" Kingston prodded Oliver.

"Thought you'd want to know as soon as I got the word. There will be no payment from Carson." Oliver laughed into the phone as though he found the whole scenario greatly amusing. "He refused. Just like you said he would. The prize is all ours."

Kingston's gaze drifted over his reluctant captive. She could only hear one side of the conversation, but seeing how her chin tilted, she obviously knew she was the subject.

"What is your expected time of arrival?

"Two o'clock," Oliver replied. "If this damn jet is ever cleared for takeoff."

"I'll speak with you then." Kingston abruptly ended the call, tossing the phone on the bedside table.

Ava's gaze tracked it. Kingston knew she debated the possibility of snatching it up and calling for help.

Help that would never come.

"Carson has officially declined to honor his debt." A rueful smile twisted his lips. "You're all mine now, little lamb. Time to pay up." Leaning forward, he tipped her chin with a blood-stained finger until their gazes clashed. "Do you understand what this means?"

"Yes. I understand." Ava bit her lip and hesitantly asked, "Y-you won't let anyone else hurt me, will you?"

The very thought made Kingston's hands flex with the desire to rip somebody in two.

"Fuck no." His eyes closed as he gathered his control so he could calmly explain things to her. "I don't want you to leave these rooms. I've got to take care of unfinished business, and at least in here, I know where you are and that you are safe."

"What business?" Her question was a whisper, but beneath it was a tremble of real fear.

Kingston's lips twitched. They both knew exactly what he was about to do.

"I'm going to kill the man who did this. And in the short window of time he has left on this earth, I will make damn sure he suffers."

Ava appeared shocked by his savagery. Then, to Kingston's consternation, fat, glossy tears began rolling down her pale cheeks. Within seconds, she was sobbing in almost uncontrollable gulps for air.

"I was so scared. Scared of what would happen. Of *him.* Scared of what you would do. Scared you wouldn't come for me." She met his eyes, fear dancing in the haunting green depths of her own.

It was an emotion Kingston was unfamiliar with but was coming to know all too well. He'd been terrified for her. Frantic with the need to carry her to safety, although Ava most certainly would never be safe with him as her jailer. He was too savage. Too possessive. Too obsessed with this untamed creature he held so violently within the calloused, bloody palm of his hand. But goddamn, he couldn't stop this.

He couldn't stop himself.

His heart swelled within his chest when Ava admitted softly, "Most of all... I was scared because I *wanted* you to come."

Fuck. He wanted to lick every single salty-sweet tear from her cheeks. He wanted to fold her close against him and feel for himself just how fast her heart was beating. Wanted to both savor and eliminate her fear.

Trembles of foreboding raced through Kingston along with a deep-seated urge to scoop her up into his arms.

His fingers tightened on her chin as he fought those unwelcome, confusing urges.

"Kingston..." she whispered tearfully. "I don't understand this. I don't understand any of it. There was overwhelming relief when I saw you. And horror as you beat..." She broke off whatever else she might say and instead asked, "How can I consider surrender? How can I want to be destroyed by you? And how can I possibly be safe with you? I'm so confused. And frightened. And alone."

Without conscious thought, Kingston sank onto the bed. He pulled her into his lap, cradling her body with bloodstained hands. Then his mouth crashed down upon hers, swallowing her feeble protest as he reinforced his claim. At that moment, nothing was more important than obliterating the memory and taste of another man's mouth on hers.

Ava fought him, the instinct to escape too overwhelming to deny, but Kingston refused to release her. Tightening his arms, he let her struggle while he continued kissing her with all the fierce confusion boiling inside him. Their tongues clashed and tangled. Their breath merged into one, and Ava whimpered in frustrated despair until something switched inside her.

Now, instead of pushing him away, her fingers clutched at Kingston's shoulders, fingernails digging into his bare skin. She kissed him back even as she wept with bitter regret.

Kingston's hand came up, his fingers wrapping around her throat and creating a necklace of restraint. When she sobbed against his lips and melted into him, her surrender so sweet and unexpected, a growl of satisfaction escaped him.

"You're fucking mine, Ava. *Mine*. And as of this moment, you are not alone. Do you understand? Everything about you, everything that you are belongs to me now. Your fears. Your dreams. Your smiles. Your body. I'll burn this world to cinders for you because your enemies are now *my* enemies. If anyone gets in my way, if anyone thinks they can take you from me, I'll slit that fool's throat. And I'll take you in a pool of their blood right before their eyes while they lay dying."

He disentangled himself from their embrace and moved Ava so she was once again seated on the bed. Bewilderment lay stamped across her face, but she obediently stayed where he placed her.

"Now, I'm going to get dressed before I visit the cells and make an example out of my former employee." Kingston smoothed a hand over her tangled hair and wiped a smudge of blood from her jawline. "You will clean yourself up while I'm gone. Wash away the scent of that animal from your body. Throw this gown and the robe in the trash. You may wear one of my shirts. Take whatever you need from my closet."

She nodded slowly, and Kingston's smile was grimly confident. "When I return, the issue of your disobedience will be addressed."

"I did nothing wrong," Ava mumbled in a momentary flash of defiance. Stubborn pride turned her cheeks a delicious pink. "I ran from you because I had to."

"There is no room for negotiation on this, Ava. You were told you could not roam the halls unattended for your own safety. But you did, regardless of your reasons for disobeying me. Even worse for you is the fact I overheard part of the conversation between you and Malcolm. You were foolish enough to attempt enlisting his help before he attacked you. This behavior will not be tolerated, and I will make damn sure you understand this."

TWENTY-SIX

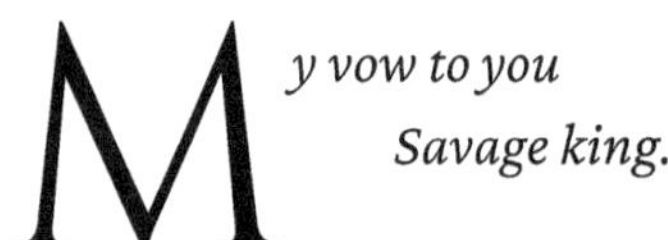

AVA DID NOT MOVE from the bed as Kingston stepped into the bathroom. The sound of water running as though from a great distance made her so sleepy.

She must have dozed off after that because it seemed like only seconds later, he was smoothing a hand over her forehead.

"I'll return shortly."

He was gone before she could gather her wits and beg him to stay. Her head didn't even lift from the pillow as the door clicked shut, indicating his departure.

Ava drifted a while longer in a fuzzy world, dangling between shock and reality before her mind slowly cleared itself. She slid from Kingston's bed and made her way into the bathroom. Turning the faucet on for the shower, she patiently waited as the water heated. Soon, steam billowed from inside the marble-slabbed stall.

Was it real life that she'd watched Kingston Winter pleasure himself with his hand around his cock and her name on his lips earlier that morning?

It didn't seem real. And yet, it was.

Peeling off her garments, she winced as pain shot up her arms. Bruises were already forming around her elbows, purplish red and in the shape of fingertips. The mirror reflected them back as she wadded the clothing into a tight ball. Everything went into the small wastebasket beside the sleek bath vanity. She even discarded the scrap of underwear. After that cretin's paws had been all over them, there was no way she would keep them.

Stepping into the shower, Ava wrapped her arms around her body and stood for an eternity beneath the stream of water. It was almost too hot to bear but she did not care. She needed the piercing, needlelike sensation of the droplets hitting her skin. It meant the ugliness of that morning was perhaps being washed away.

Eventually, she bathed and washed her hair. Both the shampoo and soap had a fresh yet masculine aroma. There was nothing floral or girly about any of it. It was all ocean breezes and evergreen woods. Spicy tea. She was drowning in Kingston, but she didn't mind. Filling her lungs with the scent, she let it cascade through her as the soapy water swirled and washed everything clean again.

Ava reflected on the display of emotions she'd seen on Kingston's face. Something profound had shifted between the two of them during her rescue. Something she didn't understand. She'd fallen into his arms, so, so glad he'd come for her. A tiny portion of her soul, the dark, shameful, scary part of her heart, wasn't really bothered that a man would likely die because of her.

Kingston would protect her. He said she belonged to him now.

Rather than fearing the man holding her prisoner in this gilded tower, Ava reluctantly acknowledged he was a sanctuary. Never mind he was the one dragging her down into black depths.

He was changing her.

"I'm crazy thinking I'm safe with him." But even her silent admonishments were useless observations. Kingston Winter wanted her, and Ava was ready to kiss the Devil himself for a mere token of the safety he offered.

But wasn't it the pinnacle of insanity to seek protection from a murderer and kidnapper?

Ava finally emerged from the shower, searching through the vanity drawers until she located a stash of new tooth-brushes. Ripping open the package, she methodically and brutally brushed her teeth until her gums were nearly bleed-ing. She rinsed and spat over and over until the sour beer flavor of Malcolm lingered as nothing more than a memory in the depths of her mind. A bad memory which could now be filed away in a little box with others.

But although she was physically clean, having scrubbed her skin to the point of discomfort, Ava wondered if anything could erase the reality of what she'd gone through that morn-ing. How could she forget? How could she continue keeping all the bad locked away?

I cannot forget everything I've endured since arriving here. Nor what happened before. Mom and Dad. Their deaths. Carson and his cruelty. It must all be faced. Challenged. Conquered. No more hiding from any of it. Even if it hurts to know the truth.

The niggling premonition that things would only get worse

sent Ava's chin tilting higher. She must be stronger than those around her expected. Even if she served as Kingston's toy for however long he wanted her, she would not break for him.

AVA KNEW she was intruding on Kingston's privacy. Even with his express permission to be there, her stomach still twisted into knots of apprehension.

Are you scared of what you might find? The secrets he keeps locked away?

Standing in the middle of the enormous, sleekly masculine walk-in closet, she stared unblinkingly at the rows and rows of pristine custom suits.

Did the man not own a simple t-shirt? A pair of jeans? Sighing, she thumbed through one of the lower racks, admiring how the luxurious fabric glided through her fingers. The suits were an extension of Kingston himself. Exquisitely made. Dark. Concealing secrets and cruelty beneath a beautiful exterior.

She turned toward the built-in drawers, but hesitated in opening them in her search, terrified of what she might discover. The souls of his victims captured inside little velvet boxes. Implements of torture. Contracts for lives that no longer existed.

Or maybe the hearts of women foolish enough to fall in love with a monster.

Ava's jaw clenched. She wasn't one of those women. She was too smart for that. Too practical. Too aware now of the darkness and how easily she could fall.

Wrenching open a random drawer, she found stacks of neatly folded Henleys in every dark color imaginable. Another drawer revealed jeans she'd never seen him wear. Yet another contained crisp, white t-shirts so blindingly bright they couldn't possibly have ever been worn.

One drawer held an impressive collection of watches. Expensive and subtle in their richness, they nestled in perfect, orderly rows on black velvet.

A tiny part of Ava hoped she might stumble upon a weapon. A gun. She could have saved herself from Malcolm's attack if she'd had one.

She shook her head at that train of thought. She didn't know the first thing about firearms, but perhaps it was time she learned. The useless pocket-sized can of pepper spray sitting in the bottom of her long-gone purse was ample evidence of that.

Having a more formidable weapon when Oliver snatched her from her hotel's elevator might have resulted in a different outcome.

Ava recognized herself in the rigid order of Kingston's private belongings. She'd always been meticulously neat. All the pieces of her life had been organized and categorized, at least until her parents died. She'd fallen apart at first, devastated by grief before realizing her emotions could be shoved into manageable little boxes. Fear went into one. Pain, another. Abandonment by her brother had its own box, as well.

Peeking into the precise perfection of Kingston's life, seeing this tiny slice of his mysterious soul, made Ava both dizzy and strangely elated. Evidence of his personal control over himself and those surrounding him echoed her own need for order. And it spoke of pain. Deep, savage pain which could only fester and swirl until it found outlets.

When a small photograph framed in black onyx caught her eye, she could not help herself.

Picking it up from the shelf, she studied it. It was a photo of Kingston and his mother. He was just a toddler and she was a gorgeous woman with long dark hair and sad blue eyes. Her arms were wrapped gently around her child. She wore a smile for the photographer, but it was an empty, meaningless emotion. Given for someone else's benefit.

That photo ripped Ava's heart in two. Kingston was chubby, his pink cheeks glowing with the innocence all babies possessed at that age. He had no idea what would happen to his mother. To his life.

Sadness swamped Ava as she replaced the photo on the neat, orderly shelf.

What did it mean when she ached to whirl through his things like a tornado? Destroying and disrupting his life as hers had been. She wanted to make him feel... *something*. But what? What good could possibly come from Kingston facing his demons? What good could come if she faced her own?

Nothing. Nothing good will come from this. And yet, I am on a collision course with this man. We will crash and twist together in violence. We will wreck each other until nothing recognizable remains in the carnage. Do not fall for this man. Do not fall for his darkness. His cruelty. His arms that hold me tighter than I've ever been held before. It's all an illusion. I can't trust it. Can't trust him.

But what else could she do? He owned her now. Like a little doll purchased in secret. He pulled her strings, and she must do as he said to stay alive and in one piece until she could escape this madness.

Sliding the towel from around her body, Ava tossed it over a low bench and stood naked. She did not glance about the closet, ashamed to see what would reflect back at her in the multiple mirrors.

Those mirrors illuminated everything, and she could hardly bear to witness the moment she accepted her fate. The moment she became Kingston Vaughn Winter's property. Like these perfect stacks of clothing and his valuable watches and exquisite cufflinks. She was nothing more than a lost, little soul hanging around like an expensive suit, waiting for her turn to be used.

Snatching a t-shirt from the drawer, Ava quickly tugged it over her head. It hung to the tops of her thighs, the fabric so soft and encompassing it was as though Kingston himself was wrapped around her. It even carried the faint, lingering aroma of his cologne beneath the crisp scent of laundry soap.

Ava quickly exited the closet and returned to the bedroom. There were two sets of double doors inside the main room. One set in the French style opened onto a lovely terrace. Paved with flagstones, it overlooked both the swimming pool and the rugged mountains in the distance. A small creek meandered below it, escaping the forest and tumbling over rocks as it flowed past this portion of the mansion.

Ava wished she could sit on that terrace. She would sip a cup of tea. Center and ground herself in the quiet stillness. Regroup her emotions and decide how she would survive this.

Those doors were locked, however, as were the second set of solid oak doors on the opposite side of the room. A keypad on the wall allowed entry, provided she had the correct finger-print. Which she didn't.

It was just as well. Those doors concealed a mystery, one Ava currently had no interest in solving. She was too tired. And too numb.

Sighing, she picked up the shattered remains of the sculp-tured chair, stacking the pieces neatly against one wall before drifting back to the bed. Then she climbed into the middle of it, grabbing a feather-down pillow and squeezing it tight. Sheets of crisp, cool cotton surrounded her, and she was so tempted to sink back into the oblivion of deep slumber.

But there could be no sleep with the threat of Kingston's

imminent return. He would punish her for running. For placing herself in danger.

And she deserved it.

He would have everything now. Her obedience. Her body. Her soul.

CHAPTER

TWENTY-SEVEN

*W*e can destroy the world
And everything standing between us

AVA HUGGED THE PILLOW TIGHTER, her heart splintering into a million pieces when the suite's outer door lock clicked. She heard him addressing another person in the main corridor and realized he must have posted a guard. Whether to keep her in or prevent someone else from entering was unknown. Whatever Kingston said to this person was a low murmur, spoken too quietly to discern the words or even who he spoke to.

Ava's entire body tightened. What would he do with her now? What punishments would be imposed? Would she be able to bear them? She glanced down at her hands. They were shaking.

Kingston sauntered into the room as casually as though returning from an unexpected errand. Formally dressed in one of those immaculate suits, his coat, slacks, and shirt were perfectly pressed and wrinkle-free. Everything was black—all of it—and the fabric concealed any evidence of blood. He was not disheveled, nor was there a single hair out of place.

He was sleek, cruel danger wrapped in a Brioni suit. And he was so devastatingly handsome, it made Ava's breath catch.

Is this what it looked like when you killed someone? This pristine, controlled persona that was deadly in its elegance? This man was too perfect to have committed murder. Too beautiful.

Kingston's eyes sparked when he saw her waiting in the middle of his bed. He carried a bundle of clothing under one arm. Ava recognized the items from the closet of the sterile, perfect bedroom she'd stayed in before.

The gleam in the dark blue depths of his intent gaze sent a shiver of awareness through her. He stalked closer. His expensive cologne teased her senses, leaving her dry-mouthed with nerves. And something else.

Relief that he'd come back.

Leaning a shoulder against the carved bedpost, he swept her from head to toe with an appreciative eye.

"Good morning again, lamb."

Ava set the pillow aside. "Good morning." She swallowed hard, her eyes closing briefly. "Sir."

She wasn't even sure why she used the title then, but it pleased Kingston. It was evident in the way his pupils blew out, the black swallowing all the blue of his eyes.

He took in the dampness of her hair and the billowy softness of his t-shirt covering her body. His mouth quirked.

"Ava?"

"Yes?" She hated how her voice trembled, but it couldn't be helped. There was something different between them now.

Something foreign and intriguing. A sense of belonging and yet, strangeness as well.

"Remove the t-shirt." His command was just that, a command, and it stung Ava like the bite of a whip.

Was this how it would be from now on? An immediate assertion of his control and dominance over her?

Her hesitation had him cocking his head.

"Your brother refused to pay the debt that held you prisoner. Need I remind you of all the reasons you are mine? Now, do as I say and remove that shirt."

Ava sucked in a breath, and with a razor-sharp motion, whipped the t-shirt over her head.

"*Tsk, Tsk.*" Kingston's chuckle was low and dark and not at all amused. "No, lamb. Not like that. Put it back on and try again. Slowly."

Ava wondered if it were possible to ignite a body with the sheer force of a frown. Because if it was, Kingston Vaughn Winter was in serious danger of igniting into flames.

Gritting her teeth, Ava did as she was told. Donning the shirt again, she slowly, deliberately teased it off her body with what she hoped were seductive movements.

"Much better," Kingston said in approval. "You learn quickly. We'll have to work on your demeanor, however. It's much too defiant."

The rumpled sheets concealed the lower half of her body, but the upper portion was now completely exposed to Kingston's gaze. She forced herself into a relaxed position, achingly aware of her nakedness. Of her breasts which swelled full and heavy beneath his perusal. Of her nipples, now puckered into tight buds of anticipation in the room's coolness.

Would he force himself upon her now? Would he shove her back into the downy soft pillows and pry her thighs apart so he could fit between them? Would she fight him? Or would she allow it?

Kingston did not move from his stance, his shoulder remaining in contact with the bedpost as he pinned her in place with diamond-bright eyes. His eyes roamed every inch of her body, rage flaring in their dark depths as he noted the extent of the bruising caused by Malcolm's hands.

"There are certain rules you will follow while you are mine."

Ava shook her hair back until the damp strands cascaded down her back. "I thought as much," she replied bravely.

The corners of Kingston's mouth kicked up a bit before he sobered. "Number one is quite obvious. I will not tolerate impertinence. Little girls with sassy mouths will find themselves punished."

Ava stiffened, her hands clenching into fists. "Am I to be punished now?"

Can I endure it right now? Will he use this opportunity to further break me? Please, God, don't let him do that just yet...

"No. That will come later. I think you've had a trying enough morning as it is. But rest assured. I've not forgotten what you are owed based on your previous behavior."

Ava did not reply, but her shoulders sagged a little with silent gratitude for his momentary restraint.

"Number two," Kingston continued. "You will do as I ask with no question or comment."

"And if I don't?" Ava asked quietly.

"Then I will refer you to rule number one." He stood straighter, crossing his arms. "Rule number three. You will refrain from any further attempts at escape. Additional freedoms I grant will depend on your willingness in following the rules I've set in place. Do you understand what I mean by this?"

Ava nodded her head. "If I do as you say, you will let me have an almost normal existence."

"Almost." Kingston smiled. "Rule number four. When we are in public, you will be referred to as my companion. And under no circumstances will you ever entertain, acknowledge, or encourage the attention of another man. You are mine and only mine while our arrangement is in place."

"Will you do the same? Ignore other women, I mean?" Ava asked impulsively. How long would he continue to stare at her naked body? The heat of his gaze left her with the disconcerting urge to rub her thighs together. Where she was cold before, it was now as though lava slowly dripped over her skin, covering her in blazing warmth. She was hot. Wound tight. Ready to burst.

"You are already violating the first rule, and I've not even finished listing them all," Kingston murmured, his expression shuttered. Moving with the quiet grace of a stalking lion, he came forward until he stood beside her. Tipping her chin up, he peered into her eyes. "During our time together, you've no need to worry about other women. My focus will be on you, Ava, and only you."

"H-how long will this arrangement last?" Her voice had gone quiet the moment he touched her, but her treacherous body roared to life. How she hated her own abdication from common sense.

"As long as it takes to repay the debt. Follow the rules and your time will pass much quicker. When it's over, and we part ways, I will ensure your future safety. For the remainder of your life, Carson will never have an opportunity to abuse you."

"And my parents' deaths... you will tell me what you know? What you alluded to once before?" Ava pressed with reckless persistence. She'd not forgotten the cryptic statement Kingston made the day he released her from the cell. How he taunted her by pointing out her naïveté when it came to her brother and his nefarious actions.

Kingston's eyes sparked with some nameless emotion. Lifting the t-shirt from the bed, he held it out to her.

Ava wondered if it was his way of offering a silent truce.

"Perhaps," he murmured. "We'll see."

Her mouth tightened at the non-committal response. Carefully, she pulled the garment back over her body until she was hiding once more beneath the soft fabric. Her nipples contracted in protest against the material, sensitive to the point of discomfort, and all because Kingston's stare had burned through her soul.

"Will we use protection?" Ava could not seem to stop asking questions. But didn't she have the right? The right to know every facet of her imprisonment? After all, it was *her* body being sacrificed on the altar of man's greed.

"I've never slept with a woman without it and I already know your sexual history." His eyes crinkled a bit at the corners. He found her questions amusing, and the realization he was laughing at her made Ava's anger rear its foolish head.

"So, that's a yes?"

His fingers tightened on her chin at her snippiness, his eyes so stormy it made her woozy.

"That's a no. I want to feel every bit of your sweet, tight pussy squeezing my cock when I fuck you, naughty lamb. Nothing will be between us."

The treacherous blood in her veins sang in delight with his words, but Ava forced herself to ask in the coldest voice she could manage, "What if I get pregnant?"

Kingston could not hide a satisfied smirk. "You won't. I made sure of that on your first day here at The Den. The shot is in full effect by now."

The room, his face, it all swirled in front of Ava.

"Y-you injected me with birth control? I can't believe…" Swallowing down her nausea was a tremendous feat of self-control. "You had no right to do that."

"It was necessary. Unless you are that eager to have a child. Are you, Ava?" His head tilted as he considered her pale features. "Eager to become pregnant for me? We can make that happen. Three months from now, I'll cancel the birth control and fuck you every day until you grow round and plump with my baby."

Ava's eyes widened with horrified panic. "No! I don't want that. I don't. How could I want such a thing when I hate you for taking away my choices? You've taken control of my body. My life. Everything!"

Kingston let out a low chuckle of amusement. "I've not taken everything, lamb. At least, not yet."

She simply glared at him, so distraught she could not think clearly. He'd done her a tiny kindness, considering his initial plans for her. But what pained her the most was having it done without her knowledge. Or her consent.

A minor point, really, when compared to abduction and imprisonment.

"All right. No babies for now," he casually conceded. Leaning over, he brushed her mouth with his own, confident she would not fight him. "And Ava, we both know you don't hate me. You most certainly will not hate the things I'll do to you now that you are truly mine. You will want the pleasure. The pain, too. You will need it. Crave it. And I intend on giving you everything you desire as long as you submit."

"Everything except true freedom," she replied bitterly.

"No one is ever really free, lamb. No one. Not even myself." His smile might have been regretful, but the lust Ava recognized in his features and the cruel grip he retained on her chin eclipsed that softer emotion. "Remember this when I'm making you come over and over. When I'm deep inside you. I am also imprisoned. Obsessed. Enraptured. Captivated. And so fucking helpless to escape my need for you. The only solution is to have you again and again until this ungodly fascination is purged."

"Are there any more rules?" Her thighs trembled from the images his words created. Such a strange contradiction to despise a person so much and yet ache for his attention. It was maddening. "I want to be sure I understand everything." Her voice was carefully subdued.

Kingston hesitated, his breathing changing with subtle nuance. Ava held her own, wondering what acts of depravity he might demand of her. How much damage would he wreak upon her treacherous body and unwilling heart?

"Just the most important one." In a voice as smooth as summer honey, he said, "Rule number five. When we are alone, you will address me as 'Sir'."

Ava's gaze dropped, her stomach flipping upside down at the reminder of his mastery. And that's when she caught sight of something previously missed. A spot of blood. It marred the pristine black of his shirt cuff where it peeked beneath the edge of his coat sleeve. Blending so perfectly with the ebony-hued fabric, she should have missed it.

She couldn't stop staring at that incriminating splotch. A trembly, "Yes, sir," automatically escaped her lips without conscious intent before she could stop it.

It was already starting. Her submission. Her capitulation. Her downfall.

Kingston frowned until he realized what had captured Ava's rapt attention. He lifted her chin higher until she had no choice but to look at him once more.

"I killed a man for you today, Ava. And I won't hesitate to do it again if it keeps you safe." His voice was a gravelly, low growl that sent shivers of terror and belonging cascading through Ava. "But don't ever mistake who I am. And who I am not. I am not a nice man. I'm not a prince in a fairytale. Nor am I a knight in shining armor. I took great delight in carving him up. I whispered your name in his ear so he would carry the reason for his death straight to hell."

His eyes bored into hers, the black pupils swallowing up the sapphire blue irises. "My men watched as I slit him from stem to stern. Now, they understand the consequences if they follow Malcolm's path. They know his death was for you. Because he touched what is mine. Because he hurt you, and only I am allowed that exquisite privilege. I removed him from this planet, and I enjoyed hearing his screams for mercy before he bled out."

Ava's eyes widened as the depths of Kingston's dark possessiveness clicked into precise, heart-pounding focus.

He would consume everything there was of her, and she would allow it. There would be no escape. No reprieve or last-minute pardon. She was his until *he* decided otherwise.

Ava wanted that as much as she feared and hated the man. Despite his cruelty, he possessed the unique ability to make her fit in as though she truly belonged somewhere. To someone. Even if it was nothing more than a glittery illusion filled with deception and painful truths about herself and her own insecurities.

Kingston had saved her. Protected her. Eliminated a true threat.

For her.

Her.

With the slightest movement, Kingston snaked his arm around her waist and lifted Ava until she was on her knees. Yanking her against his body, he fully claimed her mouth until she surrendered to his savagery with a helpless cry.

It hurt to be held so tight, but her body didn't care. She pressed closer to him, breathing him into her lungs. Breathing in the metallic tang of newly spilled blood. The salty ocean and Earl Grey tea of his cologne. The sharpness of his lust. Her hands clutched frantically at his suit coat. Pushing him away and yet, somehow holding on, too.

Holding *him*.

Kingston kissed her with tender brutality, his tongue stroking along hers, biting her bottom lip, imperiously demanding a response, and receiving it as Ava sank fully into the darkness that was Kingston Vaughn Winter.

Sealing her fate and abandoning all hope of recovering her former self. She'd never be the same girl as the one who'd arrived at The Den and found herself thrown at a king's feet.

I'm his for now.

Somehow, she would survive this. Survive him.

And maybe even find a way to ruin him, too.

To be continued...

Ava and Kingston's story continues in Book Two of The Savage Duet. Release date for A HEART SO SAVAGE to be announced. Preorder now!

HTTPS://geni.us/AHeartSoSavage

He saw me.

He took me.

He ruined me.

Now, I'm his.

I belong here with this monster, yet I still long for freedom.

I hate him, but my heart pounds faster when he kisses me.

He breaks me. Spoils me. Taunts me when I'm on my knees

before him. His punishments are exquisite pleasures I willingly endure.

Because I crave how he puts me back together again and again.

I'm nothing more than payment for a debt owed, but Kingston treats me as though I am his most precious treasure. He swears that I'm safe, but the treachery of our enemies is subtle and cruel. They won't stop until I am at their mercy and Kingston is dead from a bullet in the back.

But I'm becoming as wicked as those seeking our destruction. I can save us before all is lost. Will love weaken or strengthen us when it matters most?

I'm Ava Bella Blue. A prisoner trapped in a gilded cell of lust and secrets.

Kingston Vaughn Winter is the beast I've fallen in love with.

Crush~Conquer~Protect

It's his personal motto but I've adopted it as my own.

And I will win this king's savage heart before this is over.

Like Book I in The Savage Duet, A HEART SO SAVAGE contains adult themes intended for readers 18 years of age and older. The situations contained in these books may not be suitable for everyone. Please proceed with caution if you are affected by this type of subject matter. Read at your own risk.

Acknowledgments

As always, thank you to my readers for allowing me to experience this amazing journey. Whenever I receive emails, reviews, or notes, I just can't believe how blessed I am. To write, and have others read those words and enjoy them, is a dream come true. So, thank you from the bottom of my heart.

Huge hugs and thanks to my amazing editor, Kendra. She spit-shines every word for me—I am so grateful. Very special thanks to Cheryl Maddox for taking over PA duties and doing all the stuff to keep me on track. I adore you!

I could not do this without my sweet husband, James, by my side. He's always supportive in helping me accomplish my dreams. I can count on him—through thick and thin!

Thanks to the family and friends I can't live without. I love you all.

Special thanks to my friends in the book world. Michelle and Cindi: I love you ladies so much. Your encouragement and support mean the world to me. Thank you, Cindi, for reading this book although you hate Kingston Winter with all your heart, lol. I hope I change your mind by the end of their story. You are an amazing Alpha reader, and I'm so thankful for your willingness to dip into the darkness of my books.

To my ARC team readers: your time and support are invaluable! I appreciate each and every one of you. You are an important part of my journey as an author, and I'm blessed to have you read my words.

About April Moran

April enjoys writing both historical and new adult romance with a generous splash of heat. When not penning tales of passion, she enjoys traveling with her husband, attending rock concerts with friends, and time spent with family. Brainstorming new storylines is best done while riding her horse or during long walks with her German Shepherd. A tumbler of good whiskey helps tie all the details together and brings her characters to life.

BOOKS2READ.COM
https://books2read.com/author/april-moran/subscribe/33016

VISIT APRIL'S WEBSITE
www.aprilmoranbooks.com

SIGN UP FOR NEWSLETTER AND UPDATES
http://bit.ly/AprilMoran_BookUpdates
April Moran Book Updates

STALK APRIL EVERYWHERE

https://www.facebook.com/groups/aprilshoneybees/

https://www.bookbub.com/profile/april-moran

https://www.instagram.com/aprilmoranbooks

https://www.goodreads.com/Author-AprilMoran

https://www.pinterest.com/aprilmoranbooks

https://www.tiktok.com/authoraprilmoran

* 9 7 9 8 9 8 7 9 4 5 9 5 7 *